BLOO

Light from the sign ... door cast down on the warlock. It cut shadows under his sharp brows, eyes glittering from pools of black. He smiled, teeth a white slash in a tangle of midnight beard. He looked like a skull.

"Kill them, my children. Do not let them pass. Drink their blood. Bring me their heads."

Magick pulsed behind his words. The vampires turned, making a wall of undead flesh between us and the wizard. Stepping over and on tangled corpses they stalked down the hall toward us.

My finger squeezed thunder out of my gun as it kicked back in my hand. Three times I pulled the trigger. Three bullets smacked into the chest of the bloodsucker nearest to me, the one who had been snacking on the old man. He shuddered to a stop as twenty-four ounces of lead punched through the meat of him. They went in with a quarter-sized hole and came out his back in a spray of chunky flesh shrapnel. The vampire looked down, jaw slung open in shock.

Then his skin closed up, sealing shut in the slow blink of an eye . . .

Books by James R. Tuck

BLOOD AND BULLETS

BLOOD AND SILVER

BLOOD AND MAGICK

Novellas

THAT THING AT THE ZOO

SPIDER'S LULLABY

CIRCUS OF BLOOD

Published by Kensington Publishing Corporation

W D
AND
MAGICK

JAMES R. TUCK

KENSINGTON PUBLISHING CORP.
http://www.kensingtonbooks.com

KENSINGTON BOOKS are published by

Kensington Publishing Corp.
119 West 40th Street
New York, NY 10018

All Kensington Titles, Imprints, and Distributed Lines are available at special quantity discounts for bulk purchases for sales promotions, premiums, fund-raising, and educational or institutional use. Special book excerpts or customized printings can also be created to fit specific needs. For details, write or phone the office of the Kensington special sales manager: Kensington Publishing Corp., 119 West 40th Street, New York, NY 10018, attn: Special Sales Department, Phone: 1-800-221-2647.

Kensington and the K logo Reg. U.S. Pat & TM Off.

ISBN-13: 978-0-7582-7149-5
ISBN-10: 0-7582-7149-2

First Mass Market Printing: March 2013

10 9 8 7 6 5 4 3 2 1

Printed in the United States of America

Dedicated to the Missus.
The one woman who makes my world go round.

ACKNOWLEDGMENTS

Too many people go into the creation of a book, more than you could ever know. Thank you to my family and friends, The Missus, The Son, The Daughter, and The Kevin. Thank you to the folks at Kensington; I know there are a ton of you wonderful people whose names I don't even know, but your work is truly appreciated. Thank you to John Scognamiglio for taking a chance and keeping me straight on these books. Thank you to Lou Malcangi. Thank you to Gene Mollica and James DiNonno for bringing Deacon to life on the covers. Thank you to my critique partners in Mass Forward (lol); y'all shaped this book. Thank you to the wonderful ladies at Foxtale Books; you really know how to treat a fella on a book release party. Thank you to Dragoncon, specifically Derek Tatum. Thank you to every convention that has had me. Thank you to Stephen Zimmer and Fandom Fest. Thank you to Antonio Jones for being awesome! Thank you to all the book blogs who have totally rocked and supported this series; man, you kick ass. Thank you to my crew at Family Tradition. I have gathered a tremendous group of writerly friends whom I love dearly. Y'all inspire me to keep Y'all inspire me to keep working, keep striving, keep reaching. The other members of the Four Horsemen Of The Doompocalypse: Janice Hardy, Delilah S. Dawson,

and Carol Malcolm: John Hartness, Kalayna Price, Faith
Hunter, Jeanne C. Stein, Linda Robertson, Alex Hughes,
Annabel Joseph, Laurell K. Hamilton, Brian Keene,
Debbie Viguie, Nancy Holder, David B. Coe, J. F. Lewis,
Misty Massey, Rachel Aaron, and the ladies of both the
Word Whores and MPERWA. THANK YOU TO ALL THE
LOYALS AND TRUE BELIEVERS! You are absolutely
the most awesome fans an author could ever have. You
inspire me to write this crazy world and I love you all.

1

I should have known.

There were signs. I'm supposed to be the damn expert. I should have caught the warnings.

I should have.

But I was completely clueless until the *minute* the restaurant exploded in a wave of eldritch flame and burning glass.

"You look absolutely amazing tonight."

She really, really did. It was the God's honest truth. Tiff was wearing a black evening dress that crossed her shoulders and plunged in a scalloped V, baring her back from the base of her neck to the dimples at the bottom of her spine. I had seen that expanse of skin before, but to have it so elegantly displayed was downright damn breathtaking. The dress was a frame on a beautiful piece of art.

She turned, face close to mine, body tilted just so toward me. The front of the dress plunged sharply to below her breastbone in another deep V that was working overtime to display a gentle swell of cleavage. It was impossible for me to keep my eyes off her.

This was nothing new. I had a hard time keeping my eyes off Tiff in general, but in that dress? With her in that dress, you could set me on fire and I wouldn't notice.

Her blue eye twinkled. "You think so?"

"I know so. You are a knockout, little girl."

A tilt of her head made dark chestnut hair fall over the left side of her face. It was an unconscious move, a habitual twitch she had developed. The sweep of hair covered the eye patch she wore. I was used to the movement, but it still sent a sharp pang through my heart.

Six months ago, she stood with me in a battle against an asshole Were-lion named Leonidas. Lives had been on the line and she had gone after him and one of his gang, a Were-great white, by herself.

I got there in time to save her life, but not her eye. Where it once was she had four razor-thin scars, mementos left by Leonidas's claws.

I killed the bastard, but that didn't give Tiff her eye back.

Her hand pulled my face to hers. Soft lips touched mine with an almost electric shock. Just a brief press and then gone. Her smile twitched, voice low and breathy. "Thank you. You clean up pretty well yourself."

It was a nice compliment, but I knew better. I looked like a thug. It was the suit's fault.

Because we were out to a nice dinner with friends, I pulled out a suit I hadn't worn in over six years. It was dark gray and summer-weight. When you're my size, you wear a summer-weight suit no matter the season; winters here in the South are just too mild. Back in the day, it had set me back over five hundred dollars and had been tailored to fit.

Occult bounty hunting had made me a bit leaner in the stomach and broader in the shoulder than I had been the last time I wore it. It still fit with room for my shoulder holster and two big-bore Colt .45's.

I had taken them off a dead Yakuza assassin with a Japanese demon trapped under his skin as a tattoo.

No, I'm not kidding. Why would I make that up? I'm the one who killed him.

They were a matched set. Nickel-plated with ivory grips carved into grinning skulls. Delicate scrollwork swirled and whorled along the slide. They were pretty sweet.

What can I say? I like guns. I'm a gun guy. Go with it, it's okay.

My head was freshly shaved and my goatee slightly managed with some product Tiff had in the bathroom. It smelled like strawberries.

The suit did cover most of my tattoos. Not the ones on the backs of my hands or the ones that crawled out of my buttoned collar to spread under my jawline and across the back of my head, but most of them. Put all that together with my size and I looked like a real leg breaker.

Like I said, a thug.

Tiff began to pull away, turning back to our dinner companions. My hand snaked out, sliding along the smooth skin of her shoulder, coming to rest in the thick hair at the back of her neck. My fingers tensed slightly, pulling her back to my mouth.

Her lips parted, yielding. I pressed in, her tongue warm against mine. The sweet taste of her overwhelmed me. My head spun just a touch, making my fingers tighten in her hair. She made a little sound in her throat that vibrated up through the kiss, igniting me like a match to fuel.

"Okay, okay. You two get a room, the dessert's here."

We broke the kiss. Pulling away, I could still taste her. Dessert was going to be a disappointment now.

One long chestnut hair tangled around my finger. Shaking it off, I picked up my spoon as the waiter sat a small bowl of crème brûlée in front of me.

Looking to the couple on the other side of the table, I pointed the spoon at Larson and Kat. "All right, you two. Spill with the announcements you wanted to make after dinner."

Larson opened his mouth to speak, wavy ginger beard brushing his suit lapel. He was stopped by Kat's hand clamping on his arm.

She cut eyes at him. "Not yet. Not until after dessert."

He looked at me, shrugging in a "What are you going to do?" motion. He had filled out over the last few months, getting back to his normal weight of 140. His hair was still long, blending into a full beard like a redheaded hippie Jesus, but the weight gain had erased the dark hollows that used to rest under his eyes. He looked healthy. He looked happy.

Hell, he looked sane, which was a big improvement.

Kat rubbed his arm, affection shining in her eyes. She still had her corn-fed, midwestern, girl-next-door looks. Straightforward and simple. Even dressed up in a midnight blue evening gown, her impossibly thick honey-blond hair was pulled back in a tight ponytail.

Tiff leaned in, voice low and conspiratorial. "Now you two are just being mean." Her hand fell on my thigh under the table, palm hot through the thin material of my pants. "We're both dying to know what you have to tell us. We're betting it has something to do with a date."

Tiff and I had speculated about Kat and Larson's relationship. It was intense. Both of them had been through bad stuff, some of it together and some of it apart. I hadn't seen the two of them getting together, nobody had, but now that they were, it felt . . . inevitable. Like they had always been a couple.

Kat and Larson just grinned.

"After dessert." Kat's voice was firm. "The sooner we start the sooner we finish."

We all picked up our spoons. The crème brûlée in front of me was beautiful: caramel crust a dark roasted honey brown, with tiny bubbles of captured air marking the surface. The edge of my spoon pushed against it. It was thick, resisting the pressure. Tightening my fingers on the slim silver stem, I pushed harder. The crust split with a tiny, audible crack just like it was supposed to.

The dessert breathed out a sour, clotted stink.

It wafted up, crawling into my nose, tickling my gag reflex. The air at the table filled with it as the other desserts belched out the same rotten, sour-milk stench.

"Ugh." Kat's fingers pinched her nose shut, making her voice hum. "*That* is disgusting."

Larson pushed away from the table. His shoulders bunched, spinning his wheelchair around. "I'll be right back. I'm getting the waiter." His hands jerked harshly on the wheels of his chair, rolling him away.

Larson had lost the use of his legs almost a year ago in a battle against a hell-bitch named Appollonia and her horde of mind-controlled vampires. It was only in the last few months that he had stopped hating the chair and learned to work with it.

"That's weird." Tiff covered her dessert with the thick linen napkin from her lap. "Must have been made with a batch of spoiled cream."

From the corner of my eye, I saw a woman two tables over pull a small mirror from her purse. She held it in front of her, using it to examine a large dark spot on her cheek.

Her voice came to me as she spoke to her dinner date. "But where did it come from? I've never had a mole there."

Larson was rolling back, waiter trailing him, apologizing.

The lights blinked, flashing fever bright, flickering off and then back on.

That's when the whole world exploded.

And I had no idea it was coming until it knocked me flat on my ass.

2

My suit was ruined. Spoiled crème brûlée splattered across the front of it, clotting with dust and debris. I could feel dozens of tiny cuts littering my body. A piece of glass stuck deep in my shoulder with a cutting grind. The table had flipped over and was laying on top of me, pressing hard with weight, trying to crush me into the floor. Splinters bit my palm as I clamped on to the edge of it. My jacket ripped as I heaved and shoved, muscling my way out from under.

Tiff . . .

Scrambling, I whipped my head back and forth, searching for her. Dust and smoke filled the air. People who could move were running away from the blast. One man, bleeding from a gash in his arm that I could see bone through, smacked into me. He bounced off, stumbling away.

I kept searching.

There—laying in a tangle of skirt and wreckage. Crawling, ignoring debris that rammed and cut into my knees, I scrambled to her. She moaned as I reached her.

Dark chestnut hair was tangled across her face. A slender hand came up, sweeping it away from her good eye. "I'm okay. What's going on?"

I looked her over for injury. *Please, God, let her be okay.*

"I don't know yet. There was an explosion."

Her fingers curled around the lapel of my tattered jacket. Pulling, she sat up. My arm went behind her to help. There was a long, shallow cut on her chest running from between her breasts, across her collarbone, and up her throat. It was ragged, jagging back and forth, probably from some flying piece of debris. Dust had clotted it, there wasn't much blood, but it was already inflamed and angry. We stood up. Tiff was steady on her feet as I let go of her arm.

"You okay?"

She nodded.

I raised my voice over the chaos. "I'm going to find Kat and Larson. You find your purse."

Her purse had her gun in it. I didn't know what she was packing, but I had a feeling she would need it. This explosion wasn't a coincidence. My life didn't have coincidences in it, not since I started tangling with the supernatural.

She nodded again and I turned away to find our friends.

The floor was littered with broken furniture and broken people—a handful of them too injured to move and even more dead. We had been seated in the middle of the restaurant, which was one of the things that had saved us. There was a hole in the front of the building that you could drive a semi through. The edges sputtered with unnatural black flame that snapped and popped, sucking in light. The people who could run had gone to the back of the restaurant and out through the kitchen, leaving behind the wounded and the dead.

And me.

I spotted the table that had been beside ours. It had flipped over in the blast, tablecloth still hanging across on it. It faced away from the destruction, so the cloth was still gleaming white even though the table was charred and soot covered. Kat lay on the floor in front of it. Larson knelt beside her, feeling along her body for injuries. It looked like the table had shielded her from the worst of the explosion. Her ponytail had fallen and she was filthy, but other than that she looked perfectly normal.

Larson's hair was wild, blown to the side and singed. He had a cut on his left cheek that ran freely with blood, staining his beard dark crimson on one side. His suit jacket was scorched on one side and full of rips. The blast would have hit him from the left, knocking him sideways.

I strode to them, stepping over chunks of table, pieces of busted chairs, and bits that once were the people closer to the blast. Larson was helping Kat to her feet. "Are you two okay?"

"Nothing broken. I can't hear a damn thing out of my left ear, though." He turned his head. Blood was leaking from his ear canal in a thick trickle.

Kat reached up, turning his face back toward her. "Your eardrum is burst. It'll heal."

He nodded, making his hair fall down over the wounded ear. He stepped back and looked around the demolished restaurant.

Wait a fucking minute.

My mind chewed on what I was seeing.

Larson was standing? What. The. Hell?

A rush of something supernatural slammed into me, driving the thought out of my head by yanking the power inside me to the surface. Magick swarmed over my skin with tiny insect legs. It whipcracked across my nerves, lighting them up like a row of matches.

Since my resurrection at the hands of an Angel—yes, a real Angel of The Lord—when I first was hunting the monster that killed my family, I have been not-quite-human. I am faster, stronger, and heal quicker. Not much, but enough to keep me alive. I also have a power that lets me sense supernatural shit. It's from where the Angel gave me a transfusion of her blood, or whatever Angels use for blood. I can feel the weird and otherworldly because of it.

I hate it. It's tied to my other senses, so it comes through in jacked-up ways that are usually more distraction than information.

Right now, my power was a shark in a feeding frenzy on my senses. My mouth dried up, skin itchy with magick. No doubt about it, bad shit was coming.

Both hands went under my jacket and came out full of gun, thumbs brushing the safeties down. The Colt .45 1911 is a piece of gunsmithing genius. It shoots big ass bullets that go in the size of a dime but come out the size of saucer. They will fuck some shit up. It holds seven in a clip, eight if you carry one in the chamber.

I always have one in the chamber. Larson reached under his jacket, pulling out a Glock. The ugly, boxy semiautomatic filled his hand. Kat was removing her pistol from her purse. It was a 9mm. I know because I'm the one who gave it to her.

A touch on my arm whipped my head around. Tiff was there, a Taurus Judge in her hand.

The Judge is a big revolver that holds .410 shotgun shells. It's a bastard of a pistol that does a shit-ton of damage. It is literally a handheld shotgun. Tiff had taken to using it since losing her eye. The leeway in aiming it adjusted for the loss of parallax she suffered.

She leaned in close to me. "What's coming?"

"Don't know." I turned to the hole in the wall. "But it's going to be bad."

The words were barely out of my mouth when a woman stepped through the wreckage and into the restaurant.

She stood, prim and proper, just inside the charred ring

of the blast radius. Slowly, she pulled a pair of thin lace gloves off two chubby hands, tucking them into a small purse that hung at her elbow. It snapped shut with a click. Clasping her hands together, she settled herself with a shake of fleshy shoulders, raised her chin, and began to look around the carnage before her.

She was covered head to toe in a dress that would be dour if it wasn't made of a brilliant pthalo green fabric that shimmered in the uncertain light. It was the same iridescent color as the underside of a peacock feather. Full skirts surrounded her legs, concealing them under layers of lace and crinoline. Her top was covered with a matching waistcoat that pinched a generous middle, held together by a row of tiny ebony buttons running waist to throat in a wavy line. The sleeves were tight on her arms, stuffed in like pillows, and went from puffy shoulders to puffy wrists. A silver pentagram the size of a baby's head hung on a braid around her neck, a snarling goat head glaring out from it in satanic glee.

Her hair was pulled back into a severe bun that revealed a severe face. It was a face made for correcting schoolchildren, a face where every feature was a harsh slash on a canvas. The only thing that tilted that face from sour to interesting was a pair of poison green eyes burning with fierceness.

Two figures moved through the settling dust to stand next to her.

One was a thin blade of a man in a black cassock. Wiry hair, dark as coal, hung shaggy around his head, blending into a thick, gnarled beard. His nose hooked out between deep-set eyes. They glittered like black diamonds beneath two wide stripes of eyebrow. His fingers were covered in armor styled jewelry, jutting out wickedly in points and barbs like the claws of a wild animal. A matching pentagram to the one the woman wore, goat head and all, hung under his beard, starkly bright against the black of his overcoat.

He stood next to her, seething, shoulders rising and falling, metal claws clicking at the end of his hands. He stomped the ground with jackbooted feet, shuffling to and fro in feral agitation. His head jerked to the side, watching as the other figure sauntered up to join them.

It was a young girl. Wild, tall, and lanky, she was all long limbs and hard angles. She looked like someone had stretched her into her near six-foot height. Long hair whipped around her like a blood-red briar save for one white streak as wide as my wrist that cut through from the side of her forehead. Her face was a younger, thinner version of the lady in green, set with the same poisonous eyes. I would bet they were related.

She twisted and swayed as she moved to join her companions. Where her companions were covered nearly head to toe in clothing, this one was almost nude. Harsh angles of hipbones jutted over the waist of red leather pants so shredded they were indecent. A pentagram like the one the others had also sat on her chest, but it was lashed over nonexistent breasts with buckled straps of leather.

As she joined them, the lady in green lifted her skirts and began to walk toward us, one dainty foot in front of the other. Her voice was sharp as broken porcelain, with a clipped British accent as she spoke.

"I am Selene. We are the Wrath of Baphomet. Give us the blood or we will slaughter you and everyone who is still alive."

3

I pointed the Colt in my right hand at the witch, lining the sights up on her face. "Stop walking or I start shooting."

She drew up in a swish of skirts. Chubby hands flashed out to her sides, stopping the other two one step behind her.

"That's better. Now what the hell do you want?"

Selene cocked her head at me, one thin eyebrow arching over a poison eye. "We want the blood."

"I don't know what that means." I brought the other semiautomatic up, both pointed at her face. Tiff, Larson, and Kat raised their guns also. The three witches were covered with enough firepower to kill twenty people.

My voice pushed out through clenched teeth. "All right, Scary Poppins, you've got about three seconds to explain yourself before shit gets deadly up in here."

The warlock pushed forward, raising a steel-taloned finger and pointing it at me. His snarled voice was deeply accented with something Middle Eastern, grinding from his throat like his larynx had been crushed. "We do not have to explain anything to you. Kneel before us and beg forgiveness for your insolence."

I barked a laugh at him. "Insolence? This isn't insolence,

you asshat. Insolence might be when I stick my foot up your ass."

Ebony magick crackled from his eye sockets, olive skin flushing dark. "You DARE to insult me?"

He stepped forward, fingers weaving in arcane twists. Magick began to swell in the air, pressing against my skin. My fingers tightened on the triggers of my guns.

The skanky witch giggled, long, thin fingers waving over her lips. Blood-red hair fell across her eyes. She looked out through the white streak. "Oh, Ahriman, relax. You don't have to go apeshit over every little thing." Twirling, she danced over to him, hips leading the rest of her body. "They have no choice but to do what we want; they just don't realize it."

Snarling, the warlock jerked away from her touch. "Do not act familiar with me, Athame. I am in no mood for your games. You would do well to remember your place as third of our circle."

Athame pouted. "And you would do well to remember that you're not the boss of me." She spun on a bare foot, whipping her long hair around, hitting the warlock. She spoke to the witch in the green dress. "Isn't that right, Mom?"

Selene's tone was sharp as a knife. "The two of you be quiet and return to task."

Athame stuck her tongue out at Ahriman as she sauntered over to stand beside Selene. The dark warlock glowered. He stepped closer to the two witches with a stomp of a booted heel.

I looked at them. "Y'all done squabbling?"

Selene nodded.

"Good."

Thunder rolled as I pulled the triggers.

4

Bullets unleashed in a hail of destruction as the others joined me. The air filled with noise and the sticky-sweet smoke of spent gunpowder. We pulled triggers, slinging bullets at the witches. They all jerked and twitched under the rain of silver-jacketed lead. The warlock fell backward, hitting the floor hard. The two witches danced under the impact of the bullets. The slides locked back on my guns.

It was over in seconds.

Automatically I reloaded. Gun under arm, swipe eject button, drop spent clip, pull spare, slam it home, hit the slide release, strip a new bullet into the chamber. Cocked, locked, and ready to rock. Repeat.

It took less time to do than it did to tell.

"Well, that was easy," Larson said, replacing the clip in his Glock.

Tiff pushed the last new shell into the cylinder of the Taurus Judge. A twist of her wrist snapped it closed. "It's never *that* easy."

Magick brushed against my power like sandpaper to a match head.

My hands tightened on the grips of my guns. "Yeah, let's not break our arms patting ourselves on the back just yet."

The first one to move was the warlock. He rose, hinging back to his feet like he was hauled up on wires. Splattered silver and lead fell from his chest, tumbling down his clothes, clinking together on the floor at his feet. Steel-taloned fingers brushed through his wiry beard, pulling out bits of bullets.

The two witches rose together, shedding spent bullets that had splattered against them. The young one picked a piece of shrapnel from her teeth, using her tongue to dislodge it. She spat it on the ground. Selene simply shook out her skirts and tucked one stray strand of hair back behind her ear.

Shit.

"Did you think we came here unprepared Deacon Chalk? We are charmed against your silver. Now give us the Blood of the Trinity."

Double shit.

Blood of the Trinity? My mind clicked. They must be here for me. After my blood, or more specifically, the Angel blood that ran in my veins. It didn't matter what they wanted it for. Witches after your blood is a never a good thing.

I shook my head. "Piss off, lady. No blood for you."

Selene turned to the dark warlock. "Ahriman? You may begin."

The warlock reached under the edge of his cassock, pulling out a glass bottle. The steel talon jewelry on his fingers clinked against the glass as he pulled the stopper from it. The liquid inside was thick, lumpy, and curdled like milk left to sit out for a few days.

He turned it up, pouring the foul-looking liquid into his mouth. It splashed on his lips, sticking in his mustache and beard. Swiping the back of his hand across his mouth, he threw away the bottle. It arced up, spinning through the air to drop and shatter on the floor.

Armored jewelry flashed as his fingers wove in intricate, arcane movements. Sodium yellow light filled his eyes, spilling out of them to cut shadows around his features. His mouth chewed words, spitting them out in a garbled language never meant for a human throat.

Kat looked over at me. "What's he doing?"

"Bad shit. Dark magick. Hold on."

My power flared, running out to meet the magick filling the air. With a spark, my mind's eye opened up and I could see the warlock's fingers kneading witchcraft together, knitting lines of corrupted sorcery into a tangle between his palms. Every syllable he spat was a clot of magick that grew the spell in his hands. It was the potion, drank, activated by chanting, and regurgitated into dark sorcery. The spell was cold and clammy against my skin. Where it brushed felt hollow. Empty. Dead.

Necromancy. Awesome, that's just awesome.

The lines of sorcery tightened into a knot of energy. With a final harsh choke, he spewed the last word and flung his hands apart. The magick flew, arcing over the destruction like flaming arrows. One by one, they each struck bodies that littered the floor. The sorcery barbed in, hooking and pulling.

Ahriman's voice was a throaty whisper, the words soft and seductive. "Come to me, my lovelies. Rise. Rise and bring me the skins of my enemy."

The dead got up, ignoring their broken bodies. The ones whole enough to stand began shuffling toward us, ruptured skin flapping around gaping holes. They shambled, dead throats beginning the forlorn moan of the walking dead.

Zombies. I hate it when it's zombies.

They were all around and closing in. Between the rattling

moans was the clacking of teeth as they began biting the air in anticipation of gnawing on human flesh. My human flesh.

I counted quickly in my head. Twelve. There were twelve zombies now between us and the witches.

"What do we do?" Larson's voice had a high-pitched, brittle edge to it. I looked over. He was waving his gun around from zombie to zombie. Kat and Tiff both still had their weapons aimed at the witches, waiting on me.

I yelled at him, "Pull it together!" There wasn't time for him to lose his shit. The zombies were spread all over the front of the restaurant and coming our way.

Zombies are slow. They shuffle and shamble and drag their feet, but they are damn near unstoppable. They feel no pain. They do not get tired. They are relentless. Inexorable. The only cure for zombie-ism is to destroy the brain. They function off the cerebellum and the brainstem, which control motor functions. Destroying this part of the brain stops any kind of walking dead. Zombie, ghoul, draugr, mummy, or a wraith; it doesn't matter. Scramble the brains and the walking dead become the non-walking dead. Even ones raised by witchcraft.

I stepped around the table, rolling my shoulders to loosen them. "Stay behind me. If the witches so much as twitch a finger, you blast them. It may not kill them, but it has to hurt." I saw Tiff nod out the corner of my eye. Larson trained his Glock back on the witches. "Don't screw up and shoot me, or I'll be pissed." He knew I was talking to him. He was better than when I first met him but was still the least proven shooter.

And why the hell is he able to stand?

I pushed the thought away. First things first. Flesh-eating zombies and bloodthirsty witches before paraplegic-who-suddenly-has-the-ability-to-walk. My mind closed down, shutting off all extraneous thought. It shifted, tunneling into that soft, peaceful place that lets me do a lot of violence. The place that lets me kill. Everything falls away, becomes distant, and the only things I see are the things that need killing. My hearing went fuzzy in the staticky silence of my head.

Fourteen bullets. Twelve zombies.

Let's do this.

Pushing off, I crossed the floor. The first zombie met me midway. It was a young man dressed in a nice suit. The blast had ripped away both of his arms. He lunged at me, mouth clamping open and shut, zoom whitened teeth clacking together. The human mouth is deadly. Hinged by one of the strongest muscles in the body, it can sever flesh and break bone, especially when driven by an undead hunger for human flesh.

I shoved the Colt into his face and pulled the trigger. The .45-caliber bullet punched him just under his nose, tumbling out the back of his head in a shower of blood and brains. The body dropped to the floor like a rock.

I stepped over, meeting the next two zombies. They were one of those middle-aged couples who begin to look alike after being married for two decades. They were both pleasantly plump with frizzy, sandy brown hair. He wore a tie that matched her dress. They reached for me in unison. Crossing my arms, I stepped in and pulled both triggers at once. The bullets smacked them apart. They fell to each side of me. I stepped through and kept moving.

The world dimmed even more, adrenaline pulling my focus down to only the next target and nothing periphrial.

The couple with their son in his military uniform were dropped with three shots in a row. Mom and Pop had shielded their boy from as much of the blast as they could. Both of them were shredded by shrapnel, pink flesh screaming out against dark chocolate skin. The son was unmarked except for a wide gash across his throat that had leaked red over neat, crisp Marine dress blues.

They hit the floor. I kept moving.

Three frat boys, underdressed for the restaurant, stumbled over each other. The blast had turned two of them into charred briquettes. Skin black and cracking, they bookended their friend whose stomach was just a big gory hole I could see spine through. They dropped one after the other in a secession of shots.

The slide locked back on the gun in my right hand. Empty. I shoved it into the holster, slide hot through the leather, and switched the other Colt over to my right hand. Something bumped into my back.

Jerking around, I saw there were two zombies. Both of them were old and tiny bodies hunched from age. They scrabbled at me with thin fingers covered in loose, papery skin and liver spots. The blast had ravaged them, both missing more flesh than they had left. They were sad and pathetic, trying to eat my flesh even though the blast had also knocked both their mouths empty of dentures.

I took a deep breath and put them both down.

As they dropped I looked around for the last zombie. I was spinning on my foot when he slammed into me, riding me to the ground.

The world snapped open with a rush. The slow ballet of adrenaline broke as I was driven into the floor. *Hard.* I heard someone shout my name but couldn't tell who it was. This zombie was fast, grabbing me in a frenzy of undead strength. Fast zombies suck. The Colt clattered out of my grip. My hands pressed against the zombie's face, holding back snapping teeth. It pushed hard against my palms, beating my shoulders into the hard floor. The glass shard throbbed deep in my shoulder, an excruciating jolt that pulled my head sideways with cramped muscle. Pain shocked down in my joint; an explosion of fire-edged agony.

The zombie had lost the skin on the right side of its body and face. It was scrubbed away like road rash. What skin was left prickled my palm with embedded shrapnel. He was a big son of a bitch, a bodybuilder, thick with muscle and heavy with mass. I held him back, but just barely. My arm was weak and getting weaker each second that went by. The piece of glass ground in my shoulder, sapping my strength. Chomping teeth pressed closer and closer to my throat. Bloody saliva spattered hot on my face.

I bucked, feet scrabbling on the floor. My heel struck something, one of the walking dead I had dropped a second ago. It caught, giving me the leverage I needed to flip the big-ass zombie over. We rolled until I was sitting on its chest, hands still on its face. Leaning hard on my arm, I pinned it to the floor. The Colt lay a foot away. Snatching it up with numb fingers, I stuck the barrel between chomping teeth. Enamel cracked on nickel-plated steel as the mindless dead thing kept biting down. The head bucked once under my hand as I pulled the trigger.

The warlock began screaming. I stood shakily to my feet. His voice was the howl of a wild animal.

Selene spoke over him. "You did well."

I fought not to sway on my feet. My upper body felt sticky, covered in blood lost from a dozen small gashes. My shoulder was on *fire,* more blood running down my arm, soaking my shirt sleeve. Pain throbbed everywhere, pulses chasing each other through my muscles.

"That was nothing." I waved my hand. "You should turn around now and get the hell out of here before I really show you what I can do."

Her lips pursed. "Oh, I don't think so." She turned to the wild child witch beside her. "Athame, it's your turn."

Athame licked her lips, bright scarlet tongue slickening them in an obscene circle. Inky black magic began to pool from the corners of her eyes until they filled like liquid midnight. Her teeth lengthened into jagged enameled knives. Black horns broke the skin of her brow, curling off like those on a ram. She gave a shudder, and wide black wings opened from her back with a wet *thwap!* Her legs crooked, jointing backward as her feet transformed into black cloven hooves. A spaded tail drooped low behind her and swished between them.

Her voice was a sibilant hiss. "Oh, *goody.* I love to play."

Oh, shit.

5

Tiff moved around, coming toward me and the transformed
witch. Her gun was up, tracking the horned head. I threw my
hand up and she stopped.

"Silver bullets don't work." I knelt down and jerked up
my pants leg. My hand closed around the wire-wrapped
handle of the knife clipped inside the top of my boot. It was
a silver-coated blade, but the edges were surgical stainless
steel and razor sharp. It was a commando-style dagger with
a slim seven-inch blade, made for slitting throats or punc-
turing organs. I came up with it loose in my hand.

"That's right, your bullets don't work." Witchy lips hissed
at me. Cloven hooves clomped on the floor. Her lip snarled
as she looked at the knife in my hand. "You want to play with
sharp things? I can make that happen."

Her mouth formed a series of hisses and clicks that crawled
along my nerves. Mangled words spilled from between lips
gone black. *"Kcigam wollof ym dnammoc. Drowsluos emoc
ot ym dnah!"*

Her magick was hot against my power, sizzling inside
my skin. Black talons curled in the air. The spell rolled
down her arm in waves of crimson and ebony. Her palm

split open, a gaping and bloody wound. An onyx blade slid out, pulling free with a squelch and a shower of blood that was no longer red. Instead, it was thick and shiny, multicolored like an oil slick.

The ebony blade spilled into her hand and began to morph, growing into a full-fledged sword. Three feet of magickal midnight-black crystal, sharp on one edge, toothed on the other. The pommel sprouted wicked thorns that curled over her hand in a shiny, chitinous carapace.

"What the hell is that?"

She held the blade up in front of her face. "This is my soulsword." Her face split into a grin. "And it's going to hurt."

The demon-witch clomped toward me. She wasn't swinging her soulsword wildly through the air. No, she held it slightly out to the side, low and back. Ready to rip up and gut somebody. Somebody like me. Which meant she knew how to use the damn thing.

Great.

I started shuffling back. All I had was the knife, which meant I would have to get close. I could throw it, but that would be stupid. My eyes cast around, searching the room, looking for a better weapon.

Which is how I tripped.

My foot caught a piece of debris. I don't even know what it was—broken chair, loose brick, body part; it doesn't matter. It went under my heel and I went straight to the ground on my ass. The impact jarred through my whole body, driving air from my lungs.

I tried to bounce up, get back to my feet.

That's when Athame struck.

She drove that midnight blade deep through the center of my chest. It slid in slick and sharp. The witch behind it rushed in, pressing close, leaning her weight into it. Her eyes were wild, spinning like loose marbles of basalt. This close I could see things rippling through the inky surface, maggots under the thin skein of a cornea. Her breath was hot on my face, carrion sweet and rotten vegetable musk like compost.

Why doesn't it hurt more to have a three-foot hunk of magick blade stuck through me?

She spoke, jagged teeth clicking around the words. *"Eht tsepeed niap ouy laecnoc. Ruoy yrev luos laever!"*

I had no time to wonder what the hell she said before her spell kicked in and a jagged bolt of pain tore me in two.

6

"Hello?"

"Daddy, come home! Help us!"

"Whoa, buddy. Slow down, what's wrong?"

"There's a scary man here!" Heavy breathing from little lungs. "He's hurting Mommy!"

My heart locks up. I start running, ignoring the customer I leave half-finished.

"I'm coming. Where are you?"

"Me and Sissy are under your bed. Hurry! Mommy isn't screaming anymore, but I can hear stuff. Bad stuff."

I can't breathe. I have to run, crashing through the door.

"Hang up and call 911! I'm coming. I'm coming." In the car. Sliding around corner, overshooting the curb, driving too fast.

"I hear him. He's on the stairs. Daddy, I'm scared."

"Call 911 now! I'm coming! Hold on, buddy!"

A noise. A scream. Another noise. More screams that rise and fall, sounding hollow the farther from the phone they get.

I drive faster.

* * *

Blood. Everything has blood on it. The air is thick with it, like a humidifier has been running. Pennies laid on the fillings in your molars.

A uniformed cop runs through the door. He crashes into me, bouncing off and spinning away. Above the sounds of everyone talking I hear him throwing up over the rail of my front porch. He's splattering the azaleas. The sickly sweet smell of vomit cuts the iron tang of the blood.

A man I didn't know, Homicide Detective John Long-yard, stops me in the doorway. Past him the walls have been swept clear of all the family photos. The light blue paint is smeared with designs turning a dark, rusty red.

Just behind the coffee table that was a wedding present, I see my wife's hand. The hand I had held for the last nine years. We always laughed at the difference: mine, large and rough; hers, small and delicate. On her third finger sparkles the ring that had been worn by five generations of Chalk women.

Her hand isn't attached to her arm.

The scream claws its way up my throat, chased by a flood of stomach acid.

7

I pounded my fist into my head to clear it. Broken glass littered the floor under my fingers, tiny shards glittering in the puddle of vomit beside my hand. My ears rang like a telephone from hell, filled with a shrill sound that rolled between hot gobs of pain. The sick on the floor was spreading, moving around my hand and toward my knees.

My hands flashed to my chest, fingers looking for the hole that should have been there. My sternum felt like it had tenpenny nails driven into it but it was whole and solid. My shirt wasn't even torn. Other than the pain there was no sign I had been stabbed with a witch-sword. Sonnuvabitchin' magick. I didn't have time to think about it any more, shit was happening.

The shrill sound was someone shrieking.

"You one-eyed whore! That hurt!"

"Not charmed against an ax, are you? There's more where that came from, bitch. Just come a little closer."

Pushing off the floor shot pain through my left shoulder. Oh yeah, that piece of glass was still there, grinding inside the joint, shredding tendons and cartilage. Ignoring it, I looked up. Athame was in front of me, back turned. Wide, black wings flapped madly, and the tail that came off the base of her spine whipped in a frenzy. There was a large gash in her side that ran with oil-slick gore.

Just past her stood Tiff, holding a fire ax that dripped the same strangely colored blood.

I looked around. Selene stood where she had. She watched her witch daughter with a small smile of amusement on her lips. Ahriman stood beside her, staring wild-eyed at Tiff. Bladed fingers clicked and clacked as they flexed into and out of fists.

Searching, I found Larson and Kat. They were on the far side of the room. Larson held Kat by the arm, keeping her close. He was talking to her. I could see his mouth moving, but I couldn't hear what was being said. It didn't matter, he was keeping her out of the way.

The demon-witch in front of me took a swing at Tiff, ebony blade swishing through the air. Tiff did a quickstep back, holding the ax in front of her. The witch swiped at her three more times, driving her even farther back. Tiff swung the ax up, missing the sword that was cutting toward her. The weight of the ax slung her too far forward, just slightly off balance. It was a sign of weakness in her defense.

I had to get up.

I needed a weapon.

My hand found an unopened bottle of champagne on the floor beside the body of a young woman. The skin on one side of her body had been shredded raw from the blast. The undamaged half of her face had a smile on it, frozen in death. I picked up the bottle. It was heavy in my hand.

I rose. Shaking the bottle settled its weight in my palm, the glass cold and damp in my grip. Two big strides took me behind the witch. Her arm was up, raising her sword to strike at Tiff.

My left hand clamped on the thick edge of a wing. The glass shard screamed pain from inside my shoulder.

I told it to shut the hell up.

Swinging overhand, I smashed the thick base of the champagne bottle into the thick base of the witch's skull.

Athame howled like a captured raccoon. I held tight to her wing as she thrashed. The other wing flapped against me, stinging as it slapped my skin. Swinging back, she tried to stab me with her soulsword. I dodged to the left. The blade sang through the air where my head had been. The tip sliced into my shoulder. My head spun for a split second as memory and despair crashed into me. I was pushed back toward that night, that horrible fucking night, for just a bare moment.

The blade moved away.

Something broke inside me.

The only way I make it through a day is to keep the memory of that night pushed down. Locked away in the deepest, darkest parts of me. I hold it in a tiny cage inside of me, keeping it from breaking out and consuming my sanity. If it gets free, it will gnaw and chew away the rest of my soul.

I've spent the last five years building scar tissue over that pain, trying to deaden it, ignoring it as much as possible. This witch had come along and torn that wound open, putting me right back *there* again. Pulling all of that pain back to the surface.

But it's not just painful memories that live inside me now. No, I hold those memories, the pain of my wife and children dying at the hands of a monster, above a sea of *rage*. It bubbles and seethes deep inside me, held together by the thinnest, flimsiest dam.

That dam had smashed into a million pieces.

The bottle rose over my head. I drove it down with all my

strength, clubbing it into the side of the witch's skull. The thinnest part of the skull. The killing part.

Athame jerked. Her wing burned my palm as it slid through. I swung again, and the bottle smashed against the black horn that curled around her cheek. The glass shattered, exploding in a shower of foamy alcohol and tiny glass shards. She fell to her knees, wing slipping from my fingers. Stepping on her tail, I snatched a handful of her hair, wrapping the long red strands around my fingers. She howled a long, piercing wail. My knee drove into her back. I yanked on her hair, pulling it tight in my fist. Black talons scraped the back of my hand, but I didn't care.

I leaned in, mouth by her ear. "Quit fighting. Change back."

Her black eye rolled back to look at me. This close I could see my reflection in its squirmy, inky surface. Her voice was a hiss through clenched fangs. "Fuck you."

"No thanks."

Tiff stepped up. Her dress was ripped and filthy, hair swirled in a gnarled tangle.

The ax lifted in the air.

"He's taken." She swung the ax down, blade striking the pentagram in the center of Athame's chest. Sparks shot out as the heavy steel edge banged off it and sheared right. The cutting edge bit deep, splitting the leather bands that held it to the witch's chest. It fell away, thunking to the floor.

Athame screamed. The magick that had pressed against me snuffed out in one heartbeat. It ripped from Athame in the next. The horns on her head slipped, pulling away like they had come unglued. Thin tendrils of skin trailed as they came away. The wings shriveled like a hair in a candle flame, becoming small charcoal briquets that crumbled down her back. The tail flopped wetly onto the floor under my boot. It twitched in a widening puddle of ichor. Her feet re-formed, bones cracking and snapping loudly.

Strands of long red hair stuck to my hand as she fell away from me. Her skin was porcelain pale again before she hit the ground.

Tiff stepped around her. We both watched as the witch crawled toward Selene, human once more. Tiff stepped over to stand beside me.

"Where the hell did you get an ax from?"

A grin cracked her face. "It was by the kitchen. It said, 'IN CASE OF EMERGENCY BREAK GLASS.' I figured this counted." She held it out. "You want this? Damn thing weighs a ton."

Pain flexed in my shoulder, cramping the muscles of my chest and back, turning them into weak knots of pain. I couldn't feel the fingers of my left hand. Little flashes of pain cut through the exhaustion that pressed in on me. I was hurting.

Bad.

I still took the ax.

"Move back."

Tiff did what I said, stepping behind me far enough to be out of the way if I needed to swing. Athame had finished crawling to her mother. Her fingers clutched the green hem of those full skirts.

Selene looked down at her daughter. Her voice was an arctic wind. "Get up."

Athame struggled to stand, the fine muscles in her back trembling along a spine that jutted out. Crawling to her feet, she huddled over, thin arms crossing her bare chest. Her hair hung lank, covering her face. She shook like she was freezing.

Or coming off a meth addiction.

Magick will leave you like that. Burned down, hollowed out, used up.

I shook the ax at Selene and tried not to sway. "Two down. One left. You should hit the road before I make it a perfect trifecta."

The wail of sirens crawled into the restaurant, coming in from outside through the giant hole in the wall. "You hear that? That's the cops. You *don't* want to be here when they show." I pointed at Selene. "Ten dollars says your little girl there ain't charmed against shit without her talisman. So go on. Get the fuck out of here."

"We will not leave without the blood."

I took a step forward. "You want blood, lady? I'll gladly spill some of yours."

Those poison green eyes closed. She took a deep breath, holding it for a long second. The air thickened in the room. It curdled, becoming hard to draw in.

My mind screamed at me. It wanted me to turn out of the way.

Get down!

My body was too slow, too hurt, to move that quick. I turned, trying to put my body between the witch and Tiff. Selene's eyes flew open, blazing with satanic power, and she spat her spell at me with a single, guttural word.

The world went black.

8

I came back in a snap. One second I was out, the next I was wide awake.

And strapped to a stretcher.

I jerked against the straps, yanking at them. The metal gurney rattled and thumped against the inside of the ambulance. I hate waking up and finding myself tied down.

"Easy there, big fella. Easy."

Rolling my head around, I found myself face-to-face with a young man. He was a good-looking young man, thin but built. Almond-shaped brown eyes looked at me from a face carved in angles and flat planes. A razor-thin mustache sat above full lips. Most people would look silly in a mustache that narrow, but it fit the face I was looking at. He put one wide hand on my arm, it was warm through the thin latex glove.

He spun around to face me, sitting on the low bench next to the stretcher. "It's cool, man. Relax, I got you. I was just about to take out this big hunk of glass you've got stuck in your shoulder."

"Why am I strapped down?"

He looked sheepish. "That isn't my fault. I was just following orders."

"Who the hell ordered me to be strapped down?"

A monotone voice came from outside the ambulance.

"I did."

The man that stepped into my line of sight was normal. Completely and totally normal. Close-cropped sandy brown hair gelled close to his scalp. His face was unmarked; plain, but edging toward interesting. Completely clean-shaven, not one whisker to be seen. His eyes were wrapped in dark sunglasses. He was just shy of six foot, just shy of 200 pounds, and packaged in a black suit that didn't quite fit right, complete with a skinny black tie.

"And who the hell do you think you are?"

His hand whipped up, slapping open a black wallet. Inside it flashed a gold badge and a small card with the man's picture and some writing. "Special Agent Silas Heck, O.C.I.D." He whipped the badge back into his jacket just slow enough for me to see the black semiautomatic holstered at his hip.

"You got something to tell me, Special Agent Heck? Like where the hell my friends are, and why the hell you have me strapped to this damn gurney?"

He pointed to the straps and then waved to the EMT. The young man began unbuckling me.

Special Agent Heck leaned against the open doors. "Your friends are fine. They're finishing up questioning now. I had you strapped down because I didn't want you disappearing before we had a chance to chat." His voice had a hard tone to it, not quite an accent, but almost. Not so much the sound as the way he used his words.

The EMT finished unbuckling me and I sat up. My head brushed the roof of the ambulance. It took a second to realize that I felt pretty good. I still ached, but it was distant, one step removed from me. "Did you give me something?"

The EMT nodded. "Just a small shot of Demerol. It'll wear off in a few hours. You might want to be in bed before that happens."

Yeah right.

Turning to Special Agent Heck, I started to push off the gurney to leave. The EMT put his hand on my chest. He nodded toward my shoulder. "I still need to get that out."

The piece of glass was sticking out of my skin. It jutted up about three quarters of an inch and was coated in thick, tacky blood. Looking at it brought the hurt to the front of my mind. The painkiller kept it from being too bad, wrapping it in a fuzzy warm blanket, softening the edges to something almost abstract.

My fingers closed on the sticky glass.

Deep breath in.

Let it out.

Yank.

The glass slid free, slick and smooth, leaving behind a hollow ache. Blood pulsed to the surface, bubbling out of the gash. I let the shard fall from my fingers. It shattered on the metal floor of the ambulance.

Special Agent Heck pushed off the door. "Patch him up, Doc. I'll be right outside." He turned and walked away.

The EMT shook his head at me.

"You are *crazy."*

I waved my hand. "Not me. Just busy. Got shit to do." Like track down some damn witches. "So suture me up and get me moving."

"You sure you don't want to do it yourself? I can give you the stuff."

"Don't be a smartass. Nobody likes a smartass."

9

A few minutes later, I stepped out of the ambulance. My shirt had been ruined, so I was bare chested. The hole in my shoulder was tight, pulled closed by a haphazard row of sutures. They stitched in and out like the EMT was drunk when he did them.

Maybe I should have done my own.

There were people everywhere, moving in and around a wall of flashing lights. Reds and blues popped on and off, rolling around light bars attached to marked and unmarked police cars and emergency response vehicles. The people were in uniforms and plainclothes, all of them darting around the hole that had been blown in the side of the restaurant.

I had been caught in the blast and even I was a little overwhelmed at the amount of damage it had caused. The entire facade of the restaurant was scorched, bricks painted in dark streaks of charred stone. The hole was twice as tall as I am and probably ten feet across. A steady line of EMTs, police, and firefighters carried out streams of stretchers. I had apparently been out for a little bit because the stretchers held black body bags which means the injured had been removed from the scene and taken to medical attention.

Or there hadn't been any injured except us.

Special Agent Heck waved me over to the car he was standing by. Next to him was the man from my flashback. Detective John Longyard looked like he always did, dressed for a business meeting or a date. Hell, for all I knew, he could have been at either before this. Slick, wearing a tailored suit, this one was a dark color. It could have been blue or gray, impossible for me to tell in the flashing lights. His silk tie was pulled out, the knot hanging loose like it had tumbled free from his collar. It was unlike him. Normally, Detective Longyard is buttoned up tight. He turned as I walked up, flicking a cigarette butt to the ground.

Looking me over, he nodded up. "Deacon."

"John."

"Glad to see you dressed up for the occasion."

"You should give me your jacket. It's cool out tonight."

"I noticed that your nipples were hard."

"I'm just happy to see you."

Longyard flicked me off as he lit another cigarette.

Special Agent Heck looked at us both, lips pulled into a hard, unamused line. "If you two gentlemen are done screwing around, we can get to business."

I was all for that. I stood there in my tattered dress slacks wishing for a shirt, but I quit talking and waited. Longyard sucked on his cancerstick, blowing smoke out the side of his mouth. Special Agent Heck opened up a laptop that was sitting on the hood of the police cruiser. He began typing and clicking as he talked over his shoulder at me.

"Mr. Chalk, we are going to skip the part of this where you play dumb and act like you don't know what happened here tonight."

"Call me Deacon, and that's nice, but I *don't* know what the hell happened here."

Special Agent Heck turned away from the computer as a screen opened. It was a wide shot of the restaurant from earlier in the evening. I stepped closer, studying the moving images. The film was black and white and crystal clear. There was no sound, but I could follow what was going on.

Hell, I should be able to, the film was of me.

There I was, with my friends, in the center of the screen. I watched as Larson wheeled away from the table. After a moment he wheeled back into the frame, just in time for the wall to explode. The image wavered and blinked, screen filling with black static for a split second.

The image popped back with startling clarity to the restaurant. The room was wrecked. Tables and chairs smashed into pieces and scattered over people who had been smashed to pieces and scattered over the floor. Special Agent Heck pushed a button on the laptop, freezing the screen.

"So what the hell is this? You can see I was just eating with some friends when the place blew to hell and back. I don't know anything." I looked at the man in the black suit with a cold eye. "You're not implying that I had anything to do with this."

Special Agent Heck kept watching the computer as he began fast forwarding. Figures zipped by in a blur. "This is the feed from the security camera inside the restaurant. It was recovered a few minutes ago. You are now the third person to see it besides Detective Longyard and myself." His finger pushed the button again. "Watch this part and then we will talk."

The images snapped back to regular speed. I was closer to the camera, my back to it. I was standing with Tiff, Kat, and Larson, guns out and in our hands. The witches were distant and fuzzy at the edge of the camera angle, but I could see Ahriman gesturing.

It was weird watching him from this angle. Disconnected. I could still remember all the stuff I felt when he was casting his spell, but none of it showed on-screen. The magick was invisible to the naked eye. He flung his hands apart. Nothing happened for a second.

Then the bodies started to rise.

My stomach clenched.

Special Agent Heck didn't say anything as we watched the film version of me step toward the risen victims. On-screen they didn't look like the walking dead. They shuffled, arms reaching out, moving in herky-jerky motions. They didn't look dead. They looked like injured people reaching out for help.

And I began to shoot them all. In the head.

It went quickly. Movie-me strode through them, dropping them with an efficiency of motion. The film painted the blood black, making it stark as it splashed around. The whole thing was over in a matter of seconds.

Movie-me stood from shooting the bodybuilder in the mouth. Special Agent Heck hit the Pause button. The screen froze as I turned toward the camera, blood and gore spattered over me, face snarled from the adrenaline of battle.

I looked like a mad-dog killer.

"Twelve," Special Agent Heck said.

I looked over, judging the distance between me and him. About an arm's length. I must have made some small movement, something that indicated what I was thinking, because he stepped back, then stepped back again. My voice was hollow in my ears, hearing screwed from the tightness of my neck. "Twelve what?"

He took another step back, hand wavering dangerously

close to his hip. Close to his gun. "Twelve bodies with bullets from your gun in them."

Tension pulled the muscles at the base of my neck tighter, like a pullstring drawn through my throat. "You don't know what is really going on here."

"That's where you are wrong, Mr. Chalk. I know *exactly* what is going on here, and that's why I am not going to arrest you if you are willing to help me."

Wait. What?

Longyard reached out, stopping before his hand actually touched me. "Hear him out, Deacon."

I looked at the detective I had known for years. He was the man who helped me keep the wall of secrecy up between monsters and humans. The man who kept me out of trouble with his fellow police officers when things got out of hand. The man who had been there at the beginning, investigating the deaths of my family. I trusted him.

At least enough to listen.

"Go ahead and talk."

The man in the black suit leaned back against the fender of the car. Crossing his arms bunched up his skinny tie. "Okay, Mr. Chalk, not only am I willing to *not* arrest you for the murder of twelve citizens, but I am prepared to not even investigate you for possible collusion in a terrorist act. In fact, if you help me, I can make all of this"—he waved a hand at the frozen computer screen—"go away."

"Look, Heck, the best thing you can do is walk away and let me handle this. You have no idea what you are dealing with."

"Three witches known as the Wrath of Baphomet blew up the side of a building that you were having dinner in." His sunglasses slid down. Watered-down brown eyes, almost the color of old paper, looked over them. "I know the who and the what, Mr. Chalk. I want your help to find out the why and the how to stop them from the next thing they have planned."

I was stunned.

Monsters are *not* public knowledge. Say the word *witch* to a regular person and they think you are talking about a woman with a mean streak. This man was standing in front of me telling me that not only did *he* know, but that the *government* knew.

The whole world tilted.

My eyes narrowed. "Who the hell did you say you were with?"

"O.C.I.D. Occult Crimes Investigation Division. We are an interjurisdictional bureau specializing in stopping supernatural terrorism on American soil." He said it with a straight face.

I turned to Longyard. "Did you know about this?"

He raised his hands, cigarette still in his mouth. "Until tonight I had never heard of O.C.I.D. He was on the scene when we arrived."

"Mr. Chalk, if I may." Special Agent Heck's hand slid into his jacket. My hand automatically jerked, going for my gun. A gun that wasn't there. Dammit. I forced it down by my side, clenching it into a fist. His hand came out holding a small cell phone.

My cell phone.

I knew it was mine by the custom cover on it. Electric blue with a picture of Muddy Waters, legendary Chicago blues singer, on the back. Tiff had gotten it for me as a present for my birthday. He held it out to me. I did not reach for it.

"I'd rather have my guns back."

"Not just yet. You should make a call first; then we can discuss what your options are."

"Who the hell do you think I should call?"

"We have a mutual friend, Mr. Chalk. You should call him. Ask his opinion of me."

"Who would that be?"

"You know him as Longinus. Call him and ask about me."

I took my phone from his hand. My fingers touched the small screen in a dance, unlocking it. I scrolled through the contacts until I found the one labeled "Spearchucker" and pushed the button. The phone began to ring on the other side and I thought back a year in time.

Longinus. I'll be damned. Holder of the Spear of Destiny, cursed with immortality by God for his part in the Crucifixion, and progenitor of vampires. He walks the earth now, seeking redemption, using the Spear to hunt vampires. I get that, atonement for your sins. It's a hard gig, but it's what some of us do.

We had gotten into some shit together a while ago dealing with Appollonia. Yes. The same hell-bitch who had cost Larson his legs. She had taken the Spear and was using it to boost her powers to control other vampires. It had been a shitstorm of a night. We had come out the other side as allies. I could trust Longinus. Which made sense because, technically, the man was a saint.

The line connected and a man's voice came on. The accent was similar to an Irish lilt but more guttural, older, the words almost chewed off. It was an accent that the man was born with over two thousand years ago somewhere in what is now England. "Deacon Chalk, what can I do for you?"

Stepping away from the other two men, I kept my voice low. "Have you ever heard of someone named Heck who works for something called the O.C.I.D.?"

The line went quiet.

After a long moment, Longinus answered, "I have."

"He said you would vouch for him."

"I *will* vouch for Agent Heck. He is a good man and will

deal honorably with you. If he tells you something, you can trust it as long as it is in his power."

"He's trying to blackmail me into helping him. That doesn't feel very fucking trustworthy to me."

Longinus chuckled. "If he just asked for your help, would you give it or would you tell him to piss off, bully on, and try to solve the problem yourself?"

I thought about it. I didn't want to work with Heck. I had a few people in this world I trusted to back me up and he wasn't one of them. Dammit. Longinus knew me well enough to know that, and apparently so did Special Agent Heck. I didn't like that. Not one bit.

Longinus chuckled again. "I see I made my point."

"Yeah, yeah, I am hard to work with. Forgive me for trying to keep people out of the line of fire." I looked over at the two men by the police cruiser. Longyard was still smoking, could have been the same cigarette or a new one, stepping from one foot to another in a little dance of agitation. Special Agent Heck leaned against the police car. I couldn't see him watch me through those sunglasses he had on, but I could *feel* it. He looked calm and collected against a backdrop of activity as policemen and rescue workers continued to work at the building.

Longinus's voice pulled me back to the conversation. "What is the problem he's trying to get your help with?"

"Witches."

"I see. Need me to come your way?"

"Immortal warrior with a holy relic as a weapon? Sure, can't hurt. Where're you at?"

"Denver. I just cleared out a kiss of vampires posing as rock musicians, draining the blood of groupies." He chuckled. "You should have heard them. They were fookin' awful onstage."

Shit. Denver was hours away by plane. "You won't make

it in time. I plan to button this up quickly so I can send Special Agent Heck on his merry way."

Longinus's voice became somber. "Deacon, you can trust him, but watch your back with anyone else from O.C.I.D. Remember what I told you before I left."

I remembered. He had warned me that there were people who knew about me and were talking about me. I was on the radar, which is not where I ever wanted to be.

No, I liked working the shadows, keeping to the edges. Staying the hell out of sight.

"I'll keep it in mind. Thanks."

"You know where to find me if you need my help."

"Same to you."

The call disappeared. The phone slipped into my pocket, I didn't offer to give it back to Special Agent Heck. It was a small victory. I still wanted my guns back.

Special Agent Heck pushed off the car. Slender hands slid deep into his pockets. "Satisfied?"

"Enough to listen to your offer."

The man in the black suit nodded. "Right now we are looking at twelve bodies with fatal gunshot wounds from your firearms and video evidence to confirm you as the shooter. I can make this inconsequential if you cooperate with my investigation into tonight's attack."

My hands clenched into fists. "I don't like being black-mailed."

"It's not blackmail as such. More a reward for your assistance."

"If you have the swing to clear the evidence, then why do you need my help?"

"That's a valid question, Mr. Chalk." His hands jingled something in his pockets, a set of keys or something. "You have to understand that I am a field agent for the O.C.I.D. I have the authority to command resources, but because of the specialized and clandestine nature of what the O.C.I.D covers, agents like myself are sparse. We make due by utilizing resources outside the agency itself. It means that I need your assistance to uncover and stop the next thing these Wrath of Baphomet people have planned."

"Why don't you use the cops?"

A smile twitched the corners of his mouth. "The same reason you don't."

I understood. The police are good at what they do, I have a lot of respect for them, but taking care of criminals is nothing like dealing with monsters. The police are simply unprepared for this level of danger. Gangbangers and bank robbers? Yes. People who could reanimate corpses and destroy buildings with a word? Not even in your dreams. That's why I worked with Longyard to keep them out of the line of fire.

Turning, I found him studiously not looking at me, eyes tracking the rescue workers still clearing the scene. "Do you have any other options for me, John?"

The homicide detective sucked on his cigarette. It took him a second to think it over. With a big sigh, he stubbed out the cancerstick and shoved his hands in his pockets. His face was sour when he looked at me. "No, dammit. I can't do anything about all this. This is too fucking much for me to sweep away. Especially after the Pinetop Motel."

The Pinetop. Sonnuvabitch.

A few months back, when I had gotten tangled up in that feud between Were-lion brothers and a bunch of other lycanthropes, things had gotten bad. Especially the night we clashed at the Pinetop Motel. Bodies had been left on the ground.

A lot of bodies.

Longyard had covered it up, spinning the investigation off to a sex-ring drug deal gone tits up. He had come to me afterward. When he showed up, he implied that his help was hanging by a thin strand and about to break.

Apparently this was the breaking point.

So the choice was go to prison for multiple homicides or help Special Agent Heck. The witches were still out there. They had power. A lot of power. And they had proved that they had no problem killing people.

EMTs rolled out the last of the covered stretchers. The black bag on it was small, probably not a whole person. They carried it over to a row of body bags stretched on the asphalt of the parking lot side by side. Gently, they lifted it up and placed it next to the others. The body bag was much smaller than the one next to it.

It was child sized.

Dammit.

"Sign me up. I'm in."

"Good call, Mr. Chalk." He turned and looked at Longyard. "Please have your medical examiner transport any casualties from tonight to the morgue, but they are to leave them unexamined. An O.C.I.D. agent will come to perform the autopsies and gather any evidence needed."

Longyard just turned and walked away.

10

I felt better. I had been able to go to my car and get a shirt. It was a black T-shirt with the words GOT BULLETS? printed in white across the front. It didn't match my slacks, but it was better than being the only shirtless person at a crime scene. That's always awkward.

I walked back over to Heck. He was still by the same car. The first responders were still working. Now we had clean-cut men and women in blue windbreakers with three-letter abbreviations in big yellow block letters on the back. FBI, GBI, ATF; there were even some DEAs and SWATs scattered in there. They scurried about, swarming the scene like ants in abbreviations. Longyard and the uniforms were in a ring around the yellow tape perimeter. A crowd had gathered, buzzing around the line of officers, holding up cell phones to take pictures and videos.

Civilians.

All the body bags were gone. They had been hustled into a white box van with the Medical Examiner's seal painted on the door. I had to admit that Special Agent Heck had been good to his word so far. It still rankled me to be put in the situation, but he was the authority on-scene. There was a wide berth between him and the activity around him. He simply stood by the police cruiser, one hand in his pocket and one holding an attaché case.

He held it out to me. "This is yours."

I took it. It was heavy. I set it on the hood of the cruiser and flipped the latches. The lid raised to reveal my guns.

Hell to the yes.

I began slipping them on, immediately feeling more comfortable with their weight hanging from my shoulders. My fingers snapped the loops of the shoulder holster around my belt. I shrugged to settle the straps in place.

"You know, Heck, we might get along okay."

He moved over to the laptop that was still open on the cruiser hood. I was still on the screen looking like a crazy-eyed killer. His fingers clicked and clacked. "You'll see your people soon, Mr. Chalk, but I have things we need to discuss first."

The screen flashed away from me and brought up a still of the warlock. Heck's finger tapped a button on the keyboard, zooming in. The dark wizard's face filled the screen, framed on each side by tangles of dark hair.

"The Wrath of Baphomet has been a low-key organization up until now. Other than the name of the coven, we know almost nothing about them. They have shown up here and there throughout history, but this is the first time that they have ever done anything to directly endanger the natural world in the modern age. This one is a new member, only a part for the last three hundred years or so. He replaced another man who disappeared."

I had known the witches were ancient before Heck confirmed it, but damn. That was a long time to be gathering witchcraft and sorcery. The first thing folks who dabble in magick do is bargain for more life. It's a thing. Why deal with dangerous, demonic shit and not ask for a longer life? Plus, new practitioners would not have anywhere near the level of power I had seen tonight. That takes years, decades of incantations, spellcasting, and bargaining to achieve.

I nodded at the screenshot of the warlock. "His name is Ahriman. Not sure of the spelling. He's a necromancer. I don't know what else he can do, but that's what he did tonight. He used a potion."

Witches store magick in things—potions, talismans, fetishes, and tools. They imbue them with sorcery and use them like batteries for spell casting. Like the Energizer Bunny, but demonic and evil.

"How do you know his name?"

"The head witch used it."

"How about what his type of magick is?"

"I felt it." He gave me a look. I shrugged, pulling the stitches in my shoulder. "That's the best I can do for an explanation. Trust me, he's a necromancer." I didn't want to get into how my power works. Maybe we were going to work together, but he hadn't earned *that*. Not by a long shot. That level of sharing requires a bigger earn in. You got to ante up big time for that and that doesn't happen on your first hand of the game.

Special Agent Heck nodded and typed in the information I had given. Fingers on the keyboard, he spoke over his shoulder. "Anything else?"

"He was pretty upset at the loss of zombies he had just made. I don't know if there's anything with that."

"He raised zombies tonight?"

"Yeah, you have the movie of me putting them down."

He didn't say anything.

My eyes narrowed. "You didn't think I was shooting humans who were alive, did you?"

"I didn't give it a high likelihood."

"I don't kill humans. I hunt monsters."

"The footage was damaged. It left the situation open to speculation."

"Fuck you and your speculation, Special Agent Heck."

He nodded and clicked keys. The screen popped with a picture of the wild-child witch. She looked crazy on-screen, frozen in a half-spoken word. Her eyes were too wide, too much white showing around the iris. "This one is a shape-shifter of some kind?"

"Yep, but not a lycanthrope." I looked over at him. "You do know about lycanthropes, right?"

"Yes, the O.C.I.D. is aware of the existence of lycan-thropes."

"Just checking. Her name is Athame. Shifts into a devil form with a sword." I remembered the dunk back into the acid bath of memories of my family. Anger smouldered under my breastbone. "The sword may or may not act like a real one, but it does hella psychic damage."

"She lost her enhanced form when Miss Bramble struck her with an ax."

"She only went back to human when her talisman was knocked off."

He typed. The screen changed again and was filled with a face that was severe despite being rounded and soft. The color of the eyes didn't show in the black-and-white video footage, but they would be electric absinthe green.

"Selene. I think her and Athame are mother and daughter."

He typed. "Any idea of her power level?"

"Off the fucking charts."

He stopped and looked up at me. "Can you be more specific?"

"No." I shrugged my shoulders, stitches pulling, snagging just a little on the cotton of my sleeve. "Look, we need to have a discussion."

Special Agent Heck turned from the laptop. Selene's severe, chubby face glared out at me from it. Heck leaned against the squad car and crossed his arms. "Go ahead, Mr. Chalk."

That was aggravating. "Call me Deacon." He nodded, so I continued. "What's the plan with these Wrath of Baphomet folks?"

"I don't understand what you are asking."

I spoke slower. "What do you plan on doing with them once we catch them? Are you going to arrest them?"

"Can you think of a jail that could hold them?"

No, I couldn't, and that was my point. If Heck planned on bringing them in and putting them away, then I wanted no part of it. These three had proved they were too powerful. They could easily do what they did to the restaurant to any prison cell. There was only one way to stop them.

"So that we are on the same page, you and I are going to hunt these witches down and stop them. Permanently."

Thin fingers pulled the dark glasses off his face. Folding them closed, he deliberately placed them inside his jacket. The eyes that stared at me were emotionless. "The Wrath of Baphomet killed thirty-two American citizens tonight and injured an additional thirty-nine. I am authorized to resolve this investigation with extreme prejudice."

I looked deep at him, weighing him out. I don't get any joy out of killing, but to protect innocent lives, I will do it and I will not regret it. Not once. If what I do, no matter how horrible or bloody it is, will save a family like the one

I lost, then it is worth it. I will walk that road. That's what life has handed me, shitty as it is, and I will step up until the day I die.

Special Agent Heck may not have the same calling, but I saw nothing in him that would hold me back when the time came to pull the trigger.

It would have to do.

"Now that we have that cleared up, you need to understand something else. I don't take orders. You want my help, then we do this my way or you can kiss my ass and we part company right now."

"Mr. Chalk, one of the things I am very good at is utilizing outside resources to get the job done. I am not going to stand in your way while you do what it is that you do best."

My eyes narrowed. "Before my dad left this shitty old world, he used to say to never trust a man with all the right answers."

"He sounds like a wise man." He stood up from the car. Both of his hands rose, palms up. "Mr. Chalk, I chose you because not only are you already involved in this case, but you are the only qualified individual other than myself to handle a situation of this magnitude. The Wrath of Baphomet doesn't make moves like this. They are quiet, staying to the supernatural, never stepping out of the shadows. Tonight they made a big, public demonstration of power. They crossed the line into our world. This has to be the beginning of something bigger. The O.C.I.D. wants them stopped without any further loss of human life." His finger stabbed at me. "You are the man most suited to facilitate that." His finger turned toward himself. "I am only here to make sure you do not fail."

I took in what he was saying. It sounded good to me. "All right, then."

Special Agent Heck nodded. He moved toward the laptop again.

I flashed my hand up at him. "Stop." He did. "I've looked at enough film for the time being. I want to see my people before we go any further."

He looked at me and his lips twitched into a humorless smile. "All of them? Or Miss Bramble in particular?" Yep, nobody likes a smartass.

11

Special Agent Heck led me over to a big square transport vehicle. It sat on the edge of the parking lot like a block of used soap. Diesel exhaust coughed from it with a burnt chemical smell. Two agents in blue windbreakers stood outside. They were cut from the same cloth, or cloned from the same pod. Medium-built twins wearing cheap suits off the same rack. Both of them straightened, snapping to attention as we walked up.

The one on the left unclasped meaty hands and let them fall to his side. He stepped forward, making it clear that he was in charge. I was underimpressed. "Can we help you?"

Special Agent Heck flashed his badge at them. "Release Miss Westman and Miss Bramble from holding."

"We're not done questioning them."

He flipped his badge closed and put it his jacket pocket. "Yes, you are."

I had to give it to Agent Heck. He had style.

The agent on the left stood for a moment, glowering at both of us. I gave him my best blank stare, feeling nothing. I don't have a problem with cops or agents, or the military. In fact, I have a lot of respect for them, but they have rules they have to hold to. In my world, those rules will get you killed.

Or worse.

So I don't have much to do with them. I work around them, playing the edges, staying on the fringe. Cops protect people from other people. I protect people from monsters.

It's the difference between day and nightmare.

After a moment of pretending like he had a choice, Lefty turned and knocked on the back of the transport. The door opened immediately. He spoke to the agent inside, who looked at us over his head, nodded, and stepped back in, closing the door.

Lefty stepped back to us. "They'll be out in a minute." He took up his position again, making a point not to look at us.

I checked my watch. There was a crack across the crystal that happened at some point during the explosion or the fight. The hands still moved, second arm sweeping around. There's a reason I wear cheap-ass Timex watches. They really do take a licking and keep on ticking.

It had been roughly two hours since the attack. I must have been out longer than it felt like. We needed to get moving. Supernatural shit moves fast. It was still early in the night, but waiting was only going to give the witches more time to gain power.

The door swept open.

Tiff stepped down. She was filthy, dirt and dust smudging her skin. Her hair had gone from tousled to tangled and sat knotted up around her head. Her dress was intact, dirty but whole. Dozens of bandages spotted her exposed skin, and I could see bruises that would darken as the night went on.

She was absolutely gorgeous.

I moved, stepping through the two agents between us. My shoulder twinged as it struck Lefty and knocked him aside. He said something that I completely ignored. Tiff stepped into my arms, slipping in close. My hands slid around her trim waist moving around to her back. The dress ended and my fingers touched smooth, supple skin. Her slender arms went up and around my neck, and I swept her up, warm girl weight filling my arms.

Some hard place inside of me loosened: a fist of stress I didn't know I had been holding inside my chest.

My face pressed near her neck. I burrowed in, lips against the soft skin of her throat. Breathing deep, I drank in the warm honeysuckle scent that was Tiff. Her arms tightened around my shoulders, cheek warm against mine. Carefully, I put her down.

Special Agent Heck, Lefty, and his partner were staring at us when I looked around. I had gotten lost in Tiff for a moment. It happens. To hell with them, they were just jealous.

Tiff looked up at me, a smile pulling up one side of her mouth. "I'm glad to see you."

"Right back atcha, kiddo."

A line appeared between her brows. "Are you okay?"

"I'm fine. You?" My hand came up. Softly, my fingers touched the fall of chestnut hair over her eye. Before I could brush it aside, she ducked her head, moving just a touch, keeping it over her eye patch.

"I'm okay. Sore, but good to go." She stepped back, fingernails trailing across my back and side. A delicious thrill chased across my skin, running along the path they took. "Do we have a plan of some kind yet?"

Pride swept up in me. Tiff had joined my life almost a year ago, forcing her way in to stand by my side. She had played by my rules, done what I said, and proved herself to be capable and reliable. But after losing her eye, she had doubled down on her training, driving herself at a punishing rate. She had burned away all the girlishness and replaced it with iron. She was still just human but had become a hell of a hunter in her own right.

I grinned down at her. "Find the bad guys and kick their ass."

"So, same plan as usual?"

"Pretty much."

The door to the transport vehicle banged open, bouncing off the outside and swinging quickly back. Kat pushed through. She was barefoot, midnight blue evening gown dragging the ground, too long without heels. A man chased right behind her.

He was short, wearing a white coat pulled tight across a paunchy stomach. Thin, graying hair spiderwebbed over a shiny scalp. He held a clipboard in his hand.

"Miss Westman, wait . . ." He was breathing hard. "I need to talk to you about your—"

Kat wheeled on him, thick blond hair cutting through the air like a whip. Her voice was tight, each word pushed through clenched teeth. "I'm. Fine. I. Understand." Her finger pointed at his birdlike chest. "We are done talking, so leave me alone." Spinning back around, she dismissed him. He reached out to touch her shoulder.

My hand clamped on his scrawny arm, jerking him up before he could touch her. He goggled at me, eyes rolling behind Coke-bottle glasses. Shaking him, I growled. "What the hell is your problem? The lady said to leave her alone."

"I . . . I . . . I . . . ah . . ." He dropped his clipboard as he stammered.

I shoved him away. He stumbled, caught himself, and stood. I pointed to the way he had come. "Piss. Off."

He straightened his coat, picked up his clipboard, and left. Turning, I saw Lefty glaring at me again. His fists were clenched and so were his teeth. I might like cops, but I damn sure didn't like him. Whatever. He could piss off, too, for all I cared.

Tiff was next to Kat. I stepped over. "What was that about? You okay?"

"I'm fine. I don't know what his problem was." She looked around me. "Where's Larson?"

Special Agent Heck spoke up for the first time.

"There's something you should all see before we talk to Mr. Larson."

12

"More video?"

Special Agent Heck looked up at me. "Be patient, Mr. Chalk. This is the most important piece of footage so far."

We were gathered together outside of a huge tent that had been set up. Blue windbreakers moved in and out of it like worker ants, carrying bags and boxes of evidence inside to be processed. They all swung wide of us after Heck flashed his badge around. Maybe I should get a badge. It sure seemed to make things easier.

Nah, I would make a lousy cop.

The screen on Heck's laptop booted up to the same footage we had watched earlier. He had jumped it ahead to the point where I had the ax and was talking to Selene. We watched as the two of us talked, mouths too small to read what was said. The film flashed white, then crackled down to somewhat normal resolution. Lines cut through the footage, but you could still see what was happening.

The only people on film who were still standing were the witches.

Movie-me was sprawled on my back three or four feet from where I had stood before the flash. Tiff lay next to me, almost parallel. Kat and Larson were on the ground, Larson's body thrown over hers in a protective motion.

Heck clicked the keys. The screen expanded and moved over to focus on them. "This is the important part."

Larson and Kat lay on the screen, unmoving. Selene stepped into the edge of the shot. She squatted next to them, full skirts mushrooming around her. Her hands opened the small purse that hung on her chubby little arm.

Special Agent Heck clicked a key on the board, zooming in. There was tiny flash as the witch took something out of the purse. She fumbled with Larson's arm, pulling it into her lap. As I watched, his sleeve was pushed up and the shiny thing in her hand was pressed against the white skin in the hollow of his elbow. Blood welled up, black in the film. It ran in thin streams across his skin as she tucked the knife back in her purse and took out a small jar. None of us spoke, watching her fill it with Larson's blood.

Son of a bitch.

It wasn't my blood they were after.

Son of a BITCH!

My mind raced, playing over what had happened in the last two hours. We had been attacked by witches. Powerful, ancient witches who killed thirty-two people to get what they were after, something called the Blood of the Trinity.

The doctors had said he would never walk again, but Larson had stood up and fought after being in a wheelchair for almost a year.

The witches had taken his blood.

Motherfucking SON of a bitch.

Special Agent Heck paused the screen, catching Selene as she stood up. The picture locked in a blur like she was a ghost. He turned and looked at me, saying nothing.

Anger burned along my veins, setting my skin on fire. My hands clenched tight. I stared at Kat. She turned her face away. Tiff stepped from her, moving closer to me. Her hand hovered over my arm, not quite touching me.

"Where is Larson?"

Special Agent Heck jerked a thumb toward the tent behind him. "In there, all the way in the back in an interrogation room."

"Take me to him." My throat was tight. "Now."

Heck nodded once and turned to lead us farther into the tent.

Son of a bitch.

13

Larson looked up as I stepped through the tent flaps and into the room. He looked like shit. His hair was a dusty, lumpy mess, like he had tried to smooth it down, but the left side was singed, curled, and burned black on the ends. The cut on his cheek had scabbed over, the skin around it red and shiny from being burnt. Dark circles surrounded his eyes, making it look like someone had punched him. Twice. He pulled his hands off the tabletop and dropped them into his lap. He was too slow. I had seen the handcuffs.

Maybe I was projecting, but he looked guilty as hell.

"What did you do?" My voice rode a bubble of fury that was lodged high in my chest, just behind the hollow of my throat.

His Adam's apple bobbed up and down under his beard. "Deacon, please . . . let me explain . . ."

The bubble burst, fury boiling over. "What the FUCK did you do?"

"Hold on, Deacon. I can . . ."

My hands clamped on the table in front of him. It was a folding table, pressboard and aluminum. I threw it aside, flipping it away to thwap against the canvas wall of the room.

The barrel of my gun pressed against his forehead, safety off.

Kat behind me. "Deacon, don't! He—"

"Kat, shut up." Tiff's voice was deadly as a razor blade.

Special Agent Heck stayed silent.

Larson's eyes looked at me. They were huge in the dark hollows around them. The cornflower blue of his irises were fever bright, pulled inward, trying to see the gun against his head.

Calm washed over me, my mind dissociating, going to that place that lets me pull the trigger. Everything became distant, disconnected and fuzzy, except for the gun in my hand and the head it was pressed against.

"You have exactly one second to explain what you did that brought this shit down on our heads. Tell me *why* the witches wanted your blood." The gun barrel pressed harder as I leaned in. "Tell me why you can walk now."

He blinked, eyelashes slapping down and sweeping up. He swallowed. "I healed myself."

"How?"

He swallowed again, eyes cutting away. "With magick."

Memory flared to life in my head of the last time I'd held a gun to Larson's head. I had been using my power to try and heal a Were-dog named Sophia who had been beaten nearly to death. She was refusing to change form to kick-start her metabolism because she was pregnant. The change would have healed her, but it might have made her miscarry so she was steadfastly not doing it. Larson had convinced me to use my power to try and force her lycanthropy to work without changing form.

He had tried to help. With a spell. I stopped him by putting my gun to his head.

My hand tightened on the grip of the Colt. I was fighting to keep my finger from squeezing the trigger. "You. Did. What?"

Tears puddled on the rims of his eyes. "It gets worse. I know why they want my blood." His eyes closed, the lids driving the tears out to spill down his cheeks. "It's because of Sophia's children."

Sophia's children: Josiah, Gideon, and Samson. Three mixed-breed lycanthropes—their mother a Were-dog, their father a Were-lion. Lycanthropes can't breed across type, but somehow it had happened anyway. They were being raised by their mother. Their father was dead.

I know because I killed him.

The three children were weird. They grew faster than was normal, almost one year of development for one month of living. At six months old, they looked like four-year-olds. There was always a human child, a half-Were child, and one fully in an animal form that was a strange mix of dog and lion. Always one in each form. They switched, too; shifting forms one to another. But all three forms were always present.

Larson had been monitoring their growth, keeping check on them medically since he was the lycanthrope community's doctor, or vet. He had done hours of research on them, studying the implications of what they were.

Dammit. I should have been watching him closer.

"What does this have to do with them?"

"I used their blood to heal my spine."

When the three of them were still in the womb, I had used my power to heal a friend of mine who was dying. Sophia had been in the room. My power had brushed up against the lycanthropy of her unborn children and it sent a tidal wave of healing out. It saved my friend from dying and healed the other five lycanthropes in the room who were also injured. Larson had been there. He knew what her unborn children had done.

And now he had used it to perform witchcraft.

My foot lashed out, slamming into the chair he was sitting in. Feet and arms flailing, he slammed into the canvas-covered asphalt that was the floor of the room.

I stepped over, boots on each side of him as he lay on the ground. My gun swung around, tracking for his chest. "I warned you what would happen if you started in with magick. You didn't listen." My finger tightened on the trigger. "You brought this down on your own head."

"Deacon!" Kat grabbed my arm, yanking it. "Deacon, please. I love him. Don't do this. Please don't do this." Her eyes streamed. "For me, please let him live."

I didn't look at her. I could see her in the corner of my vision. Kat. I loved her. She was family. I had rescued her from a hellish situation, and she had joined my fight. She had been there, by my side, almost from the beginning. Reliable Kat. Serious business Kat. The girl who was as close to me as any woman had been since my wife, before Tiff had come along.

And she loved Larson.

I shoved my fucking gun back in its fucking holster. The leather straps dug into my shoulder, driving a surge of pain through it. I welcomed it. The pain drove the anger, firing it across my nerves like lightning.

Looking down, I didn't keep the fury out of my voice. "Get up. You are going to help me stop this thing you started. Then me and you are going to have a serious talk."

I stepped away as Kat bent to help him to his feet.

"And if you pull *any* more magick shit, I *will* put a bullet right in your head."

Tiff reached out, putting her hand soft on my shoulder. She didn't say anything, just looked at me, her palm warm through the cotton of the T-shirt. Her hand was on my stitches, sending a throb of hot ache through my shoulder and back, but I didn't ask her to move it.

Special Agent Heck was watching us when I looked over at him. "What now, Mr. Chalk?"

"We can assume Selene and her crew are after Sophia's children so we find them and keep them safe. The witches are probably going to use Larson's blood in a tracking spell of some kind. We have to get there first. I hope they're at home."

Kat and Larson stepped up beside us. Larson stayed on the other side of her, out of reach. He didn't have to take the precaution. He was safe. As long as he didn't screw up again I wouldn't touch him. "Kat, get the number and track Sophia down. Tiff, call the club and give Father Mulcahy a heads-up as to what is going on."

"On it." Tiff turned, pulling her phone out of her purse. Kat took hers out of Larson's pocket.

Special Agent Heck stepped up. "Anything you want me to do?"

"Send any information you have on this Wrath of Baphomet to the e-mail on this Web site." I pulled a card out of my wallet and handed it over. It was a black business card. The front had a red-foil silhouette of a monster's head on it surrounded by a bull's-eye. On the back was my cell number and Web site. He nodded and turned away, pulling a slim steel rectangle from his inner jacket pocket. Thin fingers flipped open the lid, revealing a touchscreen. Holding it sideways, he began moving his thumbs over the surface.

Larson was watching me. I looked over. He opened his mouth to say something and then thought better of it.

Good move.

Pressure mushroomed behind my eyes, settling deep inside my skull. I looked at my watch. Almost two and a half hours had passed since the attack. I didn't know how the witches were going to go after Sophia's children, but I had to assume the worst.

They had a big head start on us and probably weren't using modern transportation. When someone starts bargaining their soul and their humanity away for power, they tend to rely on magick for everything. That's the weakness they have, no matter how much power they gathered. Sometimes they don't even think of modern technology. Hell, sometimes witches even rode on brooms.

But they had used a LOT of power tonight, and magick isn't unlimited. That's why witches store it in objects to use. That's why magick has ritual and sacrifice attached to it. There is a cost. You can't just whip it up from thin air. Witches have to put effort into their spells, bargaining with demonic forces for power. Selling their souls on the installment plan.

That's why there is no "good" magick. No white witches like in the fairy tales. Magick corrupts, tainting and corroding away any goodness. It always goes wrong. Always.

I looked over at Larson. His eyes slid away from mine like he could read my mind.

Tiff broke my gaze. "Father Mulcahy is closing the club. I told him what we were dealing with. He said he would get ready for our next call."

"Good. Thank you."

She gave me a little smile. Even with all that was going on, it was hard to tear my eyes away from it. I loved that little smile. It wasn't the smile she gave to everybody else, the one that lit her face and made her shine. No, this one was smaller. Softer. This one was a little bit crooked and made her eye go soft. It was warm affection mixed with a bit of something lustful. It was a smile she gave only to me.

Kat broke our connection with a gasp. Both of us looked

over. She was holding her phone to her ear, the lines of her face drawn tight. Eyebrows creased, mouth forming an O of horror, white showing all the way around her irises.

The pressure in my skull doubled.

She had to swallow before she spoke. "It's Sophia. She and the kids aren't home."

"Where are they?"

"At the movies. By the mall."

Realization hit me like a hammer. It was Friday night. There was a new blockbuster starring a team of misfit super-heroes, a hot new romantic comedy led by the biggest celebrity couple the tabloids had ever loved, and the newest installment of a huge children's franchise that had an actual story.

The movie theater would be swarming with people.

My mind flashed to the line of body bags that Selene and her crew had left behind.

Jesus, Mary, and Joseph. It would be a bloodbath.

14

The Comet screamed down the highway, tires ripping at the asphalt, engine roaring out into the night. We started out with a police escort to move traffic, but once we hit the highway, I pushed the pedal to the metal and left it shrinking in the rearview mirror. Government issue can't compete with NASCAR level hotrodding on good old American Muscle-car. Tiff sat next to me. Her fingers moved methodically, stripping silver bullets out of magazines and replacing them with lead. Head down, hair fallen, intent on her task.

Special Agent Heck sat in the back holding on to the edge of his seat. He still had the same bland look on his face, but his mouth was so tense I could see the muscles bunch along his jawbone. My eyes flicked down to the speedometer. I guess he wasn't comfortable driving 140 miles an hour down the highway at night.

Jerking the chain-link steering wheel to the right whipped us around an SUV that was only doing eighty. We rocketed past and I smiled to myself. I couldn't help it. No matter what kind of bad shit we might be heading toward, there was a thrill in turning my car loose and letting her do what she was made to do.

Kat and Larson weren't with us. I sent them to Polecats, the club I own and use as a base of operations. We needed the room to hold Sophia and her babies, and I wanted them to go ahead and start researching the Wrath of Baphomet.

Special Agent Heck leaned up. His fingers creased the leather of the seat back, knuckles white. I reached over, turning down the stereo. AC/DC's *Back in Black* dropped to a level we could talk over.

"Mr. Chalk, do you have a plan I should know about?"

"Hopefully we're going to pull up to the front of the theater before the witches arrive. Sophia and the kids will come out, get in the car, and we'll whisk them off to safety."

"And what chance do you give that of happening?"

"Given my luck, about two percent."

Tiff snorted. "You do have shit for luck with this stuff."

"Hey! Watch it. I can let you out here." My grin matched hers.

"Don't be mad at me for pointing out your unlucky nature."

"I get lucky plenty."

"That's my good luck, not yours."

"Ahhhhh, glad you straightened that out."

"So to speak."

Dirty-minded girl.

Special Agent Heck cleared his throat. "Back to the topic at hand, what is the plan if the Wrath of Baphomet is on the scene when we arrive?"

I looked at him in the rearview mirror, taking my eyes off the road. "Then it's *The Guns of Navarone* time and we go *Apocalypse Now* on their asses."

"What about the civilians?"

"No, not them. We don't shoot civilians." He gave me a

sour look as I flipped the blinker and touched the brake, slowing for our exit. The Comet growled in protest, exhaust popping as the speedometer needle swung up and around toward the lower numbers on the dial. "We get Sophia and her kids and get gone. The witches want her, so they'll follow, taking them away from innocents. We do everything we can to minimize collateral damage, but stopping Selene and her funky bunch are the best way to do that."

Tiff slapped a freshly loaded clip into one of my Colts. Jacking the slide slipped a bullet into the chamber. Locked and loaded.

"Looks like it's *Guns of Navarone* time." She pointed out her window as we zipped down the off ramp.

The mall shone like a beacon. All the lights surrounding it blared out, enveloping it in a halo. Thick black smoke billowed, churning up to disappear into the night sky behind it.

Right where the movie theater was.

15

A teenaged girl slammed into the hood of the Comet with a swirl of brown hair and pink skirts. She had been looking behind her and ran headlong into the front of the car. Bouncing back up, she shook herself, turned, and ran away.

We were on the street. The multiplex sat below us in a depression. Chaos reigned. People ran from the theater in streams, pouring out of exits on each side. Men, women, and children scurried in herds of panicked humanity. Some of them had reached their cars and were trying to get out, get away, get gone. Both entrances into the parking lot were jammed with cars that had piled into each other. A busted ass Honda Civic had run up under a jacked-up pickup truck, both of them stuck across one opening; the other one had matching sedans, one white and one black, that had wedged against each other and the concrete marquee.

We *needed* to get down there.

"Hold on." Stomping the gas, I whipped around the Honda and the truck, tires barking as I jolted over the curb beside them. The Comet rose up for a second and then tipped forward. There was a split second where it felt like we were suspended in air, hanging in space, free-falling; then the tires slammed into grass and we were careening down an embankment. We slalomed down the hill in the blink of an eye and bounced out into the back of the parking lot. My hand hit the horn as we surged around a group of people clotted together. They bowled out of the way as we drove by. Weaving and jerking, we got to the curb in front of the theater. I slapped the gearshift in Park and threw open my door.

Here we go.

My boots hit asphalt as I stepped out of the car. My knees went weak. I grabbed the roof of the Comet to keep myself from falling back in. Magick was thick in the air, cloying and sticky. Choking. It slammed into me like a fist. The smell of struck matches dipped in spoiled milk clotted my throat, watering my eyes. Desperately I pulled in my power, shoving it deep inside. It took a second of concentration to tamp it down so I could keep moving.

Damn, these witches were powerful.

Shoving off, I moved quickly around the front of the Comet. Stepping to Tiff and Special Agent Heck, I had a moment to take in just how surreal we looked. Pandemonium was clanging all around us, people running to and fro, smoke billowing out of the doors to the movie theater, a brittle, panicked keening in the air from people screaming and alarms ringing. And here we three stood in various stages of formal wear with guns. Special Agent Heck had on his black suit and tie with a blocky plastic semiautomatic in hand; Tiff was still in that spectacular evening gown, holding a shotgun from the trunk of the Comet; and I was in the tatters of my suit, my hand full of big bore, nickel-plated Colt .45.

We were a sight to see.

"Sophia and the kids are supposed to be holed up in a

projection room if this happened. Stick together, let's find them and get them out quick."

I had wondered how Sophia and her kids had gone to a movie. The human kid she could take no problem, but the half-Were and the full-Were would be an issue. They don't look normal and don't fit in. Hell, the full-Were looks like a scary mix of a lion and a wolf. Adding in the fact that they don't hold the same form makes it impossible to take them outside the lycanthrope community.

Turns out one of Larson's patients, a Were-possum named Kenny who was sweet on Sophia, worked at the theater. He snuck them in and let them watch from the projection booth. No one was any the wiser. The kids got to see a movie, and Sophia and Kenny got to spend some time together. It was a win-win situation all the way around.

Until some ancient witches decided they need blood from the kids. Then it turned into a crowded death trap.

The doors to the theater hung askew, slammed open in a wave of stampeding humanity. They weren't designed to hold up to pressure like that and they hadn't. Tiny shards of glass crunched under my boot heel as I crossed the threshold.

The air inside was choked with smoke, everything painted with a greenish haze. The lobby was absolutely trashed. Popcorn and paper littered the floor from wall to wall. Giant displays for movies not released yet were strewn about like they had been caught in a tornado.

A wide smear of blood started on the wall next to the ladies' restroom. It wiped along the glassed-in movie posters for six or seven feet before turning sharply up, climbing the wall, and spilling onto the ceiling tiles.

It looked like a psychotic Jackson Pollock mural.

The concession counter was split in two, just cracked right down the center. One of the cola fountains spurted dark brown syrup into the air like arterial spray. The popcorn machine belched black smoke. Between the sticky sweet of cola and the acrid scent of burnt popcorn, it smelled like a carnival. In Hell.

In the center of the room was a child's sneaker. It lay on its side, pink and cute, the laces sprawled on the carpet.

I tightened my hand on my gun and started moving. Signs told me that the huge children's franchise was down the left hall in three theaters. Three choices. I crossed the lobby quickly, gun pointed forward. My eyes kept wanting to pull to the child's shoe in the center of the floor. I forced them up, but it was a struggle.

The hallway went straight for about fifteen feet, then turned left where there were more theaters. I was familiar with the layout. Tiff and I had seen *Guilty Pleasures* here a month ago. We had both liked it. Hollywood had taken some liberties and picked their Jean-Claude based on star power instead of acting, but they were spot-on in their choice to play Anita. She probably didn't agree, but I hadn't had a chance to talk to her since it had been released.

None of the signs over the theater doors had the right movie on them. That meant the one we wanted was at the end of the hall. Around the corner. Okay. Once we got Sophia and the kids, we would go through the exit that was also at the end of the hall. If my memory was right, then we would only be about twenty-feet from the Comet. Simple.

Yeah right.

Tiff and Special Agent Heck followed me as I moved quickly down the center of the hallway, the thick carpet keeping us silent.

Time pressed in on me. The longer it took us to find Sophia and the kids, the more likely it was the witches would get there first. Our only advantage was that we knew what movie they were seeing and the witches didn't. I had to hope their tracking spell wasn't very precise. We didn't have time to clear the theaters we were passing. Most of them stood closed, the doors made of wood with only a small glass window. It was surreal how quiet it was.

A woman lay in the entrance to the men's restroom in the center of the left wall. Her arms and legs were tangled together. Blood pooled under her. It had spread and was slowly wicking into the carpet at the edge of the linoleum. Eyes open, she stared at nothing. Her head lay at a weird angle, the meat of her throat torn away. Bone glistened the same blue-white tone her skin had under the florescent lights.

We kept moving.

Sounds came around the corner—quiet, wet, smacking noises. The snuffle of something eating moist food.

My chest tightened.

I stepped around the corner, gun up and at the ready.

The hallway was *littered* with bodies.

Men, women, and children lay sprawled. Every one of them had their throats torn out, blood coating them like painted-on skins.

The little girl closest to me had only one shoe. One cute pink shoe. Long black hair had been pulled into pigtails held with tiny bows that matched her one pink shoe. Blood stuck one of those pigtails to her cheek, plastering it across her jaw and mouth like a gag. It soaked her sweater, pink fabric making the blood glow brightly.

Next to her lay a young man in a theater uniform. He was still holding a broom and dustpan in his dead hands. His body was bent backward, head touching heels. From there the bodies became too tangled to tell one from the other. They lay in piles, choking the floor from wall to wall.

Midway down the hall a vampire crouched over an old man. He hugged the man's body close, hunching around it, mouth buried in the old man's throat. Blood welled around his lips, spilling out and running away. His victim shook and convulsed underneath him.

He wasn't alone.

Six other vampires held victims, engrossed in their meals, mouths buried like a starving pride of lions that had taken a herd of antelope. One by one, their heads snapped up. Fangs gleamed white in masks of gore. They rose, victims falling away like shed skin.

Ahriman stepped from the shadow of a theater door.

16

Light from the sign above the door cast down on the warlock. It cut shadows under sharp brows, his eyes glittering from pools of black. He smiled, teeth a white slash in a tangle of midnight beard. He looked like a skull.

"Kill them, my children. Do not let them pass. Drink their blood. Bring me their heads." Magick pulsed behind his words. The vampires turned, making a wall of undead flesh between us and the wizard. Stepping over and on tangled corpses, they stalked down the hall toward us.

My finger squeezed thunder out of my gun as it kicked back in my hand. Three times I pulled the trigger. Three bullets smacked into the chest of the bloodsucker nearest to me, the one who had been snacking on the old man. He shuddered to a stop as twenty-four ounces of lead punched through the meat of him. They went in with a quarter-sized hole and came out his back in a spray of chunky flesh shrapnel. The vampire looked down, jaw slung open in shock.

Then his skin closed up, sealing shut in the slow blink of an eye.

Fucking regular bullets!

I needed silver bullets for vampires. Regular bullets

hurt them, but they recover quickly. Too fucking quickly for it to do any good. Silver equalizes the damage and makes bullets work on them like they do on humans. I'd had Tiff change out my silver bullets to lead for the witches. Dammit! Sonnuvabitch! I should have known some shit like this would come up.

The vampire I shot convulsed from his feet to his head. It looked like a dance move. His mouth sprang open in a roar and he threw himself in the air toward me.

Time pulled in, shrinking around me. Adrenaline charged my nerves, jolting everything into sharp focus. The vampire flew at me, fingers transformed into talons, teeth like knives chewing the air. I ducked to the right, dropping down. He went over me, brushing along my shoulder. I hooked up as he went by, driving a punch into his stomach. My fist sank deep, pushing him over into a somersault. He crashed into the floor behind me, trash skittering away from him.

Right at Tiff's feet.

He had time to roll his eyes up before she pulled the trigger on the shotgun. It bucked in her hands, fire shooting out of the cut-down barrel. The blast took the vampire in the face. His skull became a red splat. The rest of him followed, exploding in a haze of dust and ash. Tiff racked the slide, spitting the spent shell out of the breech and sliding another one to the ready.

"Well, that worked," she said.

Yep, beheading works, whether by sword or by shotgun.

But I wouldn't be able to toss all the bloodsuckers at her feet, and that trick wouldn't work any farther away than point-blank range. The other vamps were moving toward us, slowed down by the bodies they had to step over. They would be on us in a second, and without silver bullets we were totally and completely screwed.

I needed a plan. Like right now.

Lunging forward, my hand closed on the broom held by the dead theater worker. His head lolled around like a chicken leg pulled out of its socket, dead eyes staring up at me from between his feet. His hand fell, slack and boneless, from the broom handle.

The wooden broom handle.

With a jerk, I snapped it across my knee. The wood splintered in a long, jagged point. I tossed the bristle end away, picked up my gun, and stood. I held about four feet of cheap, semi-sharp pinewood. It was the world's crappiest spear.

Or the world's longest stake.

Vampires die from stakes through the hearts. It's a holdover from their origins. Longinus, cursed by God to only be able to die at the hands of the Spear of Destiny, passed that on to his progeny. Because all vampirism comes from his original curse, it echoes with the particulars. Hates sunlight, lives off blood, and wood plus vampire heart equals dead bloodsucker.

The problem is that you can't just stick a piece of wood through somebody's sternum. No, it's just not that damn easy. The breastbone is made of thick, fibrous cartilage that's like Kevlar for the heart. Good luck getting through it with a good piece of wood, much less a busted, cheap-ass broom handle.

I had an idea.

Not a plan. I didn't have enough ass for even a half-assed plan.

"Follow my lead."

I didn't have time to see if Tiff or Heck nodded before the next vampire was on me.

He was a big bastard. You don't see a fat vampire very often, but this one was. Not just fat, but Orca fat. A pendulous belly hung low out of a shirt that was too small for him. Meaty hands reached out for me as he charged, each knuckle lost in a section of swollen finger. His arms jiggled, belly sloshing right and left with each ponderous step. Chunky blood, black in the dim lighting of the hallway, dripped off jowls, fangs sunk in a mouth made of two sets of double chins.

Time was still tight around me.

He was moving with superhuman speed, but I had all the time in the world. My gun looked huge in my fist, pointing between two swinging man udders. The first bullet punched a hole you could have stuck your thumb in and made an exit you could put your fist in. The second, third, and fourth bullets ate the edges of the entry wound, spreading it open like a blooming flower of gore. The vampire stumbled; swollen, water-balloon feet tripping over each other. I slid to the right as he dropped to his knees where I had been standing.

His back was already closing up as I twisted, driving the broom handle into the hole I had made. The pointy wood punched into the exposed heart. Dust showered me as he exploded, bouncing off the ceiling and raining down in a haze.

"Got it!" Tiff tracked up with the shotgun. "On your right!"

A vampire crouched on the wall above me, defying gravity with vampiric powers. Like a giant bloodsucking gecko, she had her feet on the ceiling and her hands on the wall, body twisted in a corkscrew. Tiny dreads of hair hung over her eyes like a veil. Greasy skin gleamed like polished teak. The blood from her victim had splashed across her face, leaving her neck clean and bare. The skin of her throat was scored with slashes that glowed faintly red. My eyes watered, the signs and sigils growing blurry as I watched.

The shotgun thundered in Tiff's hands. The blast hit the vampire in the center of her chest, peeling it apart. With a scream, she fell from the ceiling. Pivoting on my toe and pushing with my knee, I thrust the broom handle up, meeting her in the air. Her shrill scream cut off sharply with the quiet *BAMF!* Dust swirled through the air around me.

My mouth went foul with the taste of vamp ash. I didn't get it closed in time. It tasted like someone wiped their ass with a snakeskin.

Disgusting.

Special Agent Heck's voice cut across a split second before he fired his gun. "Left!" He was pointing down at the floor.

A vampire was skittering, crawling like a scorpion ready to sting. It was almost on me. An absurd rabbit fur coat twisted around its shoulders, dragging the ground. Peroxide hair poofed up with White Rain in a trailer-trash pompadour around a heavily made-up face. Thick trails of cheap mascara ran down acne-scarred cheeks, mixing with congealing blood. The same red symbols were carved in her scrawny neck.

Special Agent Heck's first bullet snapped her head back, lifting her off her hands and up to her knees. The next four grouped into a three-inch square in the center of her chest.

The broom handle slid in like a key in a keyhole.

I shook the dust off my arm.

Four down. Three to go.

Tiff stepped up on my right, Heck on my left, guns out in front of them. The vampires had stopped in a line. They stood, snarling at us, gnashing fangs together in wet chomps.

The three of them had been hobos. Tattered rags of clothing hung off them. Dirt smudged wax-pallor skin. One of them had shoes that were more duct tape than shoe leather; the other two just had the duct tape.

All of them had the same symbols cut into the filthy, whisker-stubbled skin of their throats.

I pushed my gun into its holster. "You two got your part?"

Tiff's voice came from between clenched teeth. "Hell yeah." Special Agent Heck just nodded sharply once up and then down.

My hands flexed on the broom handle, snapping it in two. "Let's do this." Pushing off, I leaped forward with a snarl of my own.

Special Agent Heck's gun cracked off four sharp reports. The homeless vampire on the left was pushed back by the impact in one jerky step. Ducking low, I shoved up with the piece of wood in my left hand, driving with my shoulder. The greasy rags that made his shirt hid the wound. The pointy end of my makeshift stake thumped to a stop on the vampire's breastbone.

I was right up on him. This close he smelled like someone had smeared him in shit. Choking back my gag reflex, I jerked my hand sideways, looking for the bullet holes before they closed up. The vamp's hand clapped on the side of my neck, dirty, broken fingernails scratching my skin. It was like a bear trap clamped on my throat. He began to pull with vampiric, superhuman strength, drawing me to his open maw. His breath stank worse than he did. A rotten, spoiled meat stink that made my eyes water. Pulling back, I fought his grip, still working the stake back and forth.

Inexorably, he drew me closer. The muscles in my back screamed as I fought. Bloody spittle misted my face. The stake slipped into a bullet hole, sinking in an inch.

Twisting my stitched-up shoulder, I shoved. The stake ground through, the resistance harsh. He exploded into dust, showering me in a sticky, gritty grime that smelled like powdered manure.

I stumbled forward, through the dust cloud. The toe of my boot clipped the torso of a dead girl who lay on the floor. Brown, almond-shaped eyes stared up at me accusingly.

You should have gotten here earlier—they said.

The loud blast of Tiff's shotgun pulled me back to the moment. I jerked my eyes up from the dead girl to see homeless vamp number two stumble to his knees. The buckshot blast had knocked a fist-sized chunk out of his shoulder and upper chest. Dim light shone through dripping gore, the skin shredded like confetti, ribs shattered into shrapnel.

The wound wasn't center chest. It was high and above the heart. I stabbed downward with the stake in my right hand, point sinking into shriveled lungs. I leaned over the bloodsucker, standing up on my toes, levering the stake in and down. The wooden point scraped along the inside of the rib cage, bumping down until it hit the heart. The vampire's head flew back, eyes thrown wide. The symbols on his throat blared crimson as he crumbled into ash, erasing as undead flesh turned gray and desiccated.

Behind me there was a flash of movement. I spun, stakes up and ready. The third vampire was on me, moving in a blur of supernatural speed. Fangs out, talons ready to tear flesh, he was a murderous undead missile moving almost too fast to see.

Tiff swung the shotgun in an arc. The butt of the gun cracked across the bloodsucker's skull, driving him to the ground. Before he could scramble up, she dropped the barrel and pulled the trigger. The shotgun bucked against her shoulder, blasting a hole in the center of the vampire's back.

Take the heart? Check.

Special Agent Heck stepped forward. His hand convulsed around the semiautomatic in his hand. Five or six bullets smashed into the vampire's skull, pulverizing the brain in a hot, pink mess.

Take the head? Check.

The vampire became a tiny sandstorm of dust, spilling across the carpet in a puddle.

I stood up. "Good job, you two."

Special Agent Heck nodded and replaced the clip in his gun.

Tiff smiled. "So I did alright?"

"You did. You can keep your job today." I laughed, tension slipping out of my shoulders.

It returned with a vengeance as Ahriman screamed out a spell.

17

Magick blasted across my skin like a hot desert wind. My lip curled in disgust, the stink of putrefaction baked in the sun rushing through the hallway. Piss yellow fog rolled up around our legs.

Spinning, I found Ahriman at the end of the hall. He stood, legs spread and arms outstretched. He was screaming, a shrill, keening sound that rose and fell, breaking into syllables an alien language.

The sound of it set my teeth on edge, grinding them together. Pain shot up my jaw and across the back of my head.

Heck covered his ears with his hands, bending at the waist, stumbling backward. Tiff's eye streamed water. She held on to the shotgun, but it drooped at the end of her arms. Her eye was shut tight against the magick boiling into the room, but the shotgun was still in her hands.

The keening grew, climbing a notch with every new syllable, brittle and shrill. Pins and needles were being driven into my eardrums. The nerve under my eye pounded like a double bass drum. Ahriman spat as he screamed out his spell, thick saliva running out of his mouth, drizzling across the front of his wiry beard. The air wavered as the spell built to a crescendo, intensifying, a fist closing around us.

I took one step toward him as the first corpse twitched.

It was a body lying just a few feet from where the warlock stood. It was a mangled, tangled wreck of a corpse, everything twisted around and in on itself. Ahriman's spell soaked into it, poison into a sponge. It herked and jerked, rising to a crawling position. Beside it another body began to push itself up, rising from the pile.

Movement swept through the carpet of corpses that littered the floor. The dead began to stand. In a few seconds there would be a wall of zombies between me and Ahriman. His spell kept growing, kept pushing against me. My skin crawled, his magick a creeping mildew across every exposed part.

The broom handle fell from my hand as I whipped out my gun. The room pulsed with magick around me, rippling reality. I was looking through air turned into a dim, shimmering screen.

Witchcraft pounded against me. More bodies pulled themselves up. Yellow spots blasted holes in my vision as I tried to draw a bead on the wizard.

I pulled the trigger as the world went dark.

The spell cut off with a choke, dropping out of the air like falling rain. The dead collapsed, puppets whose strings had been cut. Slamming into the floor, boneless as rag dolls. The carpet, soaked with their blood, *splatted* underneath them.

My vision snapped back into place with a ringing shock.

The warlock was pressed against the wall.

He stood for a second, steel-taloned hand clapped over a bleeding hole in his shoulder. His eyes were too big, white gleaming around black irises. They fluttered closed as he slumped and slid down the wall. His head lolled forward, hand dropping away to lie in his lap.

The warlock was out cold.

Getting shot will send you into shock.

Tiff stepped up, rubbing her head. "Holy shit. I thought my head was going to explode."

"You okay?"

"Yeah, the skull-splitting headache is fading."

Now that the magick was gone, so was my headache.

Special Agent Heck straightened his tie. His hand was shaking. "I really hate magick."

"I know how you feel."

"What are you going to do with Ahriman?"

"Let the sumbitch bleed out." I pulled my other gun. "We've got some more witch ass to put a boot in."

18

I knew we were in trouble the second I jerked open the door of the theater auditorium. Magick spilled out in a pink mist that grabbed my gag reflex and tried to shake it to death. I had to choke down gorge as the spoiled milk and sugarcane stench slapped me across the face.

A cacophony of sound raced around us the second I broke the seal of soundproofing by throwing the door wide: screams high-pitched and shrill, growls rumbling through the air, rolling hideous laughter that cackled out in rises and falls, the cymbal crash of a spell being cast.

Guns out, I raced down the side aisle, hugging the wall. The auditorium had stadium seating, the edge of it rising up at a sharp angle. Over it the movie was stopped, white light stuttering against the screen in retina-burning white flashes. The edge of the seating dropped away with each step, revealing the scene in the center of the stadium. Halfway down, Athame flew up in a swoop to hover in midair.

She was in full devil-lady form: curling horns; red skin; big, leathery wings beating the air in a slow, casual way. The flashing light cut her in relief from the pitch-black like a hellish disco strobe. She looked whole, like she hadn't taken a beating earlier tonight.

Dammit.

Athame's attention was in the center of the stadium seating, not on us. She hadn't seen us at all. Her head was thrown back as she laughed with satanic glee at whatever was happening out of my sight. It shook her whole body, from the tips of her curling horns to the bottoms of her hooved feet. The screeching cackle spread her flat chest wide and then contracted it in convulsive jerks of demonic humor. The pentagram was back, strapped across her chest and gleaming in the staccato light.

Staying low, I moved, sliding down the wall behind me, one short step at a time. I didn't have to try to be quiet, but movement draws attention. Carefully. One step, pause, one step, pause. One eye pinned on the devil-witch hovering in the air, one eye trying to see what she was watching.

The edge of the seating dropped slowly, one tiny inch at a time. Each small step showed me a little more.

Selene stood on the back of a row of seats. The green dress flared around her. Pudgy little hands curled into knots held in front of her like she had something in her grasp. Her mouth was open and drawing in breath.

One step, pause, one step, pause. The edge of the seats were dropping. Showing more. I could almost see what she was focused on.

One more step.

Selene's hands began to move apart. One more inch of open view. Selene spoke a word that cracked the air like a gunshot.

"Roztrhat!"

One more step and I had to watch as Selene's spell tore Kenny the Were-possum apart in a shower of gore.

19

Blood arced up as the light from the projection booth went spastic. The red fluid clicked through the air in stop-motion, rising in a wet swirl like a liquid lasso. Slick, shiny masses hung suspended as the two halves of the Were-possum fell apart, dropping to the floor in a stutter of motion. The projection light snapped into a steady stream of illumination as a howl split the night.

A dog stood in the aisle next to the spot where Kenny the Were-possum fell. Hackles up, russet fur cut down her back in a sharp ridge from skull to tail. The howl closed into a deep growl that made her entire body vibrate. Long canines gleamed. Lips pulled back into a snarl.

Sophia.

Behind her were the three kids. The half-Were crouched behind her. He was wearing a red T-shirt and a pair of blue shorts. Short fur covered his arms and legs in stripes that alternated between russet red and honey tawny. Black talons flexed at the ends of tiny fingers and toes. Long hair hung around his chubby face in a mix of colors that matched his fur. His mouth hung open, full of teeth that were too big, too sharp.

His brother stood beside him on all fours, hackles raised like his momma's. A thick mane of honey and russet fur swirled back from a leonine face that had a canine snout. A green T-shirt hugged his wide chest, the fur coming out of it striped to match his mane. Blue shorts hung around crook-shanked legs. From one of the openings a shaggy tail swished out, thick furred with a big splot on the end.

The third child was human. A blue T-shirt made his hairless arms and legs look even paler. Pudgy little fists were clenched, and his lips were pulled back in a snarl that matched the ones held by both his brothers. He stood, wide-legged, chest thrown out in challenge. His hair was the same as his brothers, hanging around his chubby face in a thick, striped shag.

All four of the family had the same pair of blazing mismatched eyes: one crystal blue, one peat-moss brown.

Selene's voice was sharp. She pointed a pudgy finger at Sophia. "Lay down, dog, or I will do to you what I just did to your defender."

Sophia answered by hunkering lower, rearing back, settling close to the ground. Low and ready to spring. A bullet in a chamber.

"Give us the Trinity, bitch." Athame swooped forward, diving toward the Were-dog. Sophia didn't move as the witch flew close, staying between the witch and her children.

Athame threw her hand out and spat a word. *"Etarenicni!"* Fire curled off taloned fingertips, scorching the air with a whoosh. Sophia leaped back in a flip. The fireball splashed the floor where she had stood, engulfing a row of theater seats that were behind the spot. The smell of burnt hair billowed up as flames singed Were-dog fur.

The witch drew back her other hand, mouth dropping to spell-speak again. Fire licked out of her palm.

I pushed off the wall behind me, moving forward, guns blazing.

20

The devil-witch jerked to the side as my bullets punched holes into her thick, leathery batwings. Canting to the left, she dropped like a stone.

Without breaking stride, I put a hand on the safety rail and vaulted over. From the corner of my eye I saw Tiff and Heck moving up behind me.

Tiff braced the shotgun on her shoulder. The black dress she wore disappeared in the darkness, making her look like a disembodied head and arms. Special Agent Heck had his gun out; the harsh light from the projection booth shined along the edges of his cheap suit, making the white shirt he wore glow.

Selene turned to face us without moving, spinning on the back of the seat she stood on. Full green skirts swirled out around her. "You!" Poison green eyes flashed. "You couldn't stop us last time; you won't stop us this time."

"You should check with your pet warlock, lady. One down, two to go."

Keeping both Colts pointed at her, I walked up the aisle, making my way toward Sophia and the kids. She had corralled them near the railing with her body, herding them down toward me.

Athame rose to her feet in a sharp unnatural movement, too fast to track. She shook her head, long blood-red hair whipping. Anger plastered across her transformed face, black lips pulled back, jagged teeth clenched, ebony eyes wide under a creased brow. Breath bellowed in and out of her as she hopped several rows of seats to land next to her mother. The light from the projection booth cut through the holes in her wings.

Magick welled up from her, mushrooming in a satanic billow. Inch-long spikes punched out of her boiled red skin, running up her arms and legs in double rows of pain. They were curved, barbed like wasp stingers. Drops of venom seeped from their needle-like tips. She pointed at me and they shook off, running like broken egg yolks across her skin. "That's twice you've hurt me. Twice! There won't be a third!"

"Wanna bet witch?"

Both trigger fingers twitched, blasting out a volley of hot lead. Tiff and Heck were a split second behind me, their guns pounding out a rhythm of death. Bullets and buck-shot flew.

Time dilated around me, clicking into focus. My eyes tracked the projectiles cutting across space toward my ene-mies. The bullets were streaks of light cutting through the stuttering light of the projector. They notched forward a click at a time. The buckshot was a gray cloud of lead tum-bling out like a jellyfish in the tide.

Athame turned away, one wing flung up like a shield. Selene didn't look at her daughter; her eyes pinned on me as she spat a word. *"Blokovat!"*

The spell whipcracked across my power. It went from nonexistent to filling the room with one word. The theater seats between me and her tore free from their moorings with a screech. They spun into the air as if flung by a child. With a bang and a clatter, they slammed together in a wall between the witches and the bullets. Lead projectiles hit the chairs in a staccato. Stuffing flew as cushions were shredded by the onslaught. The metal backing held.

My guns locked back, clips empty. Time swooshed back into place. Special Agent Heck held his gun up, slide open, too, gun just as empty. Tiff slung the shotgun over her shoulder on its strap and started helping the kids through the railing behind me.

Sophia stood beside me, hackles raised, a stripe of bristly fur along her back. Her teeth glistened in the projector light. She was staring at the wall of chairs between us and the two witches.

My hands moved, hundreds of hours of practice stripped away any thought needed, dropping the empty clips. I replaced them with my last two full ones, slipping them in like familiar lovers coming together. While I did, my mind shook out my power, tossing it around like a net.

The death stench of magick mushroomed in my nostrils, yanking on my gag reflex like a hook in a fish. My power rolled, washing up against the wall of seats, crashing against a growing bubble of demonic power. I held it against the bubble, pushing hard. It pulsed, throbbing like a raw nerve.

Whatever the witches were doing, it wasn't going to be good.

I tossed one of the Colts to Special Agent Heck. He caught it smoothly. Turning, my leg bumped Sophia, making her look up. The face was canine, but the eyes were human, one blue and one brown.

"Go. Get the kids out of here. They're after them."

Sophia nodded, the dip of her muzzle ruffling the fur along her neck. Turning, she slipped under the rail. Whipping beside her children, she gave them the quick once-over only a mother can. The sight of it flashed a memory in my head, spooling it out like razor wire.

My wife meeting the kids at the door from the school bus. Kneeling in front of them. Holding them both at arm's length while she looked them over, making sure they were both whole. Safe. Her lips parting in a small smile as she realized they were.

STOP!

Grabbing the memory, I wadded it up, shoving it deep inside my mind.

Breathe.

In through the nose and out through the mouth.

Tiff's hand touched my arm, concern in her eyes. I handed her the other Colt. She took it, leaving her hand where it was. I smiled at her and nodded. *I'm okay.*

What I said out loud was, "Take Heck, Sophia, and the boys and get to the club. Tell Father Mulcahy what's going on. Get safe. I'll make my way to you when I am done here."

Her head cocked to the side, tilting her good eye up. "What are you going to do?"

Behind me the magick in the air began to burn against my power. Not long. "Buy you some time. Now go, little girl. I'll be along shortly."

Her nails dug into my arm. The pain was sharp and immediate. Getting my attention, not trying to hurt me. She rose up on tiptoes, leaning against the railing between us. I bent down toward her. Our lips met. One warm, quick kiss, then she pulled back and turned to do her job. Gun up, she led the way down the hall toward the exit, Were-dog family in tow, Special Agent Heck bringing up the rear. They were out the door in just a second.

Tiff didn't look back.

Good girl.

I turned, put my hands together, and cracked my knuckles. They popped, releasing tension along the bones of my hands. I closed them into fists just as the magick boiled over and the wall of bullet-ridden seats collapsed.

Hells to the yeah.

Time to rock and roll.

21

I was moving when the last chair clattered to the floor. Booted feet pushing off the carpet; legs making big strides to eat the distance. Stepping up on one of the chairs, I jumped. The floor fell away in a rush as I stretched forward. My body rose. I flew at Selene in a rush, slamming into her, shoulder driving into her body.

Her skirts flapped around us as we crashed together. My body weight drove her into the seats behind her and we tumbled end over end. I fell across the seats, rolling down the incline. My arms clamped around the witch so that she took the brunt of the fall, but it still felt like I was the guest of honor at a boot party. We clanged to a stop against the handrail at the bottom.

My ribs felt like I had been beaten with baseball bats. Air had been driven from my lungs in a hard squeeze. Selene was limp in my grip. Her eyes fluttered underneath a fall of hair shaken loose from its severe bun. I pushed her off me.

My hand closed on the handrail. I had to get up. Athame was still here.

Pain flared across my back. Ignoring it, I pulled, dragging myself up. Athame swooped down on me.

"Mother!" Deadly yellow eyes cut over to me. "I will flay the flesh from your bones!"

A black taloned hand lashed out, swiping at my face. Throwing myself backward tipped me over a row of seats. Wind beat at me from her wings. I leaned back, slipping away from another razor-tipped strike. Pushing off with one leg, I twisted, snapping out my foot. Boot met jaw and the witch's head jerked back, teeth clacking against each other. I lunged forward, fingers curling around one of the horns that curved around her face. The ridges were cold and hard.

My hand clenched as I drew it back, reaching far behind me. I stretched my chest open, muscles straining to their apex.

Synapses fired, contracting muscles in a chain reaction of violence like a bullet fired from a gun. My fist crashed down like lightning, knuckles thundering against her bone-heavy brow. Pain banged into my hand. I drew back, punching her again. She screeched and thrashed in my grip.

Hot agony spiked up my side. Her talons dug into my skin, snagging and ripping. Using both hands, I shook her by the horns. Her wings *thwapped* against each other. A cloven hoof scraped across my knee, the edge of it tearing my jeans. My knee went sideways, dropping me to the floor. I shoved Athame away *hard*, bouncing her off the rail.

Magick welled up around me. Hot, sticky corruption stinging my skin. Selene rose from the floor. Her dress was twisted. Thin black threads of hair hung around her snarl-twisted, chubby face. Fury boiled out of her eyes, lighting them with witchcraft. I turned and scrambled up the seats, climbing over them to get away.

"Konzumovat!"

I clambered over the last row of seats, the only ones left from where the witches had spelled them into a shield, when her magick struck me like a bullwhip.

A giant lit match dragged across my shoulders. The

rotten-egg stench of sulfur slapped around me. Lava heat fried my skin. The sizzle of bacon filled my ears. It was my skin that was burning.

The thin cotton of my shirt wadded in my fists. I yanked at it, tearing it, trying to get it off. The heat grew sharp. My shirt was snagged, trapped by the shoulder holster that lay across it. Microseconds ticked by, feeling like hot eternity before the damned shirt tore free.

Pulling it over my head, the heat followed it. I tossed it away, eldritch green flame engulfing the shirt as it flew through the air, landing on a pile of shredded chairs.

My skin laced tight, the burn immediate and sharp. It stole my breath. I stumbled, falling. Twisting, I tried to see my enemies. Athame was in the air, blood running black down her face. Her brow was split from one horn to another. Yellow eyes glowed in the mask of blood.

Selene was rising to join her. Magick had repaired her appearance, straightening her dress and pulling her hair back into place. More fire swirled around her hands, licking into the air, growing malevolently.

Static electricity began to pop off my skin as the magick grew. Each tiny black spark was like being poked with a needle. My eyes began to water.

Athame stepped up beside her mother. Both of them thrummed with magick. The fire on Selene's hands jumped, lighting her daughter's taloned hands, engulfing them in balls of eldritch flame. The magick doubled in pressure, striking sparks that drove nails instead of needles now.

I smeared a hand across my mouth. It came away wet. I looked. My palm was coated in thin blood like watercolor. The whiskers of my goatee stunk of rusty iron. Hemoglobin and plasma thick and hardening into a crust.

Shit.

The blood ran from my nose, itching as it trickled through my goatee. It ran in hot streamers down the skin of my neck.

White light exploded from my chest.

I was blind. The world went blank and clean, my eyes robbed of sight for a long second. Blinking stuttered my vision back a little at a time. As it cleared I found the witches screaming, moving back from the light that streamed from me.

I looked down. The St. Benedict medal that always hung around my neck was painted with my blood. Holy light blasted out of it like a miniature sun gone supernova.

Holy objects glow with light around vampires. I've even seen them do it around demons, but this? This was new.

My medal had been with me since childhood. It was old before being given to me by my grandmother when my grandfather passed on. Generations of Chalk women prayed over this medal. Five priests, two bishops, and one confirmed saint, the blessed Padre Pio, had blessed it. The medal itself is a third-class relic of St. Benedict, patron saint against witchcraft.

Sometimes I can be an idiot. I should have gone for my faith first. I *knew* I was up against satanic witchcraft. I should have relied on God instead of my own power.

I stood to my feet. The holy light still cut a swath through the darkness in front of me. Both witches scurried back, past the edge of it.

My mind cast back, far back to when I was a child. Words rolled to the front of my memory, cut sharp and clear from when I was a wee boy. I opened my mouth, lips forming the prayer emblazoned from the mists of early memory. A prayer first learned with my grandmother. The prayer she first taught me at the wake for Papa.

The words fell from my lips, striking the air. A fist. A hammer. A fucking bazooka. Like they weren't spoken by me at all, even though they came from my throat. *"Crux sacra sit mihi lux! Nunquam draco sit mihi dux!"*

The words quickened, flashing lightning inside my skull. The voice of Nana Chalk translating the Latin. *The Holy Cross be my light. Let not the dragon be my guide.*

"Vade retro Satana! Nunquam suade mihi vana! Sunt mala quae libas. Ipse venena bibas!"

Begone, Satan! Do not suggest to me thy vanities! Evil are the things thou profferest. Drink thou thy own poison!

My fingers moved, tapping my forehead. *"In nomine Patris . . ."*

Touching below my heart. *"Et Filii . . ."*

Sweeping across my shoulders left to right. *"Et Spiritus Sancti."* My hand flared out toward the witches. *"Amen."*

Holy light whipped around me. The fire that danced in the hands of the witches changed, turning inward. It began to eat their clothing, chewing its way up their arms. Consuming.

Screams tore from their throats. Arms waving, they tried to shake out the fire. Satanic combustion slung off in gobbets of liquid flame, spatting down on the chairs of the theater. The flame-retardant material ignited like a match against napalm.

Acrid smoke billowed up, filling the air in an oily haze. My eyes watered, chemical-laden smoke burning across my retinas. The world blurred into green and blue flickers of diabolical flame and the white haze of the still-shining projector. I blinked rapidly.

The screams and curses of the witches were split in two by a sharp, electronic shrill. It pierced my brain, a rusty ice pick in my eardrum. Itchy pain dug into my brain.

What the fuck?

Water began to spit down on me, falling in an instant downpour. The smoke was shredded, torn apart and driven down by a sheet of stale, sour water. Water stagnant from being trapped in pipes for who knew how long. I was drenched in seconds.

Blinking away the last of the burning, I watched Selene and Athame fall from the air.

The witchfire that turned on them had guttered out. Water sluiced down their arms in runnels swirling around blisters and cracked, scorched flesh. Selene's hands were black sticks, chubbiness burned away like dross in a furnace.

Athame shook, body convulsing like she'd been dunked in a snowbank. Her skin bubbled up like plastic packing material. As the water beat down, it washed away her devil form. Horns fell from her head, shed like a torn fingernail. The spaded tail thumped to the floor, twitching at feet that had morphed, becoming thin, pale, and human.

The light from my medal dimmed, winking out to nothing.

I rolled my power out, seeking and probing the air. Queasiness roiled hot and oily in my guts, stomach lurching from the effort. My power stretched toward the witches. The swamp of magick that filled the air had been washed away, reduced to a thin aura around them. Weak. Watered down.

Realization struck me and I laughed aloud. The noise barked out of me, shaking droplets of water off my goatee. Running water.

Running water grounds magick. Not all of it, but a lot of it. There are sea witches and ocean magick, but most spells are based in earth and fire. It's why witch-finders used rivers to find out who was and who wasn't a witch during the Salem infestation.

Selene stood to her feet. The material of her dress saturated to a dark forest green. Scorch marks curved up the tattered ruins of her sleeves, blending with the dark, sodden material. Raven-wing hair had fallen, weighted by the water.

It hung over her face in a veil of black threads. Poison green eyes glowered at me.

A hand, the fingers burnt black and fragile, rose in front of her face. Her voice trembled, seething with pain and rage, as it rose to carry over falling water and screaming fire alarm. "You will pay for this. I will take from you a pound of flesh and a gallon of blood to have my vengeance."

My stomach still clenched around a molten ball of sick, head swimming just slightly with each breath. My hands clenched into fists to keep them from shaking. The skin on my back pulled tight, still burning nerve deep from the fire Selene had thrown on me. Everything felt sodden. The muscles strapped to my bones weighed a thousand wet pounds. It took everything I had to stand straight and look at the witch in her poison eye.

"Bill me, bitch." My chin tilted up, nodding toward the exit. "Get the hell out of here before I really get pissed."

Selene's charcoal hands cut a symbol into the air. A loud *BAMF!* a roil of rotten smoke, and both witches disappeared.

I collapsed into a theater seat the second they were gone.

22

Two emotions rolled around each other inside me, cutting through a cloak of pain and exhaustion. I was pissed and relieved at the same time.

The Comet sat at the curb, silver-white smoke bubbling out of her exhaust pipe in time to the rumble of the motor. The car shook just slightly as the powerful engine idled. Grass stuck out from under the bumpers in clumps, mud streaking her sides where I slalomed her down the embankment earlier.

The sight of the Comet drew me up short. My car was not supposed to be there. It was supposed to be gone, off and away, whisking Tiff and the others to safety.

The driver's side door swung open. Tiff stepped out in a swirl of long skirts, shotgun still in her hands. She looked left and right, then started moving across the sidewalk toward me. I stayed where I was, letting her come to me. She stepped up, stopped short.

My voice was choppy. "I told you to get Sophia and the kids to safety."

"Something held us up, so we waited for you."

"That's *not* what I told you to do, dammit. Do you think I'm just making this shit up as I go along?"

"Aren't you?"

"That's beside the fucking point. I wasn't in there getting my ass kicked to buy you time so you could disobey a direct order."

Her hand reached out and clamped on my arm. It was hot, the skin of her palm burning against the skin of my arm. "Don't be Mister Grumpy-face." She gave a tug. "Come see."

I let her pull me over to the car. Sophia slithered out between the front and backseat, nails *click-clacking* on concrete. She was still a dog. Her back end shook, tail wagging back and forth. She stood just shy of knee high on me, shaggy russet-colored hair in long patches on her slender frame. She sat, brown eye tilted up at me. I reached down, rubbing my fingers along her head. She leaned into it, fur silky under my calloused fingertips. I scratched behind her ear and she made that low gurgle growl of contentment that dogs make when you hit a sweet spot.

In my head, I knew Sophia was a Were-dog, but in her human form she looked completely normal, so it was weird when we interacted with her in dog form. She liked all the things dogs like humans to do—scratching behind ears, ruffling fur, petting and patting—but her mismatched eyes still held human intelligence. I shook it off and just went with it.

I straightened up, pulling my hand away. Her muzzle broke open, pink tongue lolling out.

"It's good to see you, Sophia."

One paw rose up, swiping at the air in acknowledgment. She stretched out, kneeling down, tail wagging in the air. It was a dog's way of saying thank you.

Looking up, there were three kids pressed against the back window of the Comet. Their eyes were wide, staring at me. One chubby human face, one half-Were mix of animal and human features, and one kit that was a jigsaw of canine and feline.

I cracked a smile for their benefit. The half-Were waved, the other two regarding me with the same solemn look on two completely opposite faces. I was Uncle Deacon, but since they were only six months old, I'd only seen them a few times.

They looked almost as old as my son had been when . . .

I shut my eyes.

The memory pressed *hard*, trying to break the bubble I kept it in.

Not now.

I didn't have time.

Deep breath. Push the memory down.

The sound of a car door opening pulled me back. A lifeline to a drowning man, I hauled myself to shore.

Opening my eyes, I found Special Agent Heck standing at the passenger door. He nodded at me. "Mr. Chalk."

That is still annoying.

Tiff pushed a button on the key fob in her hand. The trunk lid coughed a hollow thunk and popped up an inch or so. Her slender hand hooked the lip of the trunk lid, tendons popping as she lifted. The black metal rose up.

A duct-taped wizard lay awkwardly on the spare tire.

Ahriman.

Tape criss-crossed around his chest. Thighs and ankles wrapped in wide silver bands. His hands pressed together, wrapped in thick duct-tape mittens, covered to keep them still.

A large patch of the silver utility tape stuck to his shoulder.

It was bloody. A makeshift patch over the gunshot wound from inside.

Wiry strands of black hair from his scalp and chin were stuck in a strip of duct tape that wrapped across his mouth and around his head.

That was gonna suck for him when it was pulled off. I kept my head shaved, and it sucked the last time I'd had to pull tape off my mouth.

We had a prisoner. Now we could get information. We could find out what the witches had planned. We could make an actual plan.

Holy shit.

Tiff gave a crooked little grin and tilted her head. A sweep of chestnut hair dropped over her eye patch, hiding it from view. "See? There *was* a reason for us to still be here, so it wasn't anything to wait a few more minutes to see if you were coming out."

"You did good, little girl."

"It was Agent Heck's idea. He grabbed him on the way out."

I looked over. The O.C.I.D. man just looked back at me, face bland and impassive. I nodded, once up and then down. He did the same.

Sirens rolled through the air, coming closer.

"Is your fancy badge gonna get us out of here with Ahriman in the trunk?"

"It will as long as nobody checks the trunk."

All right. We needed to get gone before they hit the scene. I figured we had probably pushed our luck as far as we could. I looked down at the duct-taped wizard.

This close I could see his pupils were either dilated to cover his irises or they were both pitch-black. A thin ring of yellow corruption shone around them, fever bright. Stark red blood vessels laced through wide whites. Sweat beaded the dark hollows under them, forming little droplets of oily liquid that rode the edges of the duct tape.

The goat-headed pentagram gleamed dully against his black cassock.

The talisman was an object of power. My mind tripped back to Athame losing her form after losing her pentagram. Witches stored magick in an object so they could draw on it later, like a battery of satanic power.

The goat stared up at me with unblinking ruby eyes. I didn't want Ahriman drawing any satanic power off the damned thing. I didn't have time to search him fully, but leaving the talisman around his neck would be a royally dumbass move.

I try really hard not to be that dumbass.

I reached down, hand dipping toward the medallion. The last two inches of space between my fingertips and it felt like the air was made of syrup. It was thick. Sludgy. I couldn't see anything, but my fingers felt cold and sticky. Fucking magick. A staccato tingle crept under my skin, tracing along the nerves of my hand and arm. Tiny centipedes crawled under my skin. My power flared as I touched the slick metal surface of the leering goat head.

My head swam with images.

Skinless skulls coated in muscle meat and tendons. Lidless eyeballs pulling back and forth by microtendons in hollow sockets. Child-size candles made of rancid tallow rendered from human fat. The acrid stench of braided hair wicks mixing with the rich bacon smell of the candles themselves burning in my nostrils. The cold press of dead flesh. Welcoming in its lack of resistance, feeling thicker, denser, more solid than living flesh. The slippery lubrication of wet putrefaction . . .

I yanked my mind away as I tore the satanic symbol off his neck. The sensory assault stopped abruptly, leaving behind the hot taste of bile in my throat. I worked it up to my mouth and spat it out. The foulness was left behind, but the bile arced down, splattering on the ground at my feet.

I looked down at the wizard. Without a word, I slammed the trunk closed.

23

A priest smoking a cigarette was waiting as we pulled up to the front of the strip club.

This wasn't as unusual as it sounds. Polecats was my club, the good Father Mulcahy was my bartender, and he *always* had a cigarette fired up. Silver-gray smoke trailed from the side of his mouth as he limped over. I whipped the Comet by the curb, wide racing slick-back tires chirping against the concrete.

He leaned his weight over his good leg, switching the shotgun he carried over to his other shoulder. The good father loved a well-made shotgun like he loved a menthol cigarette, a cup of black coffee, or a double shot of Irish whiskey.

Or all four at once.

His free hand plucked the cancerstick from his mouth and he squinted as I stepped out of the Comet. Scar tissue masquerading as eyebrows pulled down to hang over dark eyes gotten from the Italian side of his pedigree.

His voice was whiskey smooth and honey laced, but rumbled from a deep part of his chest like a cave-in. I'd heard that voice pull tears from a hundred eyes during homily at Mass. Hell, he'd pulled tears from my eyes once or twice. Now it was edged with a bite of sarcasm. "Why is it you never have a shirt on when you come back from being out?"

"It's not my fault I live a life of excitement."

He looked past me with a grunt as Tiff slid out of the car. Sophia was out of the backseat before Tiff could pull the seat release. I watched the play of fine muscles along Tiff's arm and shoulder as she leaned the seat up for the others. Her dress was tattered, filthy from soot and dust, but it still fell open at the back, displaying the long stretch of smooth skin.

I took a step toward her, wanting nothing more than to touch the shallow valley of her spine. I knew just how it would feel, just how she would shiver as my rough fingertips skimmed toward the sway of her lower back.

I caught myself.

I settled back into being on the job as Sophia's sons boiled out of the backseat, pelted across the concrete, and flung themselves at Father Mulcahy. He dropped to one knee and gathered them into thick arms, hugging them against his wide barrel of a chest. The human child and the half-Were wrapped tiny limbs around his neck. The full-animal child slipped between them all, muzzle open in a panting laugh, tongue slurping along the priest's perpetual five o'clock shadow.

Laughter bubbled out of him. "All right, you three hooligans! Don't be so rough on an old man." Father Mulcahy tousled hair and fur as he extricated himself from the tangle of boys. Slowly, he pushed himself up to his feet, favoring his left leg.

My chest thudded closed. Realization dropped on me like a stone. Father Mulcahy was pushing sixty hard. He'd been by my side since I started down this road almost six years ago, and he had walked it before I came salong. He had a lot of scars. He was still a tough sonnuvabitch, but he had taken some big hits, suffered some big injuries, and at the end of the day, he was only human.

If I lost him . . . the man who was my spiritual father and monster-hunting mentor . . . Fuck, I didn't know what I would do.

I didn't want to think about it. That was a problem for future Deacon. Present Deacon had witches to worry about. I let out a breath I didn't know I was holding, willing my chest to ease up, and got my mind back on business.

I pushed that thought to the same place I shoved everything else I didn't deal with. Down deep. One day I might need therapy.

I never did claim to be well-adjusted.

Tiff was beside me, standing only inches away. Sophia sat in front of her. The Were-dog rolled back on her rump and kicked up a leg, scratching behind a floppy ear. The lips of her muzzle pulled back and a low-pitched purr came from her throat as she found the spot.

I looked down at the Were-dog. "Sophia, I need you human. We have to talk." She nodded her head sharply and gave a short, high-pitched yip. I looked over at Tiff. "Take Sophia and the kids inside. There should be some clothes for her to wear." Tiff nodded, chestnut tousle of hair bouncing over the eye patch it covered.

Tiff's hand fell on the side of my stomach, lightly brushing, just skimming the surface of my skin. It was a familiar touch. A delicious tickle thrilled through me. She tilted her head up, still keeping her hair over her eye patch. "I'll scrounge up some food too. Sophia will need it after changing." She stepped away, helping Sophia herd the kids into the club as Special Agent Heck moved up next to me. The three of us watched the ladies and kids go inside. The solid steel door *shooshed* shut behind them.

The moment the door closed Special Agent Heck took a step toward the priest. He shot out his hand. "Father Dominic Mulcahy? Silas Heck, it's an honor to meet you." Father Mulcahy's mitt enveloped Heck's slender hand. They shook, the Special Agent enthusiastically pumping his grip up and down. A grin split his face under the dark glasses. "I've read a lot about you."

What?

Father Mulcahy pulled his hand back. Reaching into his pocket, he pulled out a pack of Kools and his well-worn Zippo. A quick flip of his wrist opened the thin cardboard box and shook out a cancerstick. He raised it to his lips as he studied Heck. The lighter chimed open and I caught a strong whiff of gasoline before his finger flicked it to life. Orange flame licked the end of the cigarette as he worked it, pulling air in, lighting the tobacco. The cherry flared hot and bright. He slapped the Zippo closed with the same practiced motion that had opened it. Drawing in deep, he squinted at Heck, watching him carefully. His eye flicked over to me, then back at Heck. Finally, he let go the mouthful of smoke he had been holding. It trickled out, dribbling down his chin and falling softly away from his face.

"You say you're from the O.C.I.D?"

Heck nodded.

The priest's voice was hard as concrete. "I'm not going back. I'm through with you people. If you are here for that, then go back and tell Fairbanks he can kiss my Catholic ass."

I looked at the priest sharply. "Do you two know each other?"

Father Mulcahy waved his hand. "We've never met."

Special Agent Heck shook his head, grin wiped from his face. "No, we don't know each other." He pulled off his glasses, slipping them into the inner pocket of his suit. Thin brows pulled together. "I'm here to get Mr. Chalk's help on this witch situation. That is all, sir. The O.C.I.D. has a clear 'hands off' policy with you after the last time you—"

The priest cut him off. "Good. Tell them not to ever forget that. I am done with them. Fairbanks should never send anyone to contact me."

"He won't, sir. He's dead."

Father Mulcahy stopped. "When and how?"

"Four years ago. Heart attack. He went quickly."

Sadness passed through Father Mulcahy's eyes. His hand moved. Head to heart, shoulder to shoulder, the sign of the Cross. "God have mercy on his soul. I told him to stop eating so much damned fried food."

"It was a shock to everybody, sir."

"Especially to Fairbanks, I'm sure," I couldn't help chiming in. I wanted to know more about this part of Father Mulcahy's past, but we needed to get back on task. "We have shit to deal with. It'd be best if we got moving on them."

"What needs to be done, son?"

I walked over to the Comet, to the trunk. Father Mulcahy and Special Agent Heck followed me. The lock switched open with a loud click as I pushed the button on the key fob. Ahriman blinked as the light came on inside when I lifted the lid.

Father Mulcahy looked down at the wizard. He pulled on the cancerstick. "What's your plan with this one?"

"We take him inside and find out what the witches are trying to do."

"He's not going to want to talk."

"They never do."

24

Tiff held the door open. She had traded the shotgun for her Judge. It hung huge in her dainty hand. Her back pressed against the door as we carried the warlock in, Heck at his feet, me with both hands hooked under his arms. Ahriman was heavier than he looked. I had to duck walk, booted feet splaying wide to avoid stepping on the trailing tail of his cassock. His hair was wiry against my bare stomach—rough, scratchy, and annoying as piss.

The club was lit up, all the house lights turned up to maximum wattage. The bright light made everything stark, harsh shadows being cast by wooden chairs and round table-tops. Big trash cans sat here and there in the middle of the floor, full of a busy night's discarded empties and disposables. The carpet was slick, worn smooth from hundreds of feet walking through gallons of spilled drinks. I should probably have someone come out and steam-clean the damn place.

Father Mulcahy had shut down early after getting our call. When you kick out the customers of a strip club, they tend to leave a lot of trash behind. From the looks of it, the good Father had been cleaning up, probably with the help of the girls, but they weren't done. Half the club was free of debris and litter, the other half looked like a tornado had hit a trailer park.

Special Agent Heck and I walked the warlock around one of the trash cans, the yeasty smell of beer hanging over it like a fog. The stage in the center of the room was about three and a half feet high and six feet across. A ledge ran around the edge of it, broken only by three steps from the floor to the stage itself, where customers could sit with their drinks and their dollars. At each end a forearm thick brass pole gleamed from stage to ceiling.

Hoisting the wizard up, we dropped him on the wooden stage. His head made a hollow melon *thunk* against the boards.

Oops.

I turned to Father Mulcahy, digging in my pocket for the heavy thing I had there. I handed him a rag I used to check the oil in the Comet; it was wrapped around the goat's head medallion. My fingers tingled just from handling the damned thing.

"That's the symbol of his power, but be careful with him. Don't cut him free 'til you have him chained to one of these poles. And keep him gagged until we're ready to question him."

The priest flipped open a corner of the rag. The goat head leered up off the pentagram. He cursed and flipped the oily rag back over it.

Tiff spoke up. "Do you recognize it?"

He nodded, crossing himself. "I do. It's a bad, devilish symbol. A symbol for the Devil himself." He looked up. His teeth were clenched. "It's a dangerous thing to have around."

"Keep it away from him. We'll dispose of it after we get information from him."

"Do you want me to start questioning him without you?"

I studied my friend, my mentor. I didn't know all of his past. I knew some of it, but not all. I knew he hadn't always been a priest. He had been one of the Garda, Ireland's hard-boiled version of a cop, when he was young. The Garda are hard men doing a hard job, using thug tactics against outlaws. Somewhere he had served some military time. Whatever his life was before had left him a very dangerous man. But despite that, or probably because of that, Father Mulcahy was a true Catholic priest. A real servant of God.

I had no illusions. Getting information from Ahriman was going to be ugly. Really ugly. Soul-staining ugly. If I asked, Father Mulcahy would do it for me. I knew he would. He would take that burden from me.

Fuck that.

I would *never* ask it of him. Whatever he had done before I met him, whatever had brought him to the arms of the Church, it was bad enough that I wouldn't ask any more of him if I could do it myself. He had his own sin to atone for. I wouldn't lay another on him if I could. I signed up for the job, even the shitty parts.

"No, just get him ready. I'll be back to do the questioning myself."

He nodded, drawing in on the cancerstick in his mouth. The cherry flared hot orange and the white cylinder was eaten down to the filter as I watched. "Silas here can help me."

I nodded and Special Agent Heck climbed up on the stage. Both men knelt beside the bound warlock. They were a study in contrast. Special Agent Heck was close to six feet tall and on the lean side of average. His black suit bunched as he moved, pulling up his arms and legs. The cuffs of his shirt were stark white, and so were the socks covering his ankles above a pair of polished wingtips.

Father Mulcahy was almost a foot shorter than me, his

head only reaching Heck's shoulder. The priest was wide across the back, bull-thick with arms and legs like a dock worker. He probably outweighed the younger man by sixty pounds. Heck's movements were quick, hands darting to help. Father Mulcahy moved with the slower, more deliberate pace of an older man.

The difference struck me in the chest with a hollow twang.

I turned away.

Tiff was there. She held a glass of sweet tea and a plate with three microwaveable pocket sandwiches on it. She gave a small toss of her head toward the bar, spun on her heel, and began to walk over.

The smell of the food drizzled out behind her. Warm and salty bread smells. It smelled like microwave food—cheap, greasy, loaded with preservatives and chemicals; in other words, delicious. My stomach clenched, a sharp growl calling out behind my belly button.

I had that gnawing emptiness that came with depleted reserves. My blood sugar was low. I had lost blood earlier, and the burn across my back was throbbing with spikes of hot pain. A crust of lymphatic fluid ran down my spine where the blisters had burst like egg yolks. The white gauze bandage had been torn from my shoulder when I yanked my shirt off earlier. The wound was still stitched closed, but just barely. It was inflamed, swollen flesh pulling at the haphazard stitches.

Tiff had napkins laid out by the time I slid up on the bar stool beside her. Next to them were two fat bottles: ibuprofen and caffeine pills. We would need both to push through the night. Tiff had a sandwich in her hand, wrapped in a napkin. She pushed the plate toward me. "Here, eat."

I picked up one of the oblong pocket sandwiches. Heat

from it warmed my fingertips. "How'd you know I needed food?"

She laughed around the bite in her mouththen swallowed. "Well, *I* needed food, and I know your metabolism by now. You're always hungry after you've been Action Deacon."

"True." I took a bite. Salty ham and chemical, liquid cheese exploded into my mouth. I barely chewed before swallowing. Immediately, my stomach settled and the slight, fuzzy headache that sat behind my eyes faded away. Something caught my attention as I took a second bite. I leaned up, looking past Tiff.

A gorilla raised a glass full of Jack Daniels to me in greeting.

Actually, it was a Were-gorilla. Dark brown eyes looked at me blearily, his black fur greasy and shot through with silver. I nodded in return and he tossed back a mouthful. The dark amber liquid splashed into his wide-open maw. He set down the glass, wiped a hairy forearm the size of a football player's thigh across monkey lips, picked up the half-full bottle of Jack Daniels sitting at his elbow, and topped off another shot.

I leaned over the bar so I could look at him directly. "How're you doing tonight, George?"

He squinted at the bottle in his monkey paw, held it up to the light, and studied it for a long moment. The amber liquid was about even with the words *Tennessee Whiskey* on the black label. The bottle dropped with a thunk of heavy glass against polished wood. His voice was deep, a chest-rumbling growl from vocal chords that were only close to human. "Looks like I'm about halfway there. How are you doin' tonight?" The words slurred together, leaning on each other for support.

"Worse than some, better than most."

He took this in. Nodded. "I won't take up any more of your time, then." The glass lifted.

"Carry on."

George was a fixture here at Polecats. He had been since the shitstorm that had landed Sophia in our whacked-out little family. He had lost someone, a girl he loved named Lucy. She'd been a shape-shifter fighting on our side. Well, she didn't shift shape as much as she changed places with a mystic totem rhinoceros named Masego. It was part of an old family curse she'd carried because of some poaching asshole uncle somewhere in her family's past. Masego had been killed by a Were-Tyrannosaurus rex, and Lucy had died as well.

George had pretty much been drunk since then.

I didn't say anything. Normally he was here in human form being a sad but harmless drunk. Which was good. Being a Were-gorilla, he was insanely strong. Tossing cars strong. If he was a mean drunk, then it would have been really, really bad. The end of *King Kong* bad.

Silver bullet bad.

But George was quiet in his sorrow. He tossed back a bottle of Jack a night, cried a little, and then passed out in a corner. I didn't blame him. I drank an ocean of Southern Comfort when I lost my family. That kind of pain sits in you like shards of broken glass that your heart nests in. Every beat grinds that glass in a little farther, a little deeper. It cuts all the time, and the only thing you want is to somehow dull the pain.

So you pick up the booze to get a little numb, and it works. A few shots dull the pain. Just a little. Just enough. You drink some more, pushing the pain even farther away. Then all of a sudden, you've made it through the night. The problem is that once the ache of the hangover fades, everything comes rushing back, stronger and meaner than before. A rattlesnake with a hate on.

So you drink again, trying to stay ahead of the pain, and you begin the vicious cycle that leads you to wake up one day and realize you lost three months of your life at the bottom of a glass.

I didn't know where he lived now. He was here every night. Hell, he probably just lived at Polecats now. Each night after closing, he would shift, Father Mulcahy would talk with him, he would finish his bottle, and he would pass out. One of the girls would cover him in a blanket before they all left each night. He would sleep through and get up to start all over the next day.

Sometimes we got him to eat something. Sometimes we got him to take a shower. So far, we hadn't been able to get both of those things to happen on the same day.

There but for the grace of God go I.

The grace of God and killing monsters.

I turned my attention back to Tiff. She was taking a sip of sweet tea, handing me the glass when she finished. It was a new thing we were doing, sharing drinks. One day she just picked up my glass and took a drink, and we had been doing it ever since. Even out, we would order one drink to share. It felt . . . right. Just a small thing, a connection. It didn't mean anything, but for some reason putting my lips to the same place hers had touched was like a stolen secret—sweet and thrilling to keep.

She was looking at me intently. Since the incident that took her left eye, she unconsciously tilted her head when she was concentrating on something. Because her sight was only through the one eye, she would focus it, centering it on whatever it was she was looking at. Right now, that something was me.

"What's on your mind, little girl?"

"Just wondering how it's going to be when you go upstairs to talk to Kat."

"Maybe she didn't find anything out and it will be a short conversation."

Her lips flattened and her head tilted even more. She gave me a look that said, "Are you stupid?"

I held up my hands, leaning away. "You're right. It's Kat, of course she found something."

Kat was a research master. Give her a computer with Internet access and she could ferret out any information on anything. Want to know what Bigfoot's shoe size is? She could tell you. Lost your mom's PIN number? She could find that too. She was an Internet ninja. Not a hacker. No, nothing so crude, unless it was an information system. I didn't understand how she did what she did, but I have never seen anyone better.

I took another drink of sweet tea and handed her the glass. "Truth is, I don't know how it will go."

She slid off her stool with a small hop. "Just remember that she's still your friend." Her hand touched my arm, slender fingers cold and wet from the glass. "I know she screwed up, and you know she screwed up. For that matter, she knows she screwed up. She's going to be feeling bad over it. But let's get through this and deal with it on the other side."

I didn't say anything.

Her hip bumped into my thigh, warm and firm. She leaned into it, making me look at her. "You've got every right to be pissed; just keep it together until we get clear of this witch thing. Then you two can sit down and figure out where you stand." She peered at me with her crystal blue eye. "Promise me."

"I'll do what I can."

She nodded, chestnut hair bouncing up and down. I watched her, suddenly aware of just how close she was standing to me. My hand went out to draw her close. Her hands flashed up, blocking. She danced back a step. "Oh, no, you don't." She took another step away. Where she had been touching my thigh started to cool. "I'm dirty and I need a shower."

I slid forward, reaching out again. "You look and smell fine to me, little girl."

Her finger waved in the air. "Nice try, baby, but no can do. I'm going upstairs to wash off and change." She pointed at the plate by my elbow. "Finish your food. Talk to Kat. After that, you can come find me."

She turned and walked away, still wearing the heels and evening gown from earlier. The dress still framed the play of fine muscles in her back, coming down to a V that stopped on her tailbone. The heels made her sway slightly as she walked, hips swinging like a pendulum in a hypnotist's hands. My attention was locked, steel to a magnet.

I ate my sandwich as she climbed the stairs, but I didn't taste it at all.

25

Kat looked up from her monitor as I knocked on the conference room door. Her eyes were red-rimmed and puffy. Her ponytail was loose and in disarray, thick strands of honey-blond hair hanging around her face and neck. Normally she kept it as tight as a nun's knickers.

Spinning slightly in the high-backed, ergonomic chair, she faced me. Her shoulders were hunched, pulled down around herself, closed off.

She opened her mouth to speak, then stopped.

I walked in and sat in my chair on the other side of the table from her.

We looked at each other. She had changed clothes. I couldn't see her legs, but I was sure she was wearing jeans and Dr. Martens. They were below the edge of the table, but that was what she always wore. A loose-fitting Bella Morte shirt with a winged, neon-green skull wrapped around her chest.

I was still shirtless. The conference chair felt like sandpaper across the burn on my shoulders, so I leaned up, putting my forearms on the table. Silence hung between us, swollen and heavy-laden.

I've known Kat almost as long as I've been hunting

monsters. Her sister was killed by a vampire, and she took it on herself to find the bastard, planning to kill them. Playing groupie, she infiltrated a local Kiss, letting them bite and drink from her while she looked for information. Somehow they discovered her plan. They handed her over to a sick, sadistic sonnuvabitch named Darius. He turned her into a bloodwhore.

By the time I found her chained in an abattoir of blood and body parts, Kat had survived torture and abuse on a level that would have killed a weaker person.

After helping her dust that bastard, my mission became her mission.

She was like a sister to me, in some ways even closer than that. I loved Kat and she loved me. Over the years we had shared many silences. They were always easy and companionable. The type of silence that is a comfort, knowing you and the other person are connected to a point that you don't have to fill the air with words.

This silence was full of jagged edges.

It screamed out for one of us to speak, to fill it with words, to break it into a million pieces of hurt.

Tiredness fell on me like a hammer. I didn't want to do this. Not now. Not ever.

There was a coal of anger behind my breastbone, red hot and ready to flare up with the slightest brush.

But that wasn't what I wanted.

This was a crap situation in the middle of a shitstorm.

Kat stopped chewing her fingernail, looking up at me. "Deacon, I . . ."

I tried but just couldn't keep the brittle edge out of my voice. "Just tell me what you found."

Her mouth shut. A long second passed before she nodded sharply and spun her seat around. Her fingers began clacking on the keyboard. As she typed, her shoulders widened and her spine straightened. She settled back into what she knew best.

I watched the images flashing on the screen, relieved. Stick to the job. It's easier.

Kat's voice was steadier as she spoke. "The Wrath of Baphomet has been around in one form or another for the last seventeen hundred years. The first mention of them appearing in the *Formicarius* by Johannes Niders." The screen split into side-by-side images.

One was an ancient book. The leather cover worn smooth from decades of handling, shiny spots formed by hundreds of hands holding the book open to read it through the years. The thick papyrus pages were frayed along their edges, and one or two had slipped the stitched binding, pulling out to reveal thick calligraphy in tiny, precise lines across the bone-ivory paper.

The other picture was a lithograph. Millions of tiny intricate lines swirled together to form a picture. The edges of the illustration were almost solid black, boiling out of the corners and breaking apart near the center in whorls forming three figures: one man and two women. The man dripped into being from the inky darkness. Tentacles twisted where his arms should have been, and he was carried by feathered wings like an eagle. The artwork was crisp, so detailed I could see individual vanes in each pinfeather.

The two women pictured were also swooping out of the dark. One of them wore a long robe. The artist captured the swell of her chubby body under the layer of cloth, the severity of black hair being pulled back, and the scowl that pulled her face down around two piercing eyes. If the illustration had been in color, they would have been a poison shade of absinthe.

The third woman was a monstrosity, wide bat wings

trailing tails of inky blackness. The artist put a lot of work into rendering the swirl of ramhorn around a diabolical face.

The artwork was exquisite.

"Doré?"

Kat spun to face me. The flush had drained from her cheeks and her eyes didn't look as raw. "Yes, the illustration is by Gustave Doré. It's one of a set that he etched for the Vatican-sponsored, but never approved, *Malleus Maleficarum.*"

I knew I recognized that artwork. Gustave Doré was a prolific illustrator in the 1800s. He hand etched thousands of illustrations on steel and copper, making lithographs of images from a myriad of literature. Most of the images you associate with Dante's *Inferno, Don Quixote,* and the Book of Revelation are probably his.

He was one of my favorite artists. Mostly because Nana Chalk had prints of his artwork from the Bible framed in every room of her house. Whenever I would stay over, I would sleep in her small spare bedroom under a print of *The Crucifixion* that was bigger than the bed it hung over. I would turn, putting my head to the bottom of the bed, and stare up at that etching. With my nose filled with the smell of linen, mothballs, and cold cream from the handmade quilt, my young eyes would trace every meticulous line, drinking in the suffering of the Son of God.

Doré's work haunted me, driving deep into my soul. When I got older, I hunted out his work, devouring it both as an artist and a Catholic. When Nana Chalk passed on, I fought for that picture, threatening bodily injury to my cousin Sean if he tried to take it for himself. It hung over our home altar in the living room after my wife and I bought our house.

It was one of the many things that had been lost when that part of my life was destroyed.

Kat watched me with a look on her face. I had seen that

look a lot over the years. She got it every time I drifted into memory. Kat knew the story of my family. She wasn't there from the beginning like Father Mulcahy, but she had come into my life shortly after. In the years we had been friends . . . No, fuck that, in the years since we had been *family,* she had seen me through many bad times when the memories were too strong to handle. Times when the bottle and the Rosary fought to comfort me.

Times when neither one was enough.

I sat up straighter, looking at the picture on the screen. "This is the Wrath?"

"Yes."

"I see Selene and Athame, but that isn't Ahriman."

"No, that is an illustration from an earlier incarnation of the coven." She went back to the keyboard, fingers tapping quickly. "Ahriman apparently joined the coven just before they crossed the ocean to come to the Colonies in 1762."

"So they've been in America since the beginning?"

"Pretty much."

"Who's that in the illustration, then?"

More finger tapping. "He was a Russian warlock named Chernobog. He founded the Wrath of Baphomet with Selene. They were a couple, terrorizing ancient Europe for centuries. The list of atrocities connected to them is extensive. An outbreak of leprosy that threatened to destroy half of Spain in the dark ages was their fault. Athame is their daughter. She appeared with them as a child."

"What happened to him?"

"The coven was driven from Ireland after they laid waste to a monastery, a nunnery, and a children's home. The Vatican dispatched a team of witch hunters equipped with the cutting edge in weaponry at the time."

The screen flashed as the images changed. Another illustration came up. This one was an ink-wash painting, a head shot of a man with gaunt cheeks and dark eyes under the wide brim of a Puritan's hat. The expression on the face was dour, thin lips in a down-turned line, brow creased over a bladed nose.

"Chernobog was killed by this man, Solomon Kane. It was a long battle that took the lives of every witch hunter except Kane. He fought on his own for two days before killing Chernobog. Selene and Athame fled, disappearing until they arrived on this continent with Ahriman as a part of the coven."

"What happened to Solomon?"

"He traveled to Africa and never returned."

I tried to sit back in my chair. The leather was rough as I eased against it. It took a second, but I finally found a place where the burn settled to a low buzz of annoyance instead of feeling like someone was flat-ironing my shoulders. As comfortable as I was going to get, I pointed at the screen. "Okay, backtrack to the first picture."

Two clicks of a mouse switched the screen to the illustration by Doré of the three original witches. All three of them had the pentagrams around their necks. "Any hits on that symbol they all wear?"

She tip-tapped the keys. The screen filled with a picture of the amulet that all three witches wore. Blown up giant size, the face on the goat was even nastier, like it would bite you if you got too close. "The symbol was made notorious by Malachai Ephraim in the first century. Representing the 'Goat-Headed God,' it has been a symbol of use in satanic ritual throughout history."

"Goat-Headed God?"

"Yep."

"So these assholes are worshipping a demon named Baphomet who has sold them a line of shit about being a 'god.'" My fingers stabbed air quotes around the word *god*.

"Pretty much."

Witches and their kind are always getting suckered by demons proclaiming godhood. Baphomet was just the latest in a long line. Hecatae, Cernunnos, even Astaroth were all just demons. Powerful demons, arch fiends of Hell, but demons nonetheless.

The world of monsters ranges pretty far and wide, with an ass-ton of creatures claiming deity they don't deserve. Hell, I've put a number of them down myself. Delusions of grandeur or demonic deception at the end of the day, it doesn't really matter, there is one God and one God only. Everyone else is just an asshole with ulterior motives.

I thought for a second. "We know Selene and her crew are planning something big or they wouldn't have made such a high-profile move. I wonder if this is the old 'bring me to earth and rule it with me' shell game."

Demons were always trying to be pulled into this plane of existence. They traded in the chess game of temptation and torment of the mind and soul for a corporeal body with which they can cause actual death and destruction. Most of them settle for possessing people. For a demon, it's like boosting a car. They joyride around in some poor person's body, burning it up in a high-speed chase of torment and chaos.

Apparently it really blows their skirt up. They never want to let go of their host, running around in that body until the person is completely destroyed and everyone they love has been hurt.

When a demon manages to become corporeal, they don't have the limitations of a human body. It's like they hijack an F-150 fighter plane armed with thermonuclear warheads and fueled by crack cocaine.

The demon will run amok killing as many people as it can, sowing a path of destruction in its wake. For a demon, it's the ultimate high. They hunger for it like a junkie needs a fix.

Thankfully, it's next to impossible for this to happen, making the occurrence rare. If every half-ass, pimply-faced teen with a hate on for Mom and Dad could spin a record backward and call the Devil, then the world would be in some serious shit. No, it takes a convergence of ritual, power, and just the right circumstances.

Selene? She could pull it off.

That was the scary part of all the shit that had happened so far.

Kat spun her chair around. She leaned forward, elbows on the table. "Could be. When you were talking to the witches, Selene said something about the Blood of the Trinity. I did a search for that term."

"Anything pop?"

A smile crossed her face. It was small and guarded, but it was there. "Well, it's a fairly popular anime and the title of a not nearly as popular Celtic praise and worship CD."

It was nice to see my friend smile. "Somehow I don't think that's what she was referring to."

"No, probably not." Her smile widened, lifting her cheeks. Her hands moved up, fingers snagging the elastic band that held her ponytail. She pulled it loose with a tug, static electricity cracking. She gathered the loose strands up, slicking them back from her face.

Kat's hair is some of the thickest I have ever seen. Bone straight and heavy like brocade, she wears it pulled back in a single ponytail that rides high on the back of her skull. I've seen it down only a handful of times. Pulled back, it revealed her girl-next-door looks. Full lips, straight nose, and big blue eyes made a face that you would marry after meeting the girl at Sunday school in middle Ohio. Pulling her hair back, she looked almost normal.

She looked like my friend Kat, not the person I was pissed at.

"I did find this." A finger click and the screen switched to an image of a parchment page. "This is a prophecy from the *Necronomicon Ex Mortis*."

I couldn't read it. The lettering scrawled across the screen in flamelike slashes and geometric shapes. They were vaguely rune-ish, written with dark reddish brown ink on flesh-colored papyrus. Symbols and sigils had been etched in relief behind them.

The letters began to twist as I studied them, growing fuzzy and squirmy. A tickle of pain started behind my eyes, the pinprick beginnings of a headache that would blossom into a full-blown migraine. The top of my nasal cavity felt full and moist. Sloshy.

Pinching the bridge of my nose to keep it from bleeding, I looked away. "What the hell kinda language is that?"

Kat clicked the mouse and the screen went black. "Sorry. That was Kandarian."

The pressure in my skull bubbled, dissipating. "I'm assuming there's a translation or you wouldn't have brought it up."

"There is. It's a minor prophecy and some of it is indecipherable, but it mentions the Goat's Trident, the Blood of the Trinity, the Mating of Enlil and Ishtar, and the Pentacle of Heaven."

"None of that means anything to me."

"Well, the Goat's Trident could possibly be Selene, Athame, and Ahriman. Baphomet is the Goat-Headed God, there are three of them, and in witchcraft lore, a trident is a symbol of power and retribution."

I stood up, the snappy patter comfortable to me. I had my friend back for a moment and I wasn't willing to let it go. To hell with that. I didn't have enough friends not to cling to them. Push shit aside and deal with it later. I'm good at that. Hell, I'm a world champion at it.

I began to pace. "Okay, I can stretch to that. I don't know what the other references are. Enlil and Ishtar knocking boots and a Pinnacle of Heaven? I got nothing."

"That's what I'm here for." Kat typed with a smile. "The Mating of Enlil and Ishtar and the *Pentacle* of Heaven." The screen filled with a picture of space: pinholes of white and tye-dyed planets interspersed among them. It was an artist's rendition, full of purples, indigos, and magentas. "Enlil was the Kandarian king of the gods and Ishtar the goddess of fertility or love. The Romans called them Jupiter and Venus, and named the planets after them. Those two planets will align, appearing as one tomorrow."

"In other words, mating."

"Yep." She typed and the picture on the screen tilted, planets sliding up to form an artistic interpretation of someone looking down at the universe. "And when the two planets align, they form a configuration of planets that can be traced into a . . ." Lines traced between the planets forming a star shape. Kat waited on me to supply the end of her sentence.

"A pentagram. Just like the one on their amulets."

"Exactly!"

I thought about it. "I can see that. So the Blood of the Trinity seems obvious in that light too. The witches are after the blood of three children."

"Not just children, but lycanthrope children who shouldn't have ever been born. They are unique."

"Witches do love them some unique shit."

"They do. Unique means powerful."

"And we know their blood has power because . . ." I stopped short.

The unspoken words sat between us like a dead thing.

Larson stepped into the room.

"Because I can walk now."

26

Larson's hands were up, palms toward me. He had also changed clothes, now wearing a pair of jeans and a dark blue button-up shirt. He'd taken a pair of clippers to his hair and beard, shearing away all the singed pieces. Bright copper-orange hair was a short buzz, and his tangled beard had been trimmed to a neat goatee. The hollows around his cornflower blue eyes were still soot black like a domino mask.

His voice was hoarse, but strong. "Deacon, I'd like a chance to explain."

Every bit of ease I had pulled together burned away in a flash fire of anger. "Explain what? Explain how you were somehow right? That somehow you *aren't* one hundred percent to blame for the death and destruction that has been brought here? Whatever the hell you did to get your legs back, *that* is what drew these witches out of hiding and sicced them us and Sophia's children. Explain that motherfucker."

Kat spoke up. "Deacon, please—"

My finger stabbed the air in her direction. "Don't. Larson

wants to stand behind what he did, then by all means, I want to hear it."

Larson took a step toward me. His eyes flashed. "Don't you dare take any of this out on her. You're pissed at me, then fine, but you leave her out of it."

"You sawed-off little sonnuvabitch, you think you can stand there and tell me how to talk to *my* friend?" My jaw ached. Pain shooting from my teeth. "Who the *hell* do you think you are?"

Larson stepped up. His chest bumped into mine even though it was only half as wide. "I'm the man who loves her. I'm the man who shares her life and shares her bed. I'm. The. One. *She.* Loves." He pressed against me, teeth bared behind his freshly trimmed goatee. "She's the reason I did what I did."

"Oh, now you are going to blame her? See, like I said, it's not your fault."

Larson pushed away from me. "That right there, Deacon. That's your problem. You think you know what's right and wrong. Worse, you think *you* get to decide what's right and what's wrong. You stand there so convinced that there's only your way or the highway. You self-righteous asshole, life is complicated. You should grow up and realize that."

The skin on the back of my neck was hot and tight, just like the skin on the back of my clenched fists. "Listen to me, prick. There's one thing that isn't complicated: magick. It's wrong. It's pure evil."

"I had a good reason for doing what I did."

"Fuck your reason!" I lashed out. My hand hit one of the conference chairs, spinning it away, smashing it into the wall. The drywall caved around it. "There is *always* a price to pay for what you get from magick. Always. A bastard named Slaine wanted to bring a demon to earth and it cost me my family. Everything I held dear. You got your legs back and now innocent people are dead." I threw my hands up in disgust. "But their families can take comfort because you had a reason."

He glared at me, the sonnuvabitch actually glared at me. Fire blazed high in my guts, driving me forward, right up in his face. "When is it going to be enough? How many more people do I have to lose before it will be enough to pay for your sin, Larson? How much blood has to be spilled?" A string of spittle flew out of my mouth as I roared. He recoiled as if I had struck him.

Kat was on her feet. "Deacon, he didn't know. He couldn't know anything like this would happen."

"Then by God you should have, Kat. You know how this shit works and you knew what he was doing, you had to." I said it and knew it was true. "You should have stopped him or come to me. Now the blood that's been shed is on your hands too."

I swung wide around Larson. If I had touched him, I would have strangled him. My palms itched for it. I left the room without another word or a backward glance.

27

The door slammed shut behind me. My whole body felt tight, swollen with rage. My heart thudded inside my chest, banging against my breastbone in a thick knock. A whirlpool of anger and cursing swirled inside my head.

Tiff sat up on the bed.

I stopped short. She just looked at me, not saying anything. Her head tilted slightly, making her hair fall over her missing eye. Not speaking, she slid toward me. The movement caused the evening gown she still wore to fall open at the slit in the skirt. Her feet were bare, shapely calves flexing as she scooted to the end of the bed. I watched the play of smooth skin as the hem of her dress climbed. It was midthigh by the time she reached me.

The heat inside me turned, shifting from a raging inferno to smoldering burn. Her arms opened and I stepped into them. She laid her cheek against the skin of my stomach. I was acutely aware that I was shirtless. My God, the effect she had on me.

When she spoke I had to lean down to hear her.

"I take it your talk with Kat went well."

"Actually, it did. We were doing fine until Larson wanted to explain himself."

She rubbed her face against me. It was smooth and soft with a slight scrape in a thin line. *The edge of her eye patch.* "Shelve it. Work it out later. Right now it's a distraction we don't need."

"I don't think Larson will bring it up again."

"Oh, he will. That man has been trying to prove something since the minute he met you."

"Prove something?"

She sat up, pulling away. "Sometimes he wants to prove that he's worth being your ally; sometimes he wants to prove he's as good as you are. Most of the time he wants to prove that he's nothing like you." Her fingers trailed across my skin. "It's a big ball of macho bullshit, and it's gotten worse since he started seeing Kat."

"I'm confused."

She chuckled. "So is he."

"None of what you said makes sense."

"That's because you're a man. Not only are you a man, but you're a man who keeps things separated into categories, boxes where things are put and that's where they stay for you. It's how you deal with the world, not how many other people do."

"Larson accused me of seeing the world in my way or the highway."

She stood up. "And you think he's wrong?"

I stepped back. "Do you?"

"No, he got that right, but the trick is I don't think you're wrong to be that way." Her hand fell on my chest. It was a connection, a line of heat between us. "Don't doubt yourself, you can't afford it. None of us can. Your strength comes from your conviction. It's what carries you when everything goes to hell." She tilted her head. "And I think we have more hell to get through before we're done tonight."

I didn't know what to say, so I leaned down, moving toward her lips.

Her hand flexed hard on my chest, pushing back.

"Nope, not yet. You need to brush your teeth and, more importantly, I need to brush *my* teeth." Turning away, she spoke over her shoulder. "In fact, I need to shower and get out of these clothes."

She stepped toward the bathroom. Slender fingers reached under her hair, fumbling at the base of her neck. Her hands moved away. The dress parted at the halter, slipping down her skin in a quick, liquid slink. Between one step and the next she was nude save for a tiny, teasing pair of panties. One more step carried her into the bathroom and out of sight.

She left the door open behind her.

28

The bathroom was already steaming up as I stepped inside. My guns were on the bed, pants and boots on the floor with Tiff's dress. The panties she had worn were a scrap on the linoleum floor. Quickly I snatched my toothbrush from beside the sink faucet and brushed my teeth.

I watched Tiff behind the pebbled glass door to the shower. She wasn't much more than a silhouette, just the girl shape of Tiff cut against the fog, but it was enough. I finished my teeth in a hurry, stripped off my boxer briefs, and opened the door to the shower.

A blast of warm, wet steam washed over me, driving out a chill I didn't even know I had. Tiff stood under the rush of the showerhead, fingers working shampoo into her hair. The hot water ran down her back, sluicing away soapy lather that clung to her skin. It ran down, sliding past the curve of her ass and swirling around her thighs. I watched it run, my eyes drinking in the sight of her. Desire stirred, fluttering deep below my stomach.

She turned around. My eyes had been on her ass, watching the sleek muscle bunch and flex as she stretched to wash her hair. When she turned, my eyes stayed, following the turn of her hip, watching the play of smooth thighs. The hollows of her hipbones framed her. The water swept down, washing lather from the curved planes of her stomach to the gentle swell of her pelvis.

Desire hardened in an instant.

My eyes slipped up as she swayed slightly, tracing her side to the flare of her rib cage, up and over the full swell of her breasts. I wanted to reach out and cup them, feel their warm weight against my palm. Her nipples were hard, pulled into tight little peaks.

She leaned back, eye closed under the stream of water. Her hair parted as she rinsed it, revealing her face—strong but delicate jawline, full lips under a cute nose, the four thin lines of scar tissue that cut across the hollow of her missing eye.

She brought her head down and out of the running water, blowing droplets off her lips. Her bright blue eye opened and she smiled at me.

I smiled back and reached for her. Her head moved slightly to the side. She tensed as her hair, slicked by water, didn't fall. Her hand reached for it, moving to pull it down over her missing eye. I caught her wrist on the way up.

She looked at me. My heart broke just a little at the raw expression on her face. I didn't say anything, just brought my hands up, cupping her face. My fingers slipped into the wet tangle of her hair, pulling it back farther. Her teeth bit her lower lip. Slowly, softly, I leaned down and kissed her missing eye.

I couldn't feel the four thin scars that I knew were there. The skin felt smooth under my lips. I stayed for a moment, my lips pressed against that wounded part of her. I stayed there until I felt a tension leave her and she went soft under my hands.

Still moving slowly, I leaned back, pulling away gently

so I could look her in the eye. I stayed close, capturing her in my stare, holding her firm. My voice was thick when I spoke.

"You are the most beautiful woman I know, Tiffany Anne Bramble. You are absolutely gorgeous and I love you."

She stared at me. Her hands slid between my arms, cradling my face like mine were hers. With a tug, she pulled me down, lips parting under mine, hungry and insistent. Our tongues danced, slipping around each other. The connection between us charged. She made a small sound in her throat and it shot through me like an arrow.

My hands tightened, pulling her close. Her breasts brushed my chest, the point of her nipples sliding wet and hard against my skin. My head swam as we pressed close, nothing between us but the slick wet of the shower. Our skin touched in one long line of heat from thigh to chest. My hands slid down her back, slipping in the water that ran. My fingers tracing down her spine made her shiver against me, the fine tremble setting me on fire. My hand cupped her ass, fingers slipping under the crease at the top of her thigh.

Her leg rose, sliding over my hip. Her face was open and uncovered. She smiled at me, eye heavy-lidded with desire. Reaching up, she pushed the showerhead to the side, turning the stream toward the wall. It still provided steam and heat but wasn't a distraction. Her smile widened as she flexed her leg, pulling me tight against her.

My knees nearly buckled as I brushed her, the head of me swollen and hard. Her hips tilted, seeking me, rubbing herself over my hardness. Her teeth found the side of my throat as my cock found her entrance.

Bracing against the wall, I leaned in. Slick and warm, I barely slipped inside as she lifted her other leg over my hip. Her ankles locked tight behind me.

Surging forward, I drove in with one long, slow thrust.

She was tight around me, hips flexing as I pushed in. Pleasure shot up my spine, my skin tingling with it in a trembling electric thrill. Inch by delicious inch, I slid until I was fully seated inside her. We hung like that, staying lost in the sensation. She pulsed around me, each tremble shooting pleasure deep inside. No space existed between us.

Her teeth left my skin, voice throaty and breathless. "Come on, baby."

My chest hummed with a growl. I felt wicked as I looked down at her. Wanton. I flexed my hips, drawing back, dragging out of her slowly. Tight, wet, and hot, she milked against me, pulling at me greedily. Small sounds came from her throat with the delicious friction. I stopped just one scant movement from breaking the connection. Desire crackled between us. Both of us froze, both enjoying the sensation of me just inside. We rode the wave of pleasure between us.

A roll of her spine rocked her hips. My eyes shut as pleasure rippled through me. I thrust, hips rolling and bucking. Each move she made built the tension in my core. We were connected where our bodies joined, my pleasure and her pleasure weaving together. Bliss pooled in the center of me, swirling around itself, building pressure. She hung on me, hands tight on my shoulders, legs tight around my waist. Her face pressed against my chest as I drove in and out.

My hands found her hips, fingers closing, pulling her down tight against me. I bucked up, arching back, lifting her, driving a moan out of her to match my own. She was tight around me, body clenching against my hardness. We moved faster, pleasure riding us, pushing us into a frenzy. Both of us raced toward climax, her thighs trembling under my fingers. I gave one last thrust as I poured over the edge, orgasm exploding inside me, pleasure washing my mind empty. She cried out as her own orgasm took her. Both of us rode the wave to the end.

Slowly, we slipped apart, her legs lowering to the tiled floor of the shower. I held her as she stood to her feet, still pressed against me. Connected. We leaned on each other, catching our breath. I kissed her forehead as her lips found the pulse under my jaw. Her hand pressed against my chest, pushing me back a step. She smiled up at me, face open and unhidden.

I smiled back. "That was wonderful."

"Yes, it was." She pulled me down to a kiss. It was warm and sweet. She stepped past me to the door of the shower. Looking over her shoulder at me, she pushed it open. Cool air swirled past her to raise gooseflesh on my legs. "Finish your shower, you dirty old man. We still have work to do."

I reached out for the soap, smile still plastered on my face.

29

I opened the bedroom door to a crowd of people. The hallway outside my room is fairly narrow, so everyone was bunched up, pressed against each other. The first person in that group stood, fist in the air, about to knock.

She blinked at me with mismatched eyes: one ice blue, the other peat-moss brown. They sat in a face that was pale and creamy skinned. Eastern Europe was stamped on her features, like her name should be Olga or Helga, something that ended in a "ga" sound and came from a country that spoke Russian. Hair swirled around her head in a russet tangle, unbrushed since her change.

"Sophia."

Her face broke into a smile that was warm but didn't erase the worry lines on her forehead. "Deacon." She reached out to hug me. "Thank you for coming to get us earlier."

I touched my brow in a sarcastic salute. "Shucks, ma'am, tweren't nuthin; besides, you were just a few seconds away from kicking their asses." In the hallway behind her were the three kids. They looked up at me with three blue eyes and three brown eyes between them, regarding me solemnly.

The cub child sat between his brothers. A long pink tongue lolled out of his muzzle in a pant. On his right the half-Were child pulled at his green shirt with retracted claws, fidgeting against the sensation of cloth over his fur-covered body. The human child on the left looked at me without blinking. He stood on slightly bowed legs, little boy belly poking out as his back swayed so he could look up.

I smiled down. "Hey, kids."

"Hey, Unca Deacon."

"How are y'all doing?"

"We're mad."

I knelt down so that I was mostly eye level with the human brother. "Oh yeah? Who are you mad at?"

Unblinking. "Selene."

Without standing up, I turned to Sophia. "Did you tell them who was after you?"

A shake of her head. "I have no idea what's going on. That's why I'm here. I don't know anyone named Selene."

Hmmmmmm.

I turned back to the child standing before me. The eyes were the same—two different colors, wide, unblinking—but the face was different. Now it was covered in short fur that ran up into manelike hair. His nose had shifted, the nasal bones elongated into a short muzzle over lips gone thin and cleft in the center.

They had switched forms. It was the same child, they hadn't moved, but they had shifted in that moment when neither me nor Sophia was looking. They did that. Turn your back, look away, hell, just blink, and when you looked back they would be in different forms.

It was just as spooky as it sounds.

Sophia knelt down beside me. The tight spacing made her leg press against mine. "Gideon, who told you about this Selene woman?"

Unblinking eyes turned toward her. The voice was gruffer, deepened by the change in throat and mouth. "Nobody told us." Tiny, chubby, fur-covered hands reached up to cup Sophia's face. "We won't let her hurt you, Mommy." The hands fell on her.

It was like someone flipped a switch on a circuit.

My vision wiped away in a flash of golden light. White-hot power swept through Sophia, cutting into me from the patch of skin where her thigh pressed against mine. It boiled over me, singing through my veins. The world jolted, everything sparkling with clarity, sharper than it was before.

Sophia's head was thrown back, eyes fluttering under shuttered lids. Her son gleamed with a white-gold light that spilled out of his eyes. His brothers had the same burning aura, the same glowing eyes.

As one, their heads turned. They spoke, the trio of voices cutting through me in a metallic vibrato of perfect sync. *"I will be there when the blade sings and the cord cuts."*

The three of them blinked in unison and the power shut off like the slam of a door.

Sophia and I fell apart, breaking our connection.

She looked at me, her mismatched eyes wide and out of focus. "What just happened?"

Your kids were being spooky as hell, that's what just happened.

I helped her stand on shaky legs and move down the stairs. The three kids trailed behind us, silent, their footsteps in perfect unity.

Great, one more thing for me to watch out for.

30

By the time we reached the bottom of the stairs, Sophia didn't need my hand on her arm. The kids broke free, running past us as we reached the floor. I watched them sideways. They seemed normal, all indication of the super-spooky gone. Tumbling, they wrestled on the floor like normal kids were supposed to. Yes, only one of them looked human, but besides that . . .

In my world, normal is a relative term.

The stairs dumped us out in the backstage area of the club. This was where the girls relaxed between sets. The room was long, the carpet on the floor thick and heavily padded. When you spend most of your night in heels, the first thing you want to do is kick those bastards off.

Or so I've heard.

Couches lined one wall. They were well-used, broken in to comfort by people sitting on them. An electronic shi-atsu foot massager lay in front of each couch.

The opposite wall was lined with fully loaded book-shelves. Shelves sagged and bowed from the weight of thousands of pages. Books jutted haphazardly in stacks. The music of the club is too loud for a television to be worth a damn, so we provide books for entertainment.

There was also a vanity table and mirror with an array of cosmetics so the girls could spruce up before going back out to the customers.

Only one dancer was in the room right now, everyone else had been sent home. Because of her condition, this girl lived at the club just like I did. Veronica Maria Benedetta Bellini, Ronnie to her friends. Her condition? She wasn't knocked up. She was beset by spiders.

Not just any spiders, she was psychically linked to a brood of supernatural ghost spiders. They were the off-spring of Longinus and a Were-spider named Charlotte. Yes, *that* Longinus. The immortal cursed by God Longinus.

She became bonded to the murderous little yo-yos after being kidnapped by an ex-Yakuza assassin with a demon trapped under his skin.

Like I said, *normal* is a relative term.

I had saved her from the assassin, and she had saved me from the spiders by letting them imprint on her.

Now they followed her around, skittering along ceilings and walls, watching out for her, being creepy. She's their grounding, their anchor that keeps them from going on a murder spree.

It makes it hard for her to have an apartment.

The pet deposit would be outrageous.

I looked up. A few of her spiders clung to the ceiling. They hung upside down, all of them bobbing gently in unison, like they were listening to the same music. They had grown; their translucent bodies now the size of baseballs. Long, spindly legs folded out from each of them. The legs lifted, waving around in unison, all of the spiders moving as one mind.

Once again for the record, creepy as fuck.

Ronnie sat on the red velvet couch, talking to Special Agent Heck. Either he didn't notice the spiders hanging over his head or he was one ice-cube-cool SOB. Sophia stepped away from me, moving to watch her kids. I started moving toward the government secret agent and the exotic dancer. As I walked, I ran my thumbs under the straps of my shoulder holster, settling it into place.

The matched set of Colt 1911s hung under my arms in spring-steel pressure holsters. They would slip out with a good solid tug, but otherwise were held tight like a baby in its mother's arms.

The harness also held two long knives under the guns. The blades were pointed up, handles hanging down for ready draw in a split second. Both blades were ten inches, made of solid stainless steel with a silvered edge. Ten inches is a good length for monster hunting. The blade is long enough to get under most rib cages, and the edge is long enough to get through a human-sized neck. And if your monster is more than human sized, then it's still big enough to do some real damage.

The knives hung where I normally carry spare magazines, so I had them in a waist bandolier. Ten clips of .45-caliber ammunition. Seventy bullets besides the sixteen that were in the guns already. If eighty-six bullets weren't enough for me to carry, then we were well and truly screwed. Half of them were regular bullets for the witches, half were silver bullets in case we ran into any more vampires. The bandolier also held my trusty snub-nosed Taurus .44 at the small of my back, ready in case of a pinch.

I stepped up and the conversation died. Special Agent Heck looked over at my shirt. He read it. Read it again.

"I don't get it."

It was a forest green shirt with the words SPEAR MENTAL MONKEY stamped across the chest in bright blue letters. I waved his statement away. "It's from a story. If you don't get it, I don't have time to explain it." I flopped down beside Ronnie. My legs stretched out, red dinosaur-skin boots blending against the red velvet of the couch. "So what are you two crazy kids talking about?"

"Funny you should ask, Mr. Chalk. Perhaps you could clear up the issue we were discussing."

Ronnie's cheeks turned red. Ronnie is as Italian as lasagna, her skin a constant shade of Mediterranean tan. For her to blush is something else.

My eyebrow went up. "I can't wait to hear this. But first things first. Is the wizard ready for questioning?"

"Almost. Father Mulcahy will come get us. You had someone show up who is helping with the prep work."

Someone show up?

Before I could ask, Ronnie piped in. "Boothe and Josh are here. Boothe is helping Father Mulcahy."

"What's Josh doing?"

"Making coffee."

Boothe was the bouncer at Polecats. He was a Were-rabbit who I met when all the Leonidas shit was happening. Being a Were-rabbit may not sound impressive, but Boothe was one tough hombre. He could more than hold his own.

Josh was Boothe's partner of three years. He was also a tough hombre . . . for an accountant. He'd helped us with the taxes on the club this year.

Yes, we pay taxes. I can handle monsters; I would prefer to avoid the IRS. Talk about some scary shit.

"So what burning question can I answer, then?"

Special Agent Heck's face was straight and bland as an unsalted cracker. "Why do you own a strip club?"

"Why wouldn't I own a strip club? Not that it is, techni-cally, a strip club." The ordinances in this county only allow a choice between nude dancing and alcohol sales. I chose the alcohol sales, so the dancers didn't actually strip. They just danced onstage wearing very little clothing. Technically Polecats was a bikini bar.

"But why would you pick this particular business?"

"I used to work in clubs like this. They make money. Actually, they make a metric ass-ton of money. And do you know what takes a metric ass-ton of money to do?"

"What's that, Mr. Chalk?"

"Monster hunting. Bullets aren't cheap. Start putting silver on them and without a hefty revenue stream, you won't be able to afford them." I realized that he probably didn't have to worry about the cost of bullets since he worked for the government. They don't worry about the cost of thousand-dollar hammers, why would they worry about the cost of silver bullets?

"Why don't you charge people to handle their monster problems?"

The laugh burst out of me, shotgunning from my mouth in a blast. It took me a second to pull it together. Special Agent Heck just looked at me the whole time. "Oh, wait. You're serious?"

He nodded sharply.

I sighed. "Look, monsters usually stay out of sight, you know that. They try to avoid being exposed to humanity any more than they have to. If humans knew about monsters and decided to do something about them, then the monsters all know they would lose. Humans outnumber them hundreds to one. Humans can move during the day, humans can use silver, humans can pray and have faith. In short, it would be a bloody massacre, but the humans would survive and monsters would be destroyed."

Heck held up his hand. "What does this have to do with you owning a strip club?"

"It's not a strip club, but the point is that monsters stick to the shadows. They hunt the herd of humanity like lions on the Serengeti, taking the weak and the injured. They prowl the seedy underbelly of the world, preying on the people who can't or won't go to the police. People who usually won't be missed. Their victims don't have any support system, and they surely don't have any damn money. Besides, I wouldn't be able to live with myself taking money from people who had been through the hell of a monster encounter, so I have this business to fund things."

"So you have young women like Miss Bellini dance out of gratitude to you for saving their lives?"

Before I could speak, Ronnie leaned forward. "Let me answer that one."

I smiled. "Go ahead."

Ronnie turned to face Special Agent Heck. "I don't dance here out of gratitude; I dance here because I'm a dancer. I was a dancer before I met Deacon; it's what I do. And let me tell you, I have danced in some really terrible clubs." A shudder ran through her compact fame. "Here, I'm safe. Deacon, Kat, and Father Mulcahy take care of me and all the girls here. Deacon never asked. This is what I do, so now I do it to help the next girl who is in the situation I was. Monsters love strippers, so there are a lot of girls like me."

"So you choose to be a dancer?"

I raised my hand up in a "stop" gesture. "Wait just a second." I looked at Special Agent Heck. Hard. "Did you think that I run around saving pretty girls from monsters and then being like 'you owe me, now shake your ass for me'?"

He shook his head. "Not exactly like that, but it's such a strange dynamic that I am curious."

I shrugged. "Well, that's not what happens. Not at *all*. It was suggested to me by . . . well, by someone who isn't with us any longer. I needed money, and she reminded me how much money these kinds of clubs make, and the fact that they are always going to be around, no matter what. It seemed like a smart move."

I wasn't going to tell Special Agent Heck about the first year of hunting.

When my family was killed, I went off the deep end. Drank myself into oblivion for days on end, locked in the house where they were murdered. Not eating, barely sleeping, pouring tears like blood from a gut shot.

I could still see those walls. The same walls we painted that light blue in one weekend of beer and paint fumes, giddy and laughing about the silly stupid stuff that couples share. The taste of Southern Comfort washed back into my throat in memory.

Those pale blue walls, the symbols smeared on them in swaths of dark brown dried blood.

The blood of my family.

Whoa. STOP.

A warm hand touched my leg. I shook my head to clear it. I opened my eyes to Ronnie leaning forward. I could feel the hard, slick scar tissue on her palm through my jeans. Her face was soft, framed by a mass of tight, dark ringlets, dark eyes filled with pity for me.

Why did I keep going back to that day? I had pushed those memories *deep*, burying them as far as I could, layering over it to keep getting up every day. Why was it so raw and open now?

Realization clicked.

Athame.

That bitch. When she stuck me with her soulsword earlier, it ripped that memory free and threw me back to that awful day. Now it was right under the surface of my mind like a shark under bloody water–circling, swimming, hunting, waiting for the first sign of weakness to bite.

That's great. Just what I needed.

What was I thinking?

The first year of hunting.

That's right.

After I started hunting, I sold my business, sold my house, cashed out my retirement, and cashed in the life insurance policy. It was a fire sale, everything burned in my pursuit of revenge. I had a pile of cash to buy weapons and equipment.

It didn't last long. Killing the Nephilim bastard who murdered my family just about wiped it out. When I began hunting other monsters, it got hand to mouth pretty quick.

Now, monsters have to live in this world. You find a lair of vampires or Nephilim, or even rogue lycanthropes, and usually they will have a stash of ill-gotten gains to plunder. Even that doesn't last long.

I had been at the ragged edge when I met Dolly, a dancer who had great taste in clothes but terrible taste in men.

Well, not men, elves.

Dolly got a taste for the Keebler gone bad and just couldn't stay away. When I met her, she had come to Father Mulcahy for help dealing with a real mean piece of shit named Mael.

Typical story, good-hearted girl with low self-esteem and daddy issues finds some asshole who'll reinforce those feelings while drinking up the money she earns and smacking her around to make himself feel powerful.

Typical in my world, anyway.

This guy wasn't some redneck, though. He was the third son from the throne of some elven royal family. His lineage gave him a hefty dose of supernatural ability to back up his threats to kill her when she left.

Anyway, she went to Father Mulcahy after this pointy-eared bastard decided he would sell her to an ogre, and the priest called me in. I discovered that silver only hurts elves, it takes iron to kill them, so I bashed his skull in with a crowbar. After the dust settled, there was a pile of elvish gold. I tried to hand it over to Dolly so she could start a new life, but she was having none of it. That's when she proposed using the money to start a club as a way to fund future hunts.

She was even the one who named it Polecats.

We had lost Dolly a year into being open.

Not to another abusive elf. Not to anything supernatural at all.

No, Dolly was taken out on the slow train of breast cancer at the age of twenty-five.

Life fucking sucks sometimes, even without monsters.

31

"Sometimes."

I snapped out of the memory, still on the couch with Ronnie. Sophia sat on the stairs across the room watching the kids play. Special Agent Heck was standing by the bookshelves a few feet away. Tiff was next to him. It had been her voice that brought me around.

I sat up. "Sometimes what?"

She smiled at me and began to walk over. "Sometimes you drift off on us."

"Must be inconvenient," Heck said.

"It usually only happens when things are calm."

"I *am* in the room," I said.

Tiff began walking toward me. She had been gone from the bedroom when I finished my shower so I hadn't seen her since. A pair of pants that fit close and were made of heavy-duty leather hugged her hips and thighs like a jealous lover. They were tucked deep into sturdy combat boots with a tire-thick tread that laced up over her calves. A short-cropped, leather-pants–matching jacket was slung over a simple black T-shirt.

The Judge rode her hip, leaned forward for a more

natural draw. A knife hilt stuck up from her right boot and, even though I couldn't see it, I knew she had a .44 snub-nosed revolver at her back to match mine. Dressed for combat, she looked dangerous.

She looked sexy as hell.

Planting her feet on either side of my legs, her hands went to her hips. My eyes traced up her body to her face. A smile crossed her lips that was a little bit wicked. Her hair had more tousle than normal and was still wet on the ends. It fell, like always, over her missing eye.

She wasn't wearing her eye patch, though.

"Like what you see?"

I reached up for her. "Oh, hell yes." Leaning in, she planted her hands on the back of the couch. Her lips pressed to mine. Damp hair brushed the side of my face, carrying the warm honeysuckle scent of her.

Too soon she broke the kiss and stood up.

Ronnie sighed. "One day a man is going to look at me like that."

"You and me both, sister." Boothe spoke from beside the doorway. I hadn't seen him there. Then again, I'd been a bit distracted.

Tiff laughed. "You better not let Josh hear you say that."

"True. He'd kick my ass."

Boothe was taller than me, hitting around 6'7" and pushing 280 pounds of lean bodybuilder muscle. He was a fifth Dan in hapkido, which means nothing to you if you aren't into martial arts, but trust me, it meant he was a serious ass-kicker. Combine that with the strength and speed of a lycanthrope, and you have a deadly combination. That's why he was the bouncer for the club.

Josh stood about 5'6" and might top the scales at 120 pounds. He was slim and boyish. Like all the Were-rabbits, he had some martial arts training and knew how to use a gun, but he would pick doing karaoke or golf on Sunday over hitting the gym or dojo. If he was kicking Boothe's ass, it was only because Boothe let him.

"We're ready to get started with this guy in here, Deacon."

"I'll be along in a second."

He stepped back out of the room. My hand reached down, grabbing Tiff's as I stood. Our fingers entwined. Hers were slender, still soft and smooth. Mine were more scar than skin, the fingers hard with calluses. My knuckles jutted up, enlarged from being used as bludgeons. The skin was darker than hers, permanently stained with gunpowder residue. So much that it dulled the colors in the tattoo on the back of my hand.

Lifting her hand, I pressed my lips against it. Just quickly and away, a soft kiss. Her blue eye stared, a smile quirking up the corner of her luscious mouth. "What do you want?"

"Who says I want anything?"

"The way you're being sweet does."

The chuckle surprised me, rising up through my chest. "Okay, okay. I do want something. No, I need something from you."

"You want me to stay here with Sophia and the kids while you question Mr. Wizard out there. Am I right?"

"Actually, I want you and Ronnie and Special Agent Heck to stay here and guard Sophia and the kids."

"Are you putting me on the sidelines?"

I lifted my hand up. "I swear that's not what I'm doing, little girl. I have to go do this. I want you and Ronnie to keep the kids out of that room. We're going to have to do things that no child should ever see. More important, we still have two witches out loose who are after those kids."

"You don't think you kicked their ass enough to stop them from trying again?"

"I doubt it."

"Slacker."

I pushed her playfully. "Keep talkin', little girl. Your mouth is writing checks your ass can't cash."

Her smile was a beautiful thing. "Promises, promises." She waved me away with a slender hand. "Go. Get your information. I'd like to get some sleep tonight."

"You and me both."

I didn't want to leave her, but I turned and went to question a warlock.

32

The main room of Polecats was still bright as hell. The houselights filled the room with light. The main stage ran down the center of the room. The brass poles on each end ran from the waist-high stage up to the ceiling. The closest one had a warlock handcuffed to it.

He sat in a wooden chair, arms wrenched behind him around the pole. I wasn't worried about him pulling free; those poles were designed for a dancer to swing her whole body around them. They were anchored securely and weren't going anywhere. Hell, some nights we even had two girls on them at once.

Someone had put a hood over the warlock's head. The duct-tape bandage had been cut off and replaced with white gauze. The gauze was white; the blood staining it was bright red where the gunshot in his shoulder had opened up from being cuffed.

Father Mulcahy stood on the end of the stage in full priest regalia—clerical robes, rubric, the whole enchilada. He had a brass censer on a chain and was swinging it around, chanting in Latin. Thick white smoke trailed off it, smelling like chewing gum and autumn.

It smelled like Mass.

My mind tripped, falling backward to my youth. Not to a specific memory, just the feeling of being a small boy in a pew, fascinated by the majesty of Mass.

Boothe and Josh were behind the bar. Boothe held a beer, fingers wrapped around the brown glass of the long-neck. Josh sat on a stool next to him, thin hands around a steaming mug. It was probably the coffee he made earlier. Josh was a bit of a teetotaler.

Kat and Larson sat at a table in the corner, her laptop out and open. Quickly, she looked down at it as I walked through the room. She was there to instantaneously look up any information we got out of Ahriman.

Kat hid behind her screen, using her attention on it to keep from looking at me. I knew her and I knew what she was doing. That was fine with me. We could work it out later, we always did, but for now just seeing the two of them made my blood pressure rise. If she didn't talk to me, then we wouldn't fight. But one word from either of us, no matter what it was, and we would be right back at it like cats and dogs. There was a tension inside of me directed at her and Larson. A hair trigger that would trip with even the smallest touch.

Larson sat in the chair between her and the rest of the room. He had positioned himself in a way that he could shield her.

My anger at him burned hot enough to set my teeth on edge, but I still appreciated that. He could kiss my ass before I would tell him that, though.

I slid up on a barstool. Boothe lifted his bottle. "You want one?"

"Hell no. You know I don't drink that horse piss. Pour me a shot. Something dark."

"Neat?"

"It's the only way to drink it."

He nodded and turned to the row of bottles behind him. Josh raised his mug. "How are you doing tonight, Deacon?"

"Other than satanic, murderous witches? Not too shabby."

"Just another Tuesday night in Sunnydale?" His mouth flashed into a smile. It was brief, only lasting a second, but it went all the way from his chin to his eyes. He was a small, delicate man, nearly ten years older than he looked. It was an illusion helped along by a fine-boned face with a quick grin and a head full of tight curls. He pointed at Father Mulcahy. "What's he doing?"

"Blessing the room to dampen Ahriman's magick."

"Ahriman's the tied up guy, right?"

"Yep."

"Is the blessing going to help get information out of him?"

"Mostly it will limit his access to power."

"How does that work?"

Boothe slid a shot glass full of dark liquid over to me. It bumped against my fingers, a little of it splashing out over the rim. "Josh wasn't raised in church and we don't go now, so he's a little curious."

Josh grinned at him. "You love it."

"Entirely not the point."

I picked up the shot glass and held it. "It's all good."

I looked at the smaller Were-rabbit over the trembling rim of alcohol. "Magick is a bending and breaking of the physical laws of the universe. Magick trumps physics but it takes a lot of energy. Humans make magick by trading with demonic forces. It all compacts and contracts and sacrifices. Spilling blood and making deals to get power from outside the human world."

"Isn't that all religion?" Josh asked.

"Big difference between good and evil. It's not the same league. Hell, it's not even the same sport. The Angels want to save your soul, demons want to destroy it. And your body. And your mind. And your mother's soul. And you mother's body . . . etcetera, etcetera, etcetera, blah-dee-bladdiity blah."

My mind twitched. An iron band tightened across my rib cage, cinching one notch at a time with each word. "When people deal in witchcraft, somebody's got to pay. Somebody's going to suffer for it."

The memory I had been battling all night swam to the surface of my head. My heart thumped *hard* in my constricted chest. Cold sweat beaded along the back of my neck, and the shot glass was suddenly slick in my fingers. The memory darted, rushing at me, blasting right up in my head.

Mommy isn't screaming anymore, but I can hear stuff. Bad stuff.

With a flick of my wrist, I tossed the shot back.

My throat lit up in a licorice and cough syrup burn. The memory shattered, derailed as the shot smacked me across the face. Thick, mentholated vapors took my breath. I rolled the shot glass away with a flick of my hand. "Jagermeister? Seriously?"

Boothe grinned, making deep lines in the planes of his face. "It's what you get for dissing beer. I knew the holy smoke would mask the smell. Besides, you didn't specify what you wanted." He held up the distinctive green bottle. "Another?"

"Kiss my ass."

"Hey, I'm a bouncer, not a bartender."

"Good, 'cause you suck at slinging drinks and I'd have to fire you."

The brass censer made a chiming noise as Father Mulcahy sat it on the bar. He let the chain spill out of his fingers to spool around the base of it. It wasn't smoking anymore because the incense had burned out. The priest, however, was.

A cancerstick bobbed up and down from his lip as he spoke. "I'll take a shot of that."

"It's Jager."

"I don't care."

Boothe pulled another shot glass and filled it in front of Father Mulcahy. The priest tossed it back, grimacing as he swallowed.

The cigarette stayed in his mouth the entire time.

He set the glass on the bar and rolled his fingers in a "keep 'em coming" gesture. The Were-rabbit obliged. "So . . ." Father Mulcahy picked up the glass, dark green liquid shimmering at the edge of the rim. "What information are you looking to get out of this one?"

"We know the who, and we know the what. So I want to know the how, the when, and the why. Selene, Athame, and Ahriman are up to no good, but I want the information to stop them instead of having to show up just to minimize the damage."

Nicotine-laced smoke streamed out of the side of his mouth. "How hard are you willing to ask him?"

"These witches are off the deep end. They blew up a restaurant, killed a ton of people, then attacked a movie theater where they killed dozens more. They have to be stopped." I stood up. "Ahriman is a dead warlock whether he knows it yet or not. I just need information out of him so I'm willing to ask him that hard."

Josh slid his arm around Boothe's waist. "Well, that's my cue. I'm going to go find a quiet corner while you three work."

Boothe turned toward him. Standing as tall as Boothe did made Josh look even younger. If that bothered him, I couldn't see it. "Do you want to head back home? I can call when the night is over."

Josh reached up, hand on the side of Boothe's square-cut

jaw. He pulled the bigger man's face down and gave him a slow, deep kiss. I was struck by how similar it must look to Tiff kissing me. She did the hands on my face thing, and the size difference between her and I was about the same as between Boothe and Josh.

Strange. It was like watching a movie of yourself, but weirder because it was live action, only two feet away, and played with different actors.

They broke the kiss, both of them breathy on the other side of it. Both of them wore the silly smile of two lovers.

Josh spoke. "I'll stay until you leave." His hand went to his back pocket. It came out holding a paperback novel. "I've got an Andrew Vachss book to keep me company." He stepped back, his hand trailing across Boothe's hip. When he reached the end of his arm's length, he stopped and looked over at Father Mulcahy. "Sorry, Father, I forgot you were there."

The priest lit a new cigarette. "Whatever are you apologizing for, son?"

"That. Just now. I wasn't trying to offend you."

"Love isn't offensive to God."

Josh stared for a long second. "You are the coolest priest, Father Mulcahy."

"I get that a lot." He pointed at the book in Josh's hand with his cigarette. "Enjoy your book, it's a good one."

"You read Vachss?"

"Only every time he puts out a new one."

"Coolest. Priest. Ever." With that, Josh turned and walked away.

Father Mulcahy chuckled.

33

"Do you want me to move George?"

"Where is he?"

Boothe pointed at the end of the bar. I walked over, looking across the bar top. A 500-pound Were-gorilla lay curled in the fetal position on the floor. Big gray monkey mitts were wrapped around the now-empty bottle of Jack, and a line of drool ran from his jutting jaw to the mouth of the bottle.

It looked like he got all the way to the bottom of the bottle.

"Leave him be. He won't wake up even if a tornado destroyed the place."

I looked at my watch: 2:19 A.M. Had it really been six hours since dinner earlier? Holy Mary, Mother of God, it felt like forever ago.

Exhaustion fell on me. I'm nocturnal, always have been, but it had been a long damn night. Pushing off the bar, I turned to the stage. Father Mulcahy had put a black satchel, the kind doctors used to carry when he had been a boy, on the stage. It was his exorcist bag. He was elbow deep inside it, the stage littered with items. Some I recognized—vials of holy water, a jar of blessed salt, a hammer, iron nails—and some I didn't recognize at all.

That's okay. Father Mulcahy has decades of experience as an exorcist and occult expert for the Vatican.

He holds Mass at St. Augustine of Hippo, which is the Church's main cache of occult objects in North America. Vatican investigators find some scary shit, and they send it to Father Mulcahy's parish to keep it safe and out of the wrong hands.

Yeah, I trusted him.

The stage was hard against my hip as I leaned next to him. "How do you think we should work this?"

"I've got some items here you'll find helpful in getting information out of him." He handed me the hammer and the iron nails.

"Am I building a birdhouse?"

"Most magick users with any power have fae blood in their veins. It's what makes them able to do more than light candles and use a Ouija board."

"So a fairy took a dip in Ahriman's gene pool?"

"I've never read a case history where they didn't find it."

I knew that witch-finders of old had used iron nails to interrogate witches during the Salem infestation, but I didn't know why. Learn something new every day.

"This is going to get pretty ugly. Are you okay with that?" I asked because of Father Mulcahy's Catholic priesthood. Yes, he drank like a fish and smoked like a chimney. Yes, he could use a shotgun like a painter used a brush. Yes, he could knife fight like a convict, but none of that meant he didn't have limits.

Father Mulcahy was the reason I hadn't gone over the edge when I first started. He was the one who would reach out and stop me from going too far; the one who taught me to hold back with supernatural people like lycanthropes.

He stubbed his cigarette out in the ashtray beside his bag on the stage. His voice was hard. "Son, I will do anything to keep those three children safe."

The Padre had a soft spot for kids, those three in particular. He'd been there to help Sophia from the moment they had been born, changing diapers, handling feedings and bedtimes, whatever was needed. They were a lot of work not just because there were three of them, but because they grew so quickly that they were hard to keep up with. But he had been there for her. They were like the children he didn't have.

More like the grandchildren.

"And afterward? When it's time to stop them?"

"Wizards thou shalt not suffer to live." He quoted the Scripture. "If I can, I'll give them a chance to repent, but the commandment stands and I'll help you enforce it." His gray-green eyes were pieces of flint.

I nodded. Good enough for me.

Time to get started.

Time to get ugly.

34

I walked across the stage, carrying a wooden chair. My boot heels were loud, ominous on the polished wooden planks. I banged the chair down in front of the bound warlock, then swung my leg over it.

The club was silent save for the low hum of Father Mulcahy starting to pray and the muffled sound of Ahriman's breathing under the hood. I waited a long moment, just watching, letting his mind wonder what was going on. Letting his mind feed on itself, twisting around what was about to happen.

It took almost a full minute before anxiety made him move.

He twitched, the handcuffs on his wrists chiming against the brass pole. Leaning forward, I whipped the hood off his face with a jerk of my hand.

The cloth pulled wiry black hair forward. Streamers of it stuck to the sweat on his face, plastering in thin trails across his skin. The wide strip of duct tape was still across his mouth, sealing it closed.

His hooked nose flared as he tried to draw air through it. It wouldn't be enough. If your mouth is sealed shut, it makes your mind go haywire. Panic rides in heavy on thundering hoofbeats. Suddenly your nostrils feel like they are glued shut, and the only air you can get is through a tiny, clogged straw, just enough to keep you alive.

Reality is, you can breathe comfortably through your nose, but your mind forgets when it has to rely on only your nose to deliver all your life-giving oxygen. It makes you panic, your mind in a blender set to puree, unable to think straight. Your heart begins to pound and pound and pound inside your chest, burning up what little oxygen you can get. Your mouth fills with saliva behind whatever gag is breaking your jaw. It pools over your tongue, trickling down your throat in maddening dribbles. You feel like you are drowning one tiny stream of water at a time.

I've been tied up and gagged before.

Ahriman's eyes were smashed open inside dark, near-purple hollows. The pupils had dialed down to pinpricks, revealing sickly yellow irises in full. They skittered in hysteria as he tried to look everywhere at once. Red vessels had burst, splashing his eyeballs with pink from the corners to the irises.

Reaching under my holster, I drew one of the ten-inch knives.

The light of the club gleamed along the cutting edges, tracing around the blade in a thin, razor-sharp line. The warlock's eyes locked on it, still wide, still jittery, focused on only that knife. His face jerked away as I pushed the blade toward it. The chair went up on two legs. Every millimeter I moved the blade, the farther back he leaned. The cuffs chimed frantically against the pole, the sound mimicking his movement. Pressed against the pole, he couldn't go any farther.

My hand darted forward, flicking the blade down, slashing the tip against the side of his face. Duct tape parted around a slash mark that opened beside his mouth. The tape pulled the edges, making blood run freely to soak into his beard. One corner of the tape lifted, slicked free by the blood flowing from the cut, rolling back like an awning. I grabbed that corner between two callused fingers and yanked.

The tape tore free, came away covered in wiry, blue-black hair. Red irritation blossomed across his mouth and cheeks, tiny droplets of blood welling up where the hair had been yanked out.

The point of the knife pressed into the thin skin under his left eye before he could make a sound.

My voice was low and even. "There is only one rule now. If you lie to me, I will hurt you."

His eye twitched above the knife blade, trying to see the point he could feel. The sound of his voice was strangled, pitched three octaves higher than earlier. "You are going to kill me. I'm not telling you anything."

I pushed harder, blood welling around the point. That eye went spastic, like it had been hooked to a live wire. "We've got a long, hard road before we get to that. There's a lot of pain between here and there."

"Pain doesn't frighten me."

I dragged the tip of the blade downward. It snagged, bumping over his cheekbone. It stut, stut, stuttered across the bone ridge, then sliced smoothly through the fleshy part. Ahriman's teeth clenched, air hissing between them. Blood rolled out, mixing with the warlock's oily sweat to make a wide slick.

Wiping the blade on my pants leg, I slipped it back in its sheath. "What is Selene's plan? Why does she want the children?"

"I don't know—"

My fist cracked across his jaw.

His teeth clacked together, head whipping to the left. Blood from the cuts I had given him smeared across my knuckles.

I sat back down. His face rolled back toward me. Air sucked in through his mouth, each tooth outlined in crimson.

"What is Selene's plan? Why does she want the children?"

"I don't—"

My fist cracked across his jaw.

This blow caught him under the chin, sweeping up in a lazy, half-assed uppercut. His head went straight back, banging into the pole he was chained to. The chair lifted, then slammed back down onto the stage. His head lolled forward, hanging low. A line of bloody spit swung off the edge of his already swollen lower lip.

I sat back down again. "What is Selene's plan, and why does she want the children?"

"I—"

My fist cracked against his jaw a third time.

This one I stood all the way up on, bringing my whole body into it. I twisted from the waist, pulling with all my core muscles and driving my fist into him. Blood-slicked knuckles smashed with all my weight behind it.

Ahriman skewed sideways, chair tilting, legs slipping on the wood stage. He fell over, arms twisting like chicken wings, still chained to the pole. His skull bounced off the stage with a wet, melon *thunk*.

He lay there, mouth hanging open, hair falling like a ragged veil over his eyes. Blood sprinkled out of his mouth as he drew jagged breaths in. A low groaning noise came from him.

I stood over him, fists clenched by my side. I kept my voice even. Bored. "Did that one break your jaw?"

He didn't answer, just lay with his arms tangled up

behind him, groaning and bleeding. My foot lashed out, driving the pointed toe of my boot into his stomach. The groan cut off as air was evicted from his lungs. Blood sprayed in an abstract pattern across the stage.

"Answer the question."

His voice was pulled tight, strangled. "No."

My fingers tangled in his hair. It was coarse, like thin steel wool in my grip. Pulling hard, I hauled him and the chair he was taped to upright. A sour smell wafted off him. Sweat and blood mixed with the green stinking roil of fear and pain.

In the puddle of bloody spittle on the stage was a tooth. A molar.

Sliding my chair, I sat down in front of him. He hung forward, chin to chest. A purple bruise was crawling up the right side of his face. I leaned toward him, putting my elbows on my knees.

"Ahriman, just tell me what I want to know. I don't want to do this, but I will keep it up all night."

The laugh barked out of him in a spray of red droplets. "Whom are you lying to, Deacon Chalk? You love this. You enjoy hurting people."

"Tell me what Selene has planned and why she wants the children."

"You know you get a dark thrill every time you have to kill someone. You only feel normal when you are hurting someone, trying to pay back the world for taking your family away. You are every bit the monster I am."

I didn't answer him. I stood up, moving over to the other end of the stage.

"Ha! I am right! Evil is in your heart, Deacon Chalk. You're a killer. A monster who hunts and slays, reveling in every drop of blood you spill."

At the end of the stage, I picked up the hammer and a handful of nails.

Moving back, I sat in the chair again. The hammer was old, hickory handle cracked but sturdy. The head of it was patinated black with age; the wide, flat striking surface pitted and marred from driving countless nails. It was heavy in my hand.

The nails were thick, almost as wide around as a drinking straw, and about three inches long. They had a flat head the size of a dime, a cross etched into each one. The shaft of the nails had been ground to a wicked point and notched with V's to keep them from pulling out. I placed one, point down, on the meat of Ahriman's thigh.

His eyes were wide. "What are you doing?"

I hefted the hammer in my right hand.

"Tell me what I want to know."

"I will tell you nothing!"

I tapped the nail with the hammer, the face of it chinging on the head of the nail. It sank into the meat through cloth about a half inch. The warlock sucked air in through clenched teeth. I looked the question at him. He spat at me, the spray not reaching my face but splattering on my arm instead.

I drove the nail home.

A scream ripped out of Ahriman, head thrown back, tendons jutting out of his neck. Blood gushed around the head of the nail. It began to smoke, the iron reacting with the fae blood in his veins.

Somebody moved behind me, chair scraping and falling over. I didn't look, eyes on the wizard, trusting my people. Josh came around the stage, swinging wide to be as far away as possible. His hand was to his mouth as he rushed by and out the door.

The scream died, ending in a choking sob.

I let him sit for a moment.

Reaching back in my mind, I pulled in the images of the body bags back at the restaurant stacked side by side. Each bag was a person whose only mistake that night had been to go out for dinner. My mind flashed to the hallway in the theater carpeted with the bodies of people who just wanted to go out and enjoy a fucking movie on a Friday night. They started off with popcorn and Jujubes, and wound up bled dry on a theater floor. I let those images settle around me like armor, taking me to that dull, empty place where killing can be done.

"Tell me what I want to know."

I put another nail next to the one embedded in the wizard's thigh.

A spasm rattled through him as he felt the prick of the point. His head jerked, eyes wide and white under a curtain of hair. "Stop, stop. I'll tell you."

I sat back, waiting.

His head slumped, shuddering to a stop at the end of his neck. "Selene is going to tear a hole in the world."

After a long moment of listening to Ahriman suck air between his teeth, I leaned forward. "What the hell does that even mean?"

"This world is a tuning fork. Every time a convergent event happens, the fork is struck, making a ripple. Those ripples echo out, making new realities. Selene is going to tear asunder the walls that separate each of them."

"Why the hell would she do that?"

Ahriman looked away, mouth drawn in a hard line. My thumb dropped on the head of the nail still in his thigh. It was rigid in his flesh, stuck in the bone.

"Don't get brave now, witch-boy." My thumb pushed,

pressing in. He jolted back, jerking against the cuffs on his wrists. "What. Does. She. Want?"

The warlock flopped, teeth gnashing toward me. "She wants her love back! She will destroy everything to have him by her side again!"

I pulled my thumb away.

"This is the Russian dude? Chernobyl or whatever his name was?"

"Chernobog, his name is Chernobog."

"He's dead."

Ahriman sucked air in, chest shaking. "There is another reality out there in the multiverse where he is still alive. Her and her daughter will take him from there, bringing him to this world."

My eyes narrowed. "Okay, they get Daddy to come home. What do you get out of the deal?"

He spat, eyes gleaming with the feral light of a fanatic. "I will give Selene her paradise with her lover. I'll put them on some Eden in the sea and then I would have *worlds* of the dead to play with. All my favorite playthings of the past have been used up. After we open the rift I can enjoy them all without restraint. If one of them breaks I could simply pluck another from another world."

The sensory flash I had experienced when I pulled off his amulet echoed inside my head. I knew he wasn't talking about board games. No, Ahriman was one sick sonnuvabitch. He meant play in every sick, twisted, perverted way possible.

My stomach curdled at the thought.

"Tell me how to stop her."

The muscles in Ahriman's face contracted, hardening. His lips locked together, a twisted, close-mouthed snarl. I pushed the nail deeper into his leg with my thumb.

"Tell me."

His head jerked back and forth.

The hammer flashed up and slammed down on the nailhead. It drove home in a gush of blood, slipping quick and jarring to a stop in the bone. Ahriman howled, a deep-throated animal sound. I was up, arm across his throat, driving him back against the brass pole, chair and all. It shook and shimmered as I pressed him there. The howl cut off in a choke, Adam's apple hard underneath my forearm. My voice ripped out of me.

"TELL ME HOW TO STOP HER!"

Jerking my arm away, I let him fall, the four chair legs banging into the stage with a jolt. His head bounced like his neck was broken, snapping back and forth, teeth clacking together like tiles breaking. My fingers twisted his hair, yanking his face to look at me. Eyelids fluttering, he snarled, rabid like an animal. The hammer swung back over my head. Top-heavy, it pulled back on my wrist.

The air around me went icy.

The temperature plummeted. Gooseflesh chased its way up my arm. Breath rolled out of my mouth in a white fog of condensation. Letting go the warlock's hair, I stepped back. The hammer fell to the end of my arm.

Ahriman's head dropped, shoulders jerking, hitching up and down. Lank hair swayed in front of his battered face.

Laughter stuttered the air—a strangled, high-pitched cackle that chased across my nerves like racing spiders.

The wizard's head lolled, face angled like the neck was broken. His eyes had rolled back into his head, showing only bloodshot whites. Every tiny micromuscle of his face was Charley-horsed, jerking into knots, pulling his features into a horrible rictus. Those fish-belly pale eyes stared at me, seething a malice older than humanity.

Ahriman wasn't home anymore.

I looked at the demon that possessed him.

"Well, hell-boy, like my dear old daddy used to say before he left this shitty world, you just signed up for a world of hurt."

35

Father Mulcahy stepped up on the stage holding his black bag in a calloused hand. I leaned in as I passed him, speaking low out of the side of my mouth. "We still need information before you make with the casting out."

The priest nodded and kept walking toward the demon-possessed warlock. I stopped at the end of the stage and looked out at the room. Special Agent Heck had come in at some point while I was questioning Ahriman. I hadn't noticed; then again, I'd been kinda preoccupied. He perched stiffly on a barstool, black suit coat unbuttoned.

My eyes fell on Kat, Larson, Boothe, and Special Agent Heck in turn. I raised my voice. "This is where you all keep your ears open and your mouths shut. If you've never dealt with a demon before, then be prepared for shit to get extremely weird. They're master manipulators, so ignore him and let the good Padre handle it."

Behind me came a twittering laugh, discordant notes like rats scrabbling behind a wall. The skin on the back of my skull tightened. "Good Padre? What a fucking joke. If you knew what this man had done before you met him, you wouldn't trust him at all. You'd kill him where he stands."

I didn't turn around. Raising my voice, I spoke over the demon. "They tell lies and worse, they mix them with truth. They know things no one but you should know. Ignore it, every bit of it. If you listen you give him power over you."

"You can warn them all you want. They will know the truth when they hear it. Like dear, sweet Kathleen. She will know that you'll hate her for the choice she has made. For the thing she does not tell you."

Kat looked like she had been struck. Her eyes opened wide, color washing out of her face. "I . . ."

"Shut up, Kat." My voice was harsh. "It's trying to drive a wedge between us. You know better. Don't respond to it. Don't give it any ammo to use."

"See, Kathleen? 'You know better.' You heard that from him earlier. He already hates you for being with Larson. For being such a slut that you would let that joke of a man touch you. You should have been his, and instead you gave it up to someone who is so weak he could never protect you." The voice hissed. "Secret-keeper." It spat. "WHORE!"

Kat turned away as if someone had slapped her in the face. Larson's skin boiled red. He rose in his chair, fists clenched. I held my hand out to him, palm up in a "STOP!" motion. He stood there shaking with anger.

I spoke over my shoulder to Father Mulcahy. "Sooner would be better." The priest kept working, kneeling over his open bag. He had to be precise, ritualistic. Ritual is where the power is. We just had to hold it together until he was ready.

A cackle cut the air. "Yes, priest. Hurry your fucking ass up, some of us still have throats to slit tonight."

Larson began to sink back in his seat. The demon spoke again. "Sit down, you coward. Do what Deacon Chalk tells you to do. He knows best. He's three times the man you are; just ask Kathleen." The demon's voice dropped, an insidious whisper. "You *know.* You have seen the way she looks at him. He could have her in a second. You are just the one who will, not the one she wants."

Larson's chair flipped as he leaped to his feet. Kat's hand grabbed his arm. "It's not true, Larson! I love you."

"Oh, the whore has spoken." The demon's voice was sibilant, the S's sliding into each other, long and drawn out. "Not just a whore but a liar as well. You know you love Deacon Chalk, you have for years now. It burns deep inside you, but you know he has NEVER looked at you like that. He found you in your filth and shame, used like the slut you are. Used like you asked for by going to find Darius in the first place. You've always been a whore, and Deacon Chalk knows it." Kat burst into tears. "Cry all you want! You know being with Larson has turned his pity for you into disgust!"

I was tensed, ready to stop Larson from coming on the stage. I wasn't prepared for Boothe.

Boothe cleared the bar with a leap, lycanthrope strength carrying him over. In a flash of unnatural speed, he was on the stage, gun in hand and pressed against Ahriman's temple. His face curled in anger, cheeks mottling scarlet, eyes narrowed in fury. "Shut up. Shut up. SHUT THE HELL UP!" The gun barrel shoved Ahriman's head sideways. "Say one more thing about her and I'll kill you!"

Two strides put me across the stage. My hand clamped on Boothe's arm. I leaned back, using my body weight to yank him away from the warlock. Ramming into him with my shoulder, I shoved him off the stage. "Everybody stop. Right. Now."

The demon's cackle whistled through Ahriman's teeth, cutting the air. The shrill "tee-hee-heeing" crawled like an earwig, burrowing deep into my brain. It was maddening. The nerve under my eye fluttered like a butterfly that'd been pinned alive. "Y'all are playing into his hands. Knock it the fuck off."

Boothe shook his head. Slowly, he put his gun away. "I can't handle that damned laughter, Deacon. And the shit he's saying to Kat is . . ." He turned and roared. Anger ripped from his chest, splitting the air like a crack of thunder. His hand flashed down against a barstool, crumpling the metal and vinyl into a tangled wreck. Breath bellowed in and out of the Were-rabbit, his sculpted chest rising and falling. "He just needs to shut the hell up."

"And now we hear from the sodomite! You should keep your disgusting mouth shut, faggot. Nobody cares what you say." The air was brittle, crackling around the edges with tension and pain. The demon leaned forward, stretching Ahriman's arms in a disjointed tangle as it leered at Boothe. Rolled back eyes gleamed under a veil of scraggly hair. "They all know you only come to Kathleen's defense because of guilt. The lust in your heart for Larson. You jump because you burn for what she has."

"ENOUGH!" Father Mulcahy rose up. His arm swung, an aspergillum clenched in his fist. Droplets flung, splashing in a line across the demon's face. The blessed liquid sizzled when it struck the demon-possessed warlock, raising blisters like it was hot bacon grease. The demon howled in pain. "I bind you in the name of Jesus Christ. Hold your tongue." Ahriman's jaw clamped shut, muffling the curses of the demon.

I looked around the room again. Boothe was still standing by the stage, muscles corded in his shoulders, hands clenched into fists. His eyes were slitted as he seethed, staring at the demon-possessed warlock.

Kat hunched over, hands covering her face. She shook as she sobbed. Larson hovered over her, hands moving toward, then away. Almost touching her for comfort, then stopping. His face kept turning, looking at her, then looking up at me. The expression he wore kept changing, making him unreadable.

Special Agent Heck sat on the same stool, unmoved. He hadn't fallen into the trap and had kept his mouth shut. The demon hadn't spoken to him. Not at all. Was it because he was a pious man, with no sins to pull out and use against him? Or was it because of something else? Something darker? Was it possible that Special Agent Heck was collaborating with the witches?

My skin went cold.

I didn't know anything about the man in the dark suit. He'd shown up and I had taken him in, letting him join me in this. My head swirled with the implications. Before I realized it, my hand was halfway to the pistol under my arm.

Stop.

Stop.

Hold on just one damn minute.

I hadn't just taken Special Agent Heck on his own recommendation. Longinus had vouched for him. Longinus who I had fought side by side with. Longinus who I had bled with. Longinus who was a living, breathing saint with a holy relic for a weapon.

Son of a bitch.

The demon had done its work well. Spreading filth and corruption, half-lies and twisted truths, to drive us apart. Realization struck me like a cannonball. By not saying anything about Heck, that damned demon had made me doubt him.

Special Agent Heck turned as if he felt my intent. His eyes went to my hand, hanging still in front of me, angled toward my gun. They flicked to my face.

He nodded at me once, dipping his chin down, then up slowly.

My hand dropped to my side.

God damned demons.

36

The demon glared at Father Mulcahy with blind eyes. The muscles around the eyes bunched, thickening the brow and sharpening the cheeks. Capillaries had burst in the sockets, spreading plum-colored bruising around them like a mask. It gnashed Ahriman's teeth together in a grind that could be heard across the room.

The priest stood tall, holy water shaker in one hand, crucifix held in the other. The cross swung toward the demon's face. "Who am I speaking to?"

The demon snarled, the sound ripping out of Ahriman's throat like guts torn from a caught fish. Father Mulcahy slashed down with the aspergillum, slinging holy water across the demon's chest. "In the name of Christ Jesus, I command you to speak your name."

The demon's mouth opened, words spilling out of it in a guttural language. The syllables were harsh, chopping the air. Each consonant felt like someone panging two pans together. They vibrated behind my molars, drawing my jaw painfully tight.

Father Mulcahy pointed with the holy water shaker. "Speak English, hellspawn."

Ahriman's beard dripped, soaked with spittle and blood. The demon's voice was strangled. "I am the Keeper."

"Not your function. Give me your name."

The demon spat. "I am the Keeper. My name and function are one."

"How many of you are there?"

"There are many of us. Too many to name. Too many to count."

"In the Name of Christ, tell me how to stop Selene."

Ahriman's mouth stretched in a deranged grin. "Silly little man with your weak little faith. You cannot stop Selene. She is indomitable. She will have her will and her way. Give up now! Lay down and die—"

The priest cut him off with a chop of his hand. "Be quiet. In Christ's Name, be quiet." The demon looked away, jaw locked. Father Mulcahy leaned in. "You will tell me what I want to know, or I will call upon St. Michael the Archangel to come down from Heaven and smite you."

A growl rolled out of clenched teeth. "I will tell you nothing!"

"Speak the truth in the Name of Christ or suffer torment."

"I am already tormented!"

Father Mulcahy shoved the crucifix against the demon's skull. The Keeper jerked and shook Ahriman's body like a live wire was struck against it. Smoke curled under the priest's hand, a loud sizzle cut through the demon's howl. The priest wrapped a thick arm around Ahriman's head, shoving it forward against the crucifix in his hand. White light shone brightly around his hand, so bright it outlined the bones like an X-ray.

The demon jerked the warlock's body, bouncing Father Mulcahy on the balls of his feet. Face red and veins swollen, the priest squeezed his arms, pressing against the demon-possessed wizard. His voice was harsh as he screamed, "Tell me how to stop Selene! I command you by the Sacrifice of Christ! Speak the truth!"

"The window is small! She can only perform the Black Mass when the time is right!"

Father Mulcahy staggered. The Keeper slumped against the cuffs that held him to the brass pole. Moving quickly, I put my arm around the priest. He sagged against me, head even with my shoulder. Sweat soaked his salt and pepper hair, slicking it to his skull. The crucifix and the aspergillum vibrated in his hand like he'd been struck with a palsy. I could feel his heart thudding inside his chest through my arm across his back.

My own chest tightened. Father Mulcahy felt so small in my arms. Fragile. He looked at me. The color had washed out of his face, leaving it gray and pallored. Deep creases marked the corners of his eyes, lines cut with age. He took a breath, held it, then let it out. I wanted to send him away. To tell him he had done enough and he didn't have to do any more.

"Are you all right?"

He blew breath out between clenched teeth. "I could use a fucking cigarette."

I wanted to make him sit down. He should be in his own room, wrapped in a blanket, reading the newest Andrew Vachss book. Safe and sound.

That's what I wanted. It's not what I could have tonight. Nobody could do what the priest could do.

"I'll light up with you after you send this asshole back to the pit where he belongs."

He nodded, straightening, pulling away. Squaring his shoulders, he took a step toward the demon-possessed warlock. I swore in my heart that when this was all over, I was going to do what I had to to make sure Father Mulcahy took a step back. He'd done his service and deserved some rest.

Something broke deep inside of me with the thought that one day he wouldn't be here. He was too committed to the fight, and too stubborn for me to shut out altogether, but age and past injuries were slowing him down, making him vulnerable.

I pushed it all out of my mind. Do the job. Get through the night. Deal with the rest later.

Father Mulcahy's voice rose up in a cadence. "I cast you out, unclean spirit. I cast you along with every satanic power of the Enemy, every spectre from hell, and all your fell companions. In the name of our Lord Jesus Christ, begone."

The Keeper jerked Ahriman's body in the chair, bouncing the legs off the floor, banging it against the brass pole. The wood striking metal rang out like a bell. The demon screamed out, air vibrating around his head. "No! Fuck you, priest! I have held this body too long! You will not remove me! I own Ahriman body and soul!"

Father Mulcahy kept chanting, ignoring the demon. "Hearken, therefore, and tremble in fear, Satan, you enemy of the faith, you foe of the human race, you begetter of death, you robber of life, you corrupter of justice, you root of all evil and vice; seducer of men, betrayer of the nations, instigator of envy, font of avarice, fomentor of discord, author of pain and sorrow. Why do you stand and resist, knowing as you must that Christ the Lord brings your plans to nothing?" His hand flicked out, slinging holy water across the demon-possessed warlock in a sizzling slice.

The demon cackled, the laugh high-pitched and sharp. It bounced in the chair like a gleeful child, cracked lips pulled apart, rolled back eyes wide and excited. "You are too late! Ha! You fools!"

A tingle crawled across the base of my neck.

Uh-oh.

"Father Mulcahy . . ."

The priest ignored me, keeping his back turned. Tension shook his shoulders. His voice rose up in a shout. "I adjure you, profligate dragon, in the name of the Spotless Lamb who has trodden down the asp and the basilisk, who overcame the lion and the dragon, to depart from this man!" He swung the crucifix down, striking it across Ahriman's brow.

The demon jerked under the blow but kept laughing. The cackles, like fingernails plucking a steel string, jarring along my bones. "It has been done, you stupid humans! The end is nigh for you!"

Dread crouched in the pit of my stomach. My hand went out, hovering by the priest's shoulder, not touching him. "Padre . . ."

He kept speaking, calling out the exorcism.

"Tremble and flee, as I call on the name of the Lord, before whom the denizens of hell cower. The Word made flesh commands you." His hand swung in the sign of the Cross over Ahriman's head, causing him to jerk and foam at the mouth.

"The Virgin's Son commands you." He made the sign of the cross again. "Jesus of Nazareth commands you, and when He had cast you out, you did not even dare, except by His leave, to enter into a herd of swine. I adjure you in His name."

The lights in the club flickered.

His hand swung up, down, and then left and right in the

sign of the Cross. It whipped down, crucifix pointed like a sword. He roared, "Begone!"

The last word cracked through the noise of the Keeper's howl, cutting it sharply like cloth in shears. The silence swept through the room, filling it like the aftermath of a sonic boom. The world hung suspended for a long moment. My skin was tight, heart heavy in my chest. No one in the room moved, each of us holding our breath.

Waiting.

Someone knocked on the front door.

My gun was out and in my hand, safety off, finger on the trigger. Its heavy, comforting weight filled my entire grip. The heft of the chrome barrel pulled forward just a little. The ridges on the trigger were sharp against the tip of my index finger. Familiar.

Special Agent Heck slid off his stool, his own gun out in a two-handed grip pointed at the ground. He was looking at the door, face blank.

Boothe moved up beside him quickly, feet rolling silently heel to toe, his gun up and pointed forward as he moved. He stopped even with Heck, both of them waiting on me.

Across the room Larson stood in front of Kat, pistol in hand. He didn't move away from her, just shifted from one foot to the other.

I stepped off the end of the stage, taking the shock through my knees. Looking back, I saw Father Mulcahy stumble a step. He dropped the aspergillum to grab the chair that was still beside him. It clattered to the ground, dribbling a puddle of holy water. Ahriman slumped behind him, hanging boneless and limp. Father Mulcahy gripped the chair, tendons stringing up along his forearm, using it to steady himself. His other hand rose, waving me on.

Slowly, I walked to the door. Each step the dread inside

me grew, building stone by stone until it threatened to tear a hole in my guts and spill me out on the floor.

I felt detached, like I was watching someone else. Like it wasn't my hand reaching for the lock. The cold finger down my spine felt hollow and staticky. Numb, my fingers twisted the latch, releasing the bolts that held the door shut.

I pulled the handle.

The vampire standing there smiled widely, fangs gleaming long and deadly in the club lights. Her voice was a throaty purr.

"Hello, Sugah, miss me?"

37

My mind crashed around the sight of the vampire in front of me.

Blair.

I had run into her twice before. The first time she was working in a jack shack on the shit side of town. That time I'd had to let her go. The second time was at a no-tell motel on the other shit side of town. That time she had slipped away.

Her arm rose up and draped the side of the door as she cocked one curvy hip to the left, framing herself for display. Long, spray-tanned legs stretched up to disappear into a pair of Daisy Dukes cut higher than lingerie. Her top was a camouflage shirt that looked like it should belong to toddler. It was stretched to capacity, thin cotton straining over a pair of breasts that could only be described as outrageously fake. Her face was pretty, doe-eyed and delicate, with thick lips made for sucking blood, and a head full of thick bleach-blond hair.

"Y'all hiring, Sugah? I think I could work at a joint like this." She drew in air she didn't need, expanding her already expansive chest. "I shouldn't need an audition. You've already seen me dance."

My gun whipped up, barrel pointing at her forehead. Crystal blue eyes raised to look at it, lifting her small, pointed chin. There were marks carved red and raw into her throat. Just like the vampires at the movie theater.

The vampires that Ahriman had controlled.

Aw, shit.

Behind me the Keeper began to giggle.

Aw, double shit.

My finger pulled the trigger.

Faster than my eyes could track, Blair ducked under my gun, the bullet zinging through thick, hair-sprayed locks. Taloned hands slammed into my chest like a baseball bat, lifting me off my feet and throwing me through the air. Time stretched around me as I hung in the air, flying backward. My gun slipped weightlessly out of my fingers, spinning lazily through the air and away from me. I watched three other bloodsuckers zip in the door behind Blair. I tilted, losing sight of them.

Vampires need invitation to go in someone's home.

This was a business. Damn.

My shoulders crashed into the floor, snapping time back in place. My feet kept flying, flipping me heels over head. I rolled into a line of tables and chairs, jarring to a stop with my face against the carpet.

The air I sucked in smelled like a beer-soaked ashtray someone had wiped their ass with. *Get the carpets steam-cleaned, asshole,* ran through my head as I fought off the vertigo of being slammed around.

I had to get *up.* My ears opened in a whoosh, the room shockingly loud around me. Bangs and crashes. Cracks of gunfire. Animal growls. Screams.

Shoving my palms against the floor, I pushed myself up. A table that had landed on my back rolled off, taking what felt like a yard of skin off my kidneys with it. I raised my head to utter chaos.

Larson had thrown the tables around him and Kat onto their sides, making a hedge. They both crouched behind them, guns out. Larson had a holy object in his hand, holding it in front of him. I couldn't see what it was through the glow coming off it. It was holding off the two vampires who were so angry they were hopping at the edge of the holy light.

Special Agent Heck was on top of the bar, gun out and blasting at Blair. He wasn't hitting her, just keeping her off him. He moved nimbly, staying one quickstep ahead of her.

Father Mulcahy was using the crucifix and the aspergillum to hold off the fourth vampire. Holy light shone around him, spilling over the slumped form of Ahriman. The vampire, a football player–sized Indian, darted in, trying to dive under the edge of the light. Father Mulcahy flicked the aspergillum, cutting a line of holy water across the bloodsucker's back.

Boothe had shifted. His head was larger, oval, and covered in short gray fur. Bright crimson eyes the size of saucers glared under ears that had lengthened and now waved on top of that oval skull. His legs had broken, now double-jointed and crookshanked. They raised his height to over seven feet. Thick bunches of muscle padded his new form.

He was getting his ass kicked by George.

The Were-gorilla stood toe to toe with Boothe. The coarse black and silver fur that covered his body jutted up like bristles on a brush. He stood upright on thickly bowed legs, long arms knotted in muscle whipped through the air. Hammer-like fists pounded the Were-rabbit's sides. George's eyes were rolled back into his monkey skull, the whites of them shining out over a monkey face pulled into a gleeful, murderous leer.

The Keeper's twittering cackle rolled out of his gibbon lips.

The demon had pulled a fast one on us.

Tiff and Ronnie came running into the room as Boothe fell under a thunderous blow from George's big right hand. The possessed Were-gorilla turned, thick tongue sliding around his lips, leaving a wet, dripping mask of saliva.

The Keeper's voice singsonged out of him as he leered at the girls. "Oh me, oh my, sweet as pumpkin pie!"

I started slinging bullets across the room.

38

Four bullets thundered out of the end of my Colt .45. They zipped across the room, cutting between Blair and Special Agent Heck, zinging over Boothe's fallen form, and smashing into George's back. Blood spurted out like broken sprinklers as the bullets stitched him from one shoulder to the other. The impact knocked him forward. He spun with a scream, big arm banging against the bar.

The whole bar shook, knocking Special Agent Heck off balance. He tumbled, disappearing behind it. Blair leaped over the bar after him. I fired after her, but she was moving with vamp speed and I was in motion, heading toward Tiff.

The bullets went wide, missing Blair and shattering bottles that lined the back of the bar. The slide locked back on the Colt. My thumb brushed the magazine release, dropping the empty clip as my other hand yanked a full one from the bandolier around my waist and slapped it home. A flick of my thumb released the slide, stripping off a fresh round and putting it in the chamber.

Tiff came up by the stage, gun out. She had hit the ground and rolled when George turned toward them. The Judge jerked in her hand. She popped off a handful of rounds. Her shells punched into his side, knocking out gouts of blood.

The bullets were hurting him, but not dropping him.

Sonnuvabitch! We were still using lead bullets for the witches. They were almost worthless against a lycanthrope, especially a lycanthrope jacked up on demon juice.

"Switch to silver!" I dropped the clip I had just put in out of my pistol, reaching around my side for one full of silver. It slid home with a click as I jumped over Boothe's fallen form. He was still shifted in Were-rabbit, which meant he was still alive, but he was out cold. The side of his face swelled like someone was filling a water balloon.

Tiff gave a sharp nod, slender fingers working her cylinder release. Empty shells clattered to the floor. She pulled a speedloader off her belt.

The vampire Father Mulcahy was holding off whipped around the end of the stage. Tiff jerked away as his hand flashed out, cuffing her across the jaw. Her reflexes made it a glancing blow; if they hadn't, it would have broken her neck. Still, it drove her to the ground, knocking the gun out of her hand.

The vampire careened off, snatching Ronnie up in his arms. He picked her up, lifting her into the air so that her feet dangled in front of him. His head went back, jaw knotting to distend long, wet fangs. His skull hinged, opening his mouth as wide as possible so that he could get the deepest bite radius. Neck muscles corded, he was ready to strike.

The second before he struck was the second the spiders fell on him.

They dropped like hailstones of judgment, pelting him with translucent bodies. I couldn't count how many there were, they were so fast. They stuck to him, swarming over undead flesh, pouring into his mouth, clogging his throat, choking off his scream. They skittered over his eyeballs, spindly little legs needlepointing through undead corneas. A gossamer net of webbing began to sheen over his skin, binding him.

Then the venom started to take hold.

Hundreds of tiny spider bites began to smoke, filling the air with the smell of rotten curried goat. Ronnie stumbled away as the vampire let go in a spasm of agony.

George turned, demonic lycanthrope speed making him faster than my eye could track. My hand exploded in pain as he slapped the gun out of it. A roar tore out of me, ripping from the bottom of my guts as my left arm became a forest fire of agony. It made me trip on my own feet, stumbling to my knees in front of him. I knelt there, cradling my injured arm across my chest.

A scream came from behind me. I could see Tiff from the corner of my eye. She was shaking her head, trying to clear it. The scream wasn't from her.

The Keeper stood in front of me wearing George's body. His cackling voice was different through the Weregorilla's vocal cords. It was lower, and it dropped some of the consonants at the ends of words, but it still had that nerve-grating quality. It still sounded like someone grinding the edges of glass shards against each other.

"The mighty Deacon Chalk, at my feet. Well, not my feet, feet that I am using." He ran hands the size of catcher mitts down George's arms. "I like this body. I've never possessed a lycanthrope before. It's not often that we can. This one lost his faith in God when his woman was killed. You remember Lucy, right? The girl you *murdered* by using her as a weapon in your sad little war. This one has never forgiven you. He holds a burning ember of wrath inside his chest for you. That's why he has given away pieces of his soul for the addiction of alcohol." Rolled back, fish-belly white eyes looked down at me. A line of drool ran from the corner of George's mouth where the demon pulled it into a disturbing grin. "It's funny, Deacon Chalk. Because of *your* actions I have the perfect vessel to destroy you with. This is your fault."

My voice was gravel in my throat. "Go to hell." Anger coursed through me, setting my veins on fire, rushing over the pain.

The Keeper cackled, raising gooseflesh on my arms. "I am about to kill you, Deacon Chalk. I am going to use the body of your ally to strike you dead." He paused and looked over at Tiff. "I think after I kill her I will go back into Ahriman and have him resurrect her. He'd like that. He is such an overachiever when it comes to pretty girls and his necromancy. You wouldn't believe the things he comes up with, even without my help." The Keeper raised George's hairy arms up, lifting them over me. Those heavy gorilla hands clenched into fists the size of cinderblocks.

The knife in my hand slashed out, edge biting into the knot of scar tissue that was George's knee. Scar tissue I made with a silver bullet the first time I met him. The gnarled flesh parted bloodlessly, the weight of George's body pulling the edges apart. The blade grated on bone and cartilage deep inside the joint.

Pushing, I rose, jerking the knife free. My hand flashed, driven by rage, and drove down again. The point of the knife sank into the Were-gorilla's thigh. Hot, moist monkey breath misted my scalp as the Keeper roared. My left arm hung down, weak and nearly useless. I drove that shoulder into George's chest. Twisting the knife in my hand, I scooped out a chunk of thigh meat. The blade came free in a splash of blood that scalded across my arm. A jerk of my arm drove it up and into the Were-gorilla's guts.

Blind, fish-belly eyes widened in surprise. The ten-inch blade sank to the hilt, cutting off the Keeper's brittle howls.

Shoving with my whole body, muscles screaming in my lower back, I ripped up and out with the blade. George's intestines tumbled over my arm like slick rubbery sausages. The air between us filled with a sick, green stink of perforated bowel.

My stomach tried to climb out of my throat.

The Keeper stumbled, big mitt hands fumbling with the loose body parts. It was gross and fucked up, but even this wouldn't kill George. It hurt him, and therefore hurt the demon possessing him, but his lycanthropy would fix it given enough time. I had to stop him while he was being ridden by the demon; he was too powerful to leave standing. It would be like leaving a thermonuclear device in the hands of a cracked-out terrorist.

Numb fingers closed around the handle of the .44 Magnum in my waistband. The .44 Magnum loaded with silver hollowpoints.

I didn't want to kill him, but I would be damned before I let the demon use him to kill anyone else.

That's when Blair slammed into my back, knocked my hand away, and rode me to the ground.

39

Blair drove me face-first into the sopping carpet. I was slicked from waist to forehead with foul-smelling Were-gorilla gut blood. Talons dug into the muscle of my shoulders, sticking deep into the meat, tearing into the swath of burn from earlier. I shoved with my arms, spinning against her weight, using the gore as lubricant to buck my way onto my back.

Blair crouched over me, thick blond hair wild around a face gone feral. Her pupils had dilated widely, covering the middle of her eyes, the corners puddled with crimson. Fangs distended from her gums, jaw knotted with muscle as she hissed at me. The symbols cut into her throat shone with magick as she threw back her head to strike like a cobra.

I slashed out with the knife, the keen edge splitting the skin under her breasts, across her rib cage in a wash of black, clotted, room temperature blood. She yelped, tearing down with a taloned hand. It ripped across my forearm, splashing blood from four identical slashes.

Adrenaline crystallized everything, slowing time. I watched my blood arc up, globules of it spinning and twisting in a stream. It splashed across the symbols on her throat, coating them. Soaking into them.

The effect was a metaphysical lightning strike.

My power roared to life, ripping out of me and smashing into Blair. It was a boiling ocean sweeping through her. A connection forged, tumbling into the space between us. With a jolt, it locked into place. I felt her dead heart start up. It spasmed, jerking to life, starting to thump in her chest. It pounded in heavy, hard beats, knocking around for a second before evening into a smooth, solid rhythm.

Beating in time to mine.

Her face smoothed into her human guise. She looked at me with wide blue eyes, lips slightly parted over sheathed fangs.

The magick that had controlled her broke like spun sugar in the hand of a child.

My voice was harsh through clenched teeth. "Get the hell off me, bloodsucker."

Blair flew off me, literally flew. She rose into the air with a swift jerk like she had been pulled by strings. She landed, crouching on top of the bar like a cat.

I stood. The connection stretched between us. I could feel her in my mind, like that thing you don't want to forget so you shove it into a corner of your skull for later. I pushed a thought out at her.

Raise your right hand.

A long-taloned hand rose up, lifting over her head and staying there.

Scratch your ass.

With one hand still over her head, the other one went behind her, moving in a back-and-forth motion as she did what I thought.

Stop.

The vampire froze in place. The connection was strong, humming between us.

Kill yourself.

Blair shook, body convulsing from head to toe like she had hypothermia. The connection between us flared hot, rolling back on me like a desert wind. My nostrils filled with the smell of vampire, a reptile smell of snakeskin and venom. The connection cooled off. Blair was still undead on the bar.

Apparently I couldn't command her to do that.

"Deacon!"

The world came back to me with a crack. Sounds rushed into my ears. I spun to find Ronnie and Tiff helping Boothe to stand. He had shrunk, still in his hybrid form, but more man than rabbit. One side of his head was swollen, eye squeezed closed by a bruise the size of my foot.

Special Agent Heck was on the other side of the room. His white shirt was splashed with blood, blazing pink from collar to midchest in a crimson tie-dye. The blood came from a gash on his neck. His gun was blazing, pumping bullets into the chest of a vampire that jerked and convulsed under the firepower. It took a second, but the vamp finally fell, exploding into dust before it hit the floor. An orb bounced off the carpet. It was revealed as the bloodsucker disintegrated around it. The softball-sized orb looked like it was made of solid crystal.

My mind blinked. *What the hell?*

A few feet away from him Larson lay in a heap, limbs crumpled and tangled. He looked dead, but I couldn't see any blood. The cross he had been holding lay in his open palm, glowing. My eyes tracked around him, looking, searching.

On the other side of him a vampire was wrapped around Kat.

The vampire pressed himself against her on the ground, its face buried against her throat. Wet, snuffling sounds came from the bloodsucker. It had a scrawny arm wedged into Kat's mouth, forcing her jaws apart. Black blood ran from four slashes down that arm. It slid, pouring into Kat's open mouth. Pouring down her throat.

Everything else shut away as I pushed off, moving across the floor, jumping on the stage, sliding across the boards on my hip. I bounced off the edge on the other side, feet on the floor again, moving. Two more strides and I was on them, fingers closing in the vampire's permed hair. It was brittle, breaking in my hand, crumbling.

I couldn't pull the vamp off with his fangs locked in her jugular, not without ripping Kat's throat out. The bloodsucker rode her, pinning her to the floor with his body, grinding into her. His arm bent her head back, stretching her neck under his sucking mouth. Kat's eyes were wide, panic raw inside them. Her screams were muffled against undead flesh, choking wetly down into gurgles, drowning on vampire blood. She fought weakly, struggles slowing to shudders.

Kat was dying while I stood there.

I had to get the vampire off her.

The blade in my hand slid into the hollow under the vampire's ear. I shoved deep, wedging the point between the jawbone and its socket. Cold blood jetted over my hand. I jerked up and then down, severing the tendons that held the vampire's jaw in place. Prying with the blade and pulling up broke the seal of the vamp's mouth on Kat's throat. He came away with a sloppy, wet, sucking sound.

Rage roared from deep inside me. It blasted through my

chest, spilling into my arms. The vampire was weightless as I jerked him into the air, holding him by his fried hair. He dangled in my grip, kicking and screaming through a jaw that hung askew. His tongue flailed, loose jawbone banging against collarbones. I rammed the knife in its bloody mouth, sawing back and forth. It took a second before the head popped off, coming away in my hand. The body turned to dust before it hit the ground at my feet.

A second crystal globe thudded to the carpet.

What the fuck?

It rolled away, zigging and zagging until it tapped to a stop by the stage.

Kat reached up, arm limp. Blood spurted from the wound on her neck weakly in slow beats. The part of my mind that stays detached realized her heart was slowing down. Under the smears of blood and gore, her skin was colorless. She tried to turn, eyes looking, searching.

Larson crawled to her, scrambling to get there. His hand closed on hers and he pulled her close. There was a lump the size of a baseball on his head. He looked up at me, anguish raw on his face, tears streaming. The pupil of his right eye had blown, eating all the blue of the iris. The eye had also gone lazy, drifting to the corner unanchored.

Head injury.

"We have to get her out of here! Deacon, please! She's dying."

The Keeper's voice came from behind me.

"She's not the only one."

40

The Keeper stood in George's body on the stage. The demon had scooped up the Were-gorilla's entrails and now they draped over his shoulder in a lumpy, bubble-gum pink bandolier. The wound across George's stomach yawned open like a toothless maw. It was starting to seal but still gaped. The knee I had sliced apart had knit itself back together.

Damn lycanthrope healing.

The brass stripper pole lay on the stage, wrenched from its moorings. Ahriman was still unconscious, draped head down on George's other shoulder.

Father Mulcahy dangled from one of the possessed Were-gorilla's hands.

The demon cackled. "Bring me the mix-breed bastards or I will kill the priest."

Larson screamed at me from the floor. He struggled to lift Kat. Failing. "Deacon! We have to get Kat out of here!"

The world shrank, everything becoming fuzzy. Disconnected.

Tiff and Boothe had guns out, pointing at the Keeper.

Special Agent Heck was walking with his gun raised.

Blair still crouched on the bar like a statue, eyes jerking wildly around the room, the only movement she made.

My hand slid along my lower back, my nails skimming the thin cotton of my shirt. The grip of the snubnosed .44 Magnum slipped across my palm like a lover. It was heavy in my hand as I pulled it from the holster. The front sight dragged across my kidney as I swung it out and around, raising it up. One eye closed, sighting down my arm and over my hand, I lined the blade of the front sight with George's head.

The world opened back up in a rush.

The Keeper jerked Father Mulcahy between himself and our guns. "You can't shoot this body without hitting your precious priest. Give me what I want and I will go away."

I widened my chest, cheek almost touching my outstretched arm. The front sight looked as wide as a street. "You know what your problem is?"

"I have the advantage here!"

Larson screamed at me again. I ignored it, concentrating on the possessed lycanthrope holding the priest and the warlock.

"You don't understand a damn thing about us. The man you're using as a hostage would rather die than let you have those kids."

The Keeper twisted George's face into a mask of hatred. He danced back and forth on bowed legs. "But are you willing to kill him to stop me?"

My mind flashed to every talk I had ever had with Father Mulcahy. All the times we had discussed the nature of evil and how it was our responsibility to stand in the gap. That protecting the innocent, no matter the cost, was the reason we had both been put on our paths. I thought about how he would get worked up, honey and whiskey voice deepening as he got animated. He would talk to me about righteousness with a fervor that belonged to a Pentecostal instead of a staid Catholic priest. The speeches would always end with the warmth of sentimentality and scotch and the feeling that this man, who I loved like a second father, was proud of me and the work we did together.

I thought about all the times he had stood with me, shoulder to shoulder against the vile forces of hell itself. He stood, unflinching, even though he didn't have Angel blood to make him stronger. He stood with only the strength of his body and the protection of his Faith.

I thought about his love for Sophia's kids. Conviction burning fever bright in his gray eyes as he said he would do whatever it took to keep them safe.

I thought about the gun in my hand. A .44 Magnum full of bullets powerful enough to sever limbs and blow fist-sized holes in people. I carried it as my last resort. The gun guaranteed to kill something. If I shot a human with it, there would be no surviving. No flesh wounds.

The Keeper barked at me. "I know how much you love this man, Deacon. He's the father you don't have anymore. Are you willing to trade his life to save three mixed-breed mongrels?"

The gun roared as I squeezed the trigger.

The effect was instantaneous. Faster than the eye could see, the bullet crossed the space between me and the demon. It went past Father Mulcahy at 1100 feet per second, cracking the sound barrier.

It was at maximum velocity when it blasted into Ahriman's skull, began to tumble, and tore his head apart like a water balloon filled with gore.

The Keeper's voice ripped out of George's throat, a tornado of glass shards. He screamed inhumanly, the sound so loud and high-pitched it made the bones of my arm vibrate. The air filled with the stifling reek of sulfur.

Demonic power exploded, rolling over me in a tidal wave of honey hornets, sticky and stinging and crushing. My vision went blurry, eyes watering desperately to wash out the acid sting.

Blinking, I barely had time to react when the Keeper leaped off the stage at me, swinging Father Mulcahy like a weapon. The priest's body whipped toward me. I tried to turn and catch him, to take the blow, absorb the damage, so he wouldn't be hurt.

It was like getting slammed into by a city bus.

Air drove from my lungs, scattering black specks across my eyesight like birdseed at a wedding. I wrapped my arms around him as I fell, trying to pull him out of the demon-possessed Were-gorilla's hands. The Keeper let go, shoving both of us away. I held on to Father Mulcahy as we skidded across the carpet. Rug burn splashed across my arm, raw and nasty. We banged to a stop with him lying on top of me.

Gunshots cracked from the other side of the club. I couldn't see, but I knew Tiff, Boothe, and Heck had begun shooting at the Keeper.

The priest weighed a thousand pounds as I pushed, sliding him off me. He rolled bonelessly to the floor. My chest sprang up, free from the burden, dragging air back in my lungs. It burned going down my throat, raw and splintery. Each gasp lightened my lungs, making them feel like they were reinflating, filling them with small sips of sweet oxygen.

Father Mulcahy lay still and limp on the floor. I reached for him, my hand touching his shoulder.

Not breathing.

My heart lurched, clenching tight like a fist.

No. Not now. Please God. Not now. Not yet.

A tremor ran under my hand.

Father Mulcahy hitched in a breath.

Oh, Holy Mary, Mother of God. Thank you. Thank you, Lord. I owe you.

The priest sat up with a groan. He looked around. His eyes were out of focus, glazed over. "What's happening?"

Pushing myself to my feet, I pulled him up. He was steady enough to stand. Larson screamed at me again.

Kat.

My eyes cut over. Larson was still cradling Kat, she was still breathing, chest jerking up and down. Blood had stopped shooting from her neck but still dripped off her. She had lost a lot of blood, skin the color of paper. I had to get her out of here or she wasn't going to make it. That brick crashed back in my chest.

Movement turned my head.

The Keeper had Ahriman's corpse by the leg. He was jumping away, leaping and swinging toward the back of the club. Tiff, Boothe, and Heck were still shooting. The demon-possessed Were-gorilla stopped at the door leading to the employees' lounge. A roar tore out of his throat as he spun and tossed the dead wizard across the room toward Tiff, Boothe, and Heck.

The body whipped through the air, scattering them like bowling pins.

"I am the power behind the magick! You destroyed my vessel, so I will use this one, but I will still help Selene crack the skin of this world." He lowered his eyes to me, glaring. Monkey lips cracked open, spitting out one word.

"Detonate."

He spun, disappearing through the door. His last word spun magick through the room. It swept in like a pollen cloud. My mouth filled with the taste of vinegar and iron.

At my feet, the crystal orb from the dusted vampire

began to pulse with a sinister red light. The magick in the room spiked with each throb of the crystal.

Oh, shit.

"Everyone get out!"

Pushing off, I turned and propelled Father Mulcahy. He stumbled toward the door. Tiff was there, shoving her head under his arm and pulling it across her shoulders for support. She began to run, dragging him along with her. Special Agent Heck was right beside them. Blair had disappeared from the top of the bar.

The magick spiked faster and faster, cycling up and down, building in intensity. Every time it spiked it felt like someone was shoving a hot poker in my spine. We had seconds, maybe less.

I shouldered Larson out of the way, sliding my arms under Kat. She was dead weight, limp and heavy. I tripped and fell to my knees. They banged the floor in a sharp crack of pain that ran up the bones of my thighs. Magick spiked, driving pain, then fell. I shoved, pulling my legs under me to stand. Kat's head lolled against my chest. The thin cotton of my shirt soaked through with her blood. One foot in front of the other, I pushed to the door.

Magick spiked, pain drove, magick fell.

Special Agent Heck held the door for me, waving me through. A glance over my shoulder showed Boothe disappearing through the curtain toward the back of the club.

He's going after Josh.

I knew it was true. If Tiff had been in the back of the club, I would have gone that way too. I kept running through the door, holding Kat in my arms. Special Agent Heck slammed it shut behind me.

I took twenty steps before Polecats exploded, throwing flames into the night and me ass over teakettle into the parking lot.

41

I shoved Larson out of the way. He banged against the side of the Comet with a thunk. "I've got her! Go get prepped!"

Raw, red anger flashed across his face. His mouth twisted in a snarl. Whirling on him, I snarled right back, a low, wet, animal sound that pulled from my gut. Jerking up, he shook himself and ran to the door of the clinic, pulling keys out of his pocket with a jangle.

No hospital, not with a damn vampire bite to try and explain.

I leaned in the backseat of the Comet, heart in my throat.

Kat's eyes were filled with a wild, animal panic. The only color in her face was the bruised purple hollows under her eyes. Her breath was shallow gasps, sips taken by a drowning woman. The blood slathered on her throat and chest had begun to congeal, turning into a burgundy jelly that coated her from cheekbones to waistline.

My hands went around her. Gentle as I could but still hurrying, I slid her across the leather interior and pulled her into my arms. It put my face close to her throat while I lifted.

The wound, the fucking wound on her neck was deep,

edges ragged. It looked sticky, coated in syrup, like that cheap gunk they use to make fake blood for special effects. This was all too real. It didn't smell like candy and red food coloring number forty.

It smelled like rust and iron and meat. And cut just under the edge of that was the musky, reptile taint of shed skin and venom.

Kat was limp, heavier than she looked. Her weight was all dead, bones disconnected in her skin. She flopped and I held her tight to my chest, hurrying across the lot, up the ramp, and into the clinic. Each footstep jostled her head against my chest, making her eyes flutter.

"Stay with me, Kat. Just hold on."

She didn't respond. A twitch started in her. I could feel it under my hands as it ran up her spine and into her neck, making her head jiggle and her wound chew open and closed.

God, I know I said I owe You, but don't You fucking take her. Don't make her my price.

I moved through the lobby and down the hall, steps getting faster, stride getting longer. *Hurry. Fucking hurry.* I stepped into the exam room and went straight to the table where Larson was frantically pulling equipment. I laid her down. Larson grabbed her arm before I could pull away and deftly sank a needle into the waxy, pale skin. A thin plastic tube coiled off it, flushing red as he twisted a clamp; blood began to flow freely through the IV.

He was working with a level of concentration that kept his hands from shaking, but not the tears out of his eyes. They spilled, running down freckled cheeks, soaking into his goatee and making it darken. He came around the table, ramming into me with his hip. His fingertips held round, sticky pads.

His voice was a strangled growl. "This is my area, get out of my way."

I stepped back, letting him work. He pressed the pads to Kat's chest, clipping thin bundles of wires to each of them. The heart monitor kicked on with a shrill beep that sliced me to the nerves making me jump.

It began beeping and tracing little mountains on its screen. The green peaks and valleys were slow coming, long stretches of flat green between them. The beeps that marked her heartbeat were erratic. They staggered around, sometimes clumping into a short, tight group, then stretching out and coming very slowly. The ones that stretched out seemed to be getting longer.

One one thousand, two one thousand, *beep.*

One one thousand, two one thousand, three one thousand, *beep.*

One one thousand, two one thousand, three one thousand, four one thousand, *beep beep beep.*

Larson pulled over a tray full of shiny instruments. He snatched up a big yellow flashlight, shoving it toward me. "Shine this here." He pointed at Kat's wound. "I need more light and I have to get her sewn up or she'll just pump out any blood I give her."

The flashlight was heavy, full of D batteries. My thumb pushed the button and white light seared out. It bathed the wound on the side of Kat's throat, harsh light stripping away some of the color, making the blood look almost blue. Larson took a bottle from the tray and squirted the wound. My nose filled with the smell of saltwater and blood as the stream washed gore away, leaving just the wound. It still bled, just a dribble, but now it looked like what it was, mangled torn flesh.

Larson shoved his fingers in Kat's neck, one hand was empty but the other held a curved needle threaded with thin black filament. He began sewing together edges inside her wound. The thin needle flashed, weaving in and out.

Kat's eyes rolled. I watched them focus on me with the familiar crease between her eyebrows. The same crease she always got when she was concentrating on something. Her jaw moved a fraction of an inch, and she made a small sound in the bottom of her throat.

I kept my voice soft. "Shush, Kat. You can't talk, Larson is working."

"Have to . . . tell you . . ."

"It can wait. It can wait until you're better. Let Larson work."

"No . . . now . . ." Her words slid off in a whisper. Her hand lashed out, latching on to my arm, jerking the light down. Her hand was like ice from blood loss. She pulled, lifting herself up. Larson moved the needle away a second before he would have rammed it all the way into her neck.

Kat's eyes were wild, full of fevered pain. Her words came through clenched teeth. "I'm . . . sorry. I'm so sorry I didn't . . . tell you . . ."

A convulsion struck, twisting her body like someone wringing a washcloth. Her eyes rolled back in her head under fluttering eyelids.

The machine began a long, plaintive wail of a flatline.

Larson grabbed my arm, pulling me over Kat. "Start CPR!"

I put my hands on her chest, her skin icy under my palms. *Twenty or thirty?* I couldn't remember how many times I was supposed to push in her chest. *Start! Go until it feels right!* Driving the heel of my palm into her sternum, I pushed, counted off twenty, then kept going. Each push bounced her on the table. Her arm slid sideways, dangling off the edge of the table, fingers loose. The heart monitor continued its shrill alarm.

I pulled away at thirty and slipped my hand under her neck, thumb brushing through crusted blood. Her mouth fell open. I sealed my mouth to hers. Her lips were spongy and ice-cold. I blew air into her lungs, making her chest rise. The corner of my eye saw a tiny spot in her wound where air bubbles made of blood hissed. A fang had pierced her trachea. I blew another breath into her as those little bubbles stacking on top of each other filled my vision, becoming my whole world.

My heart was a brick in my chest.

I pulled back, the air I had shoved down her throat and into her lungs leaked back out. Larson crashed into me, hands full of humming defibrillator paddles. Wires trailed off them, dragging a square hunk of machinery closer to the bed. I stepped back, stumbling against the rolling tray of equipment. My eyes cut away for a split second and when they returned Larson had the paddles shoved against Kat's rib cage. His thumbs hit the buttons and Kat's body arched at the spine, drawing her up like a bow. The crown of her head was on the table and so were her heels, but nothing in between. He jerked the paddles away, cutting the current. Kat slammed back down on the table with a bang.

The monitor continued to scream its flatline.

Larson's scream of anguish drowned it out.

The paddles banged back against Kat's chest. Veins corded on Larson's arms. His face a mask of red, freckles standing out like burned spots. His thumbs hit the buttons on the paddles again. The buzz of them climbed into a *CRACK!* as they jolted electricity through Kat, lifting her off the table again. He pulled them away and she fell as if her strings had been cut.

Larson's mouth began to move.

The words fell like stones in a pool of poison, splashing corruption into the air. Guttural and harsh, they slapped out. Magick filled the room, my taste buds seared with the flavor of raw honey and spoiled meat.

Larson was casting a spell over Kat.

My fingers hit my empty holster.

I had lost every gun I had at the club. I drew out the ten-inch knife that was still there.

Larson turned to me. His face was contorted in anguish, red blooming to purple in his pain. Tears sheeted his cheeks with saltwater, dripping off his goatee. His eyes were wild, wide with panic and pain, the whites shot through with blood. They bounced from the knife in my hand to my face.

"Let me do this! Let me save her!" His chest hitched, a sob jerking out of him. "Please . . . she's dying. It's Kat and our baby, Deacon!"

I stopped. "What did you just say?"

"It's what we were going to tell you at the restaurant! Kat's nine weeks' pregnant."

His words slapped me. Kat? Pregnant? With Larson's baby? Everything that had happened tonight rushed back at me. The doctor that checked her out at the crime scene, the way she and Larson held back when the witches attacked . . . it all made sense in one giant click, the snap of a bone break.

It was so sharp it almost buckled my knees. My hard words to her fell on me like a ton of bricks. The things I had said to my friend. I hadn't known . . . There was no way I could have . . . not at the time. But that didn't make one damn bit of difference.

"Let me save them. It's Kat! You love her as much as I do!" He choked, voice strangling down to a whisper. "I can *do* this, if you'll just let me." His eyes were raw, full of pain and anguish. "Please, I can't live without her."

God forgive me, I stepped back and let him.

42

Larson stood over Kat, hands on her face. The air was clotted, curdled with magick. It hung around us like a fog, laying on my skin, sticking to me. The words he said weren't in English. Hell, most of them didn't sound like they were in human. They ripped out of his throat in noises like an animal being gutted, splatting out and gushing through the air to fall on Kat's slack face.

My nerves were on fire, my power reacting to the sorcery despite every effort to shove it down and hide it away. Acid scorched the thin lining of my esophagus, splashing up from my roiling stomach.

I hate magick. I truly fucking despise it. Magick was the reason my family were killed. Magick was the reason my club was burning in the night. Magick was the very reason Kat lay on that table.

But if it could bring her back.

I loved Kat; I had for a long time. I loved her stubborn streak that made her stay after a task until, by God, it was complete. I loved her even personality, sometimes up, sometimes down, but mostly just steady and calm. She could be annoyed, but she rarely got mad. I loved her wiseass remarks about almost everything; her sense of humor dry, but sharp.

For a few years it had been me, her, and Father Mulcahy fighting the good fight, killing monsters, keeping people safe. There'd been many nights of talks, many of laughing, some of crying. We had shed blood together, both our own and others.

She was my friend.

Hell, she was my family. The sister I never had and, in some ways, replacing the daughter I had lost. There's the family you are born with and then there's the family you choose, but it's all family nonetheless.

Larson stuck his thumb in his mouth, wetting it with a gob of saliva. A rope of spittle hung as he pulled it free and used the body fluid to paint a symbol on Kat's forehead.

The magick closed like hands around a throat.

Kat's eyes flew open, her mouth coming apart like she was gasping for air, but no air was drawn in. The heart monitor continued its long, lonesome wail, the green beep a steady flatline.

She sat up in a smooth motion, hinging from the waist. Larson threw his arms around her, pulling her tight. Tears still streamed down his cheeks, but his mouth was a wide grin of joy. He whispered into her hair as he held her tight. "It worked, baby. Thank Acheron, it worked. I'll *never* let you go again."

The nerve under my eye started to twitch.

Kat sat there, being held by Larson. She stared at me, eyes wide and empty. She wasn't blinking, just staring. The suture needle hung by the black thread in her neck wound, laying like a baitless hook against her shoulder, bouncing as she twitched. Crimson boiled, spreading from the corners of her eyes. The pupils dilated out, covering the iris completely.

My hand clamped on Larson's arm. Kat's head snapped back, fangs bursting from her gums in twin spurts of blood. I yanked Larson away as she struck. Her fangs clacked together as she missed.

In a blink, she was crouched on the table like a feral animal. Shoving Larson behind me, I stepped forward. Holy light flared as I yanked my St. Benedict medal from under my shirt. A long hiss rolled out of a mouth full of murder.

Kat blinked, shying back from the light. Her voice was shaky, lisping through extended fangs. She looked confused as she scooted away from the light of the saint medallion.

"Deacon?"

"Kat?" I lowered the medal, still keeping it between us, but moving the light out of my line of sight. "Do you have control of yourself?"

Larson pressed against me, pushing toward Kat. "Of course she does! Look at her!" My hand balled in his shirt. I shoved him backward, harder than I had the first time. He stumbled before catching himself. I pointed back in his direction while keeping my eyes on Kat.

"Kat, is that you?"

She wrapped her arms around herself. A tremor ran through her body, shaking her hard enough to make teeth rattle. When she spoke, she had to draw in air deliberately to do it. "It's me." Her face twisted around a mouthful of fangs and pink, blood-stained tears began to run from her eyes. "I think it's me."

Her fingers went to her mouth. They trembled, hanging in the air before slowly and softly touching her teeth. Her fingertips moved across the fangs. Horror, naked and raw, crawled over her face. "No, no, no, no, nonononononono."

"Kat, keep it together."

"What did you do to me?"

Larson spoke up. "Baby, I can explain . . ."

"WHAT DID YOU DO TO ME!"

This time the words came in a roar that shook the skin on my face. My power flared. Icy needles jabbed my skin. The cold, dead tingling you get when your arm falls asleep, but over my whole body. My nostrils went painfully dry, cracking deep in my sinuses with the smell of shed skin and tainted venom.

Kat threw herself off the table. She flew farther than a human could have. Especially a human with a fist-sized chunk of meat gone from their throat. She hit the far wall high up over the cabinets and stuck there, clinging like a lizard. Her tears were streams of red pouring off her face.

She fell off the wall to the floor with a thud. Scrambling, she pressed herself into a corner trying to fold in on herself. Knees to her chin, arms wrapped around her legs, she rocked back and forth. Back and forth. Back and forth. A low-pitched mewling slithered from deep in her chest.

My bones weighed a thousand pounds, too heavy for me to carry. My chest was hollow, scooped out.

Larson stood next to me. "What's wrong with her?"

"She's stuck. You kept Kat here, but she still turned anyway."

"That's impossible."

"Fuck you. Being impossible doesn't stop shit from happening."

I've seen people rise as vampires. When they come back, the person is completely gone. It's just a body that's been re-animated as an undead bloodsucker. The vampire inside them uses their brain as a template, accessing memories and even personality traits, but it is a completely new entity. A demonic, bloodthirsty, vicious entity.

"But it's still Kat?"

"Seems to be."

A smile lit his face. "Then the spell worked. She's still alive."

I whirled on him, driving my forearm into his chest, ramming him back against the heavy metal table. The knife blade in my hand gleamed as it lay across his throat. "Do you not know anything about her? About her past? About what happened to her?"

He gulped. The movement cut a small slice across the skin of his throat. It was tiny, barely a nick. A bad mosquito bite.

The second his blood hit the air the noise from Kat switched to a high-pitched keening.

She rocked faster, slamming her back into the wall behind her. I pointed at her with the hand that held the saint medal.

"You see that? *That's* what I'm talking about." I pressed closer, my face less than an inch from his. "I was there. I saw what the vampires had done to her. The spell worked?" My voice jumped an octave. "The spell worked? You sonnuvabitch, there's nothing you could have done to her that would be worse than turning her into a vampire."

Anger boiled low in my guts, a snake twisting in on itself, coiling and uncoiling in a whisper of slick-scaled skin. It would be so easy. Pull the knife. Slit his fucking throat.

I shoved off him, pushing away before murder took root in my mind. Slowly, carefully, I walked toward Kat. Each step the snake twisted harder. I knelt in front of her, St. Benedict medal loose in my hand. The holy light of it spilled between us, her just on the outside edge.

Her head turned away from the light. She stopped rocking. Her eyes were slitted, watching me from the corners, bloody tears drying on her cheeks. They had become normal again. They looked like Kat's eyes.

I kept my voice a gentle as I could. "How ya doin', kiddo?"

Her voice was a tremble, the words twittery and broken as they came out. "I don't . . . know. I can hear it in my head. The vampire. It's in me. It is me." She began to bang her forehead on her knees. "I'm thirsty, Deacon, so damn thirsty . . . and all I can smell is Larson's blood, blood, blood. . . ." The rocking came back as she kept babbling, the word *blood* glitching over and over until it became nonsense.

She looked up sharply. "All I want to do is to tear your throat out and let your blood rush down my skin. The vampire in my head is whispering to me, it wants to do all the things that were done to me to somebody else." Eyes wide, she stared at me. "And I want to do that to somebody else. Somebody innocent."

In a blink, she was on her knees. It happened faster than I could see. I jumped, bringing the saint medal up between us. She recoiled against the wall.

Too close. Too *stupid*.

"You have to kill me. You can't let me become this! You can't let me be this thing!" Her hands grew into talons. She slashed at her arm. The skin laid open in four deep gashes. No blood welled up, the muscle underneath was gray and dull and dead. She held it out to me. "See! The only thing keeping me from tearing out your throat is that damned medal in your hand."

She drew to her feet like she was pulled up by strings. "I'm already dead, Deacon, keep me from being a monster."

I stepped backwards, moving carefully until there was space between us. I put the medal under my shirt.

Kat shook from head to toe, a quick convulsion that rolled through her. Her head snapped up, fangs unsheathed, eyes gone to black and crimson pools of murder. A long, sibilant hiss rolled out of her mouth.

She dropped low, crouching, and stayed like that a long moment. I could see her tense before she sprang. She moved like a human. It felt like hours of warning.

I ducked to the left as she slammed into me. My arm came around, clamping on her forehead. I jerked her close, spinning and pressing her back to my chest. Leaning, I lifted her by her head, stretching her throat in a long line.

My mouth was close to her ear. Tears spilled from my eyes, running down my face in hot trails. "I love you."

She growled, lost in animalistic, vampire thirst.

The blade bit deep as I jerked it across.

It took four times before she crumbled to dust in my arms.

43

"WHAT DID YOU DO?"

Larson seethed, face red, veins bulging.

I ignored him. Dust shook off me, Kat's clothes peeling away like a ghost as I pushed the knife into its sheath. The snake in my guts was crawling, slithering into the hollow place in my chest.

Kat's dead.

I just killed my friend. My sister.

I started walking to the door.

"Answer me! What did you do? You killed her, you sick, sick bastard! You're a monster, Deacon Chalk." Larson's voice was a scream, high-pitched and metallic. "You killed the woman I love."

The air crackled. The hairs on my arms lifted up. Larson began chanting in the same guttural, inhuman language he had used before. The pressure in the room grew, building with each rotten syllable that fell from his lips.

I turned.

He stood in the middle of the room, in the pile of dust that used to be my sister Kat. Muscles knotted his jaw as he chanted, eyes rolled back in his head. His finger pointed at me like a claw. In his other hand was something that was beginning to glow with a corrupted yellow light that spilled out between his fingers.

The air around me popped with stinging magick. Tiny, biting mouths of sorcery washing over me in an ozone-laden sweep. The lights flickered and dimmed. The taint of death magick hung heavy like curdled incense.

The snake climbed higher.

Reaching down inside, I grabbed my power. Shoving out, it cut through Larson's magick like a scalpel. I drove it deep inside him. My mind's theater clicked on and I could see the magick in him. It clung, hanging like malignant fruit, swollen full of rot and corruption. Like a chain of cancer running through him, he was stuffed with it. My power wormed deep inside, looking for something specific.

Outside, I could feel the spell growing. It wouldn't be but another moment or two before he completed it. Whatever he was casting felt immense, violent, and deadly. It would fall on me like an avalanche of hellfire and damnation. Racing the clock, I pushed harder, looking until I found it.

There.

Running through his blood was a thin silver thread. Father Mulcahy said all powerful magick users had fae blood somewhere in their family. I had just found Larson's. My power clamped down on that silver thread and pulled, tracing the line of fae blood until it led me where I wanted to go.

In my mind's eye, I saw Larson's spine. Magick throbbed around it, wrapping the injury in a sticky pustule of sorcery. Liquid sacks of corruption held his backbone together, giving him the ability to walk again.

The snake twisted.

My power crashed into the magick brace around Larson's spine, tearing it away in one swift, vicious yank.

I watched it happen.

His eyes widened, showing white all around. His breath stuck in his throat as he felt the vertebrae go. His chest slid forward in a jarring motion over his hips, like he was a game of Jenga whose pieces were starting to fall. I saw the vertebrae slip sideways in my mind's eye. He crumpled to the floor.

The spell died, breaking apart, dissolving into nothing.

Stepping over, I crouched in front of Larson. He lay slumped on his side, legs sprawled out. Useless. His face was white with pain, fat droplets of oily sweat standing out on waxy skin. He breathed in small sips, taking in little bits of oxygen. Cornflower blue eyes rolled over, wide and skittery. They locked, focusing on me while he fought for air.

I leaned in close, making sure he really saw me through the pain.

"Disappear. Find some cave and drop off the face of the earth. Don't be around people. Don't be anywhere, because if I ever lay eyes on you again, I'll fucking kill you."

I stood up and walked away, leaving him lying helpless on the floor.

The snake twisted some more.

44

The taint of magick sloughed off, falling away like a thick sheet of dead flesh, as I stepped over the threshold of St. Augustine of Hippo Catholic Church. My body felt lighter, but my soul was just as heavy. The rage snake lay in my belly, coiled, not moving. It wasn't time yet. It could wait.

I was met inside the door by a nun with a gun.

She sat on a small bench off to the side of the heavy wooden doors, wearing a full black habit. The toes of polished combat boots peeked out from under the hem. A starched coif and veil covered her head, draping down and framing a smooth face with narrow eyes. The gun pointed my way was a small, square bundle of death. A MAC-10 holding thirty rounds of .45-caliber righteousness it could spit out in seconds.

Her finger was on the trigger.

We stared at each other for a long moment.

She stood, submachine gun disappearing inside a wide sleeve. The habit was modest, draping from head to toe. She wasn't fat, but she was fleshy in that way some women are where they can fluctuate thirty pounds in any direction and still have guys following them home from the club. Not that nuns go to clubs.

Then again, not that nuns hide submachine guns in their robes either.

A silver pectoral crucifix hung from her neck on a braided black cord. It was big enough to be a breastplate. A rosary made of what looked to be polished teakwood beads the size of my knuckles hung from little hooks at her waist. She was a nun from top to bottom and looked like she could knock heads or break balls.

"It's good to see you again, Deacon. It's been too many years."

Wait? What?

I looked at her face hard, racking my brain. She was young, especially for a nun in a traditional habit. Nuns nowadays wear modern clothes. It's a sign of a Sister's hard-core dedication to the Church to wear the old-school full habit.

She could still be in her teens or pushing thirty. Her narrow eyes were set in an unlined round face with a wide nose and a pair of undefined cheekbones. Her chin had a small dimple sitting below a wide bottom lip.

"I'm sorry, Sister. It's been a helluva night. We've met before?"

She stepped around me, moving to the door. I caught a whiff of bleach and starched linen that always reminded me of nuns. Those full habits took some serious laundry, and every Sister I have ever met who wore one smelled exactly the same.

She spoke over her shoulder, free hand turning bolts into place and locking the door. Her right hand, the one with the submachine gun, stayed inside her sleeve.

"We met almost five years ago. I was just a kid."

"No disrespect, I'm not trying to be a pain in the ass, but if you could narrow that down just a little more."

She turned to face me. "Kaylee Ann Dobbs."

The name was a slap.

When I first started hunting, I ran across my first lycanthrope, a real scum-sucking piece of shit named McMahon. He had been a crack-dealing, child-snatching cannibal.

And a Were-polar bear.

Hand to God, I shit you not.

He kidnapped little Kaylee Ann Dobbs while she was on a field trip at school. I was hired to find her. The search led me to a ghetto where McMahon lived in a crackhouse, using his lycanthropy to protect the business.

I met a little girl named Mary who was being dragged to McMahon by her mom to be traded for crack. I put a stop to that. I was too late to save little Kaylee Ann Dobbs, all I could do was avenge her, but Mary I had taken out of there. I dropped her off with Father Mulcahy to find a home for her.

"Mary?"

She smiled. It was a small, quick thing. "Sister Mary Polycarp now. I took my solemn vows last year. I work here with Father Mulcahy."

"Congratulations." I looked around. My heart beat faster. "They did make it here, right? We were supposed to meet."

"They're here. Follow me."

We walked to the end of the narthex, stopping at the fountain of holy water in the center so that I could dip my fingers in and cross myself. No matter how hellish the night had been, it couldn't break a lifetime of habit. We continued to the other side where there was a hallway. I followed her, my mind swirling.

Polecats was gone. Twenty-foot flames had been shooting into the night sky when I tore away in the Comet, racing

to get Kat to help. We had roared by fire trucks as we flew
down the highway. They were heading in the direction of the
club with lights flashing and sirens wailing. They couldn't
have gotten there in time to save anything. The explosion
had been too big, the flames too high.

Plus, I had a basement full of stuff that would go bang
and boom in a fire.

The club had no chance.

Sadness panged through me. I loved that club. It was
my home and was full of people I had come to love. Now
the girls who had worked there would have to find their own
way. I would have to find a new income.

If I lived through the night.

The Wrath of Baphomet was powerful and deadly. They
had cost me my club. They had cost me my friend.

No more.

It was time for some witches to die.

Sister Mary pushed a button on the elevator at the end of
the hall. The doors *shooshed* open. Stepping in made the
elevator car shake, banging against the frame it rode in with
dull metal thunks. Normally that would bother me. Tonight,
I didn't care.

The elevator descended with a lurch. The interior filled
with a low, grinding noise.

It took me a minute to realize it was my teeth.

We shuddered to a stop. The doors *shooshed* open, revealing another hallway. Sister Mary stepped out, leading me
down the hall. With every step, she made a rustling *click-
clack* noise of her rosary rubbing and bouncing against her
hip. The MAC-10 swung freely in her hand and I realized I
still didn't have a gun. That was going to change. Like soon.

The end of the hall was a vault door that took up the
whole wall. It stood shut, large stainless-steel wheel in the

center like an old bank vault. It was the secret stash. The good stuff. The real shit.

The Vatican keeps strongholds around the world. Places where they store occult items for safe keeping and anti-occult weapons for preparation. St. Augustine's was the main one in North America.

The vault was the center of a five-foot-thick block of solid concrete and set under the pool of holy water from upstairs. The walls were inlaid with crucifixes that were blessed thrice daily, and the ground the vault sat under had been consecrated for generations. The stuff locked inside it was as safe as could be.

Why didn't the Vatican just destroy it all?

Because of the demons. When an object is made into an occult weapon, it is imbued with power through ritual, sacrifice, and being used in an evil or blasphemous way. These actions draw demons to it and trap them inside where they lay dormant, becoming a power source for spells and witchcraft. If the object is destroyed, then the demons are released.

The Vatican is not in the practice of releasing demons.

Instead, the Holy See locks them away to keep them out of the hands of wrongdoers.

Halfway down the hall, Sister Mary took a sharp left into an alcove set back in the wall. She knocked sharply on the door, then opened it.

I walked into a roomful of people who were staring at me.

Boothe and Josh sat together on a low-slung couch. Josh was tucked under the big man's arm, his head on Boothe's shirtless chest. Boothe had dozens of adhesive bandages stuck to him, and his shoulder had the pockmarked look of road rash.

Shrapnel.

Josh was wrapped in a blanket, his head swathed in a thick gauze bandage like a turban, but his eyes were bright and clear. He tried to sit up as I walked in, but Boothe pulled him back down.

Ronnie sat cross-legged in a chair that matched the couch. She was rocking back and forth, making thick ringlets of hair shimmy and shake. Scattered on her and the chair were several of the ghost spiders. They jumped up as I walked in, zipping up and away on near-invisible monofilaments of webbing. Her eyes were wide and unfocused as she turned toward me.

Special Agent Heck and Father Mulcahy stood in one corner, turning as I entered. Both of them were smoking, cigarettes in their hands while they had been talking. Special Agent Heck had a wide burn across his forehead, the skin red and blistered. His whole body looked singed, black suit ragged with holes burned through the material.

Father Mulcahy leaned heavily on a crutch. A brace wrapped his leg from midthigh to shin. It was the leg he limped on. The leg that hadn't been the same since being slashed open by a vampire slave of that evil bitch Appollonia last year.

He still looked gray, his complexion wan and washed out. A large bruise crawled up his face, making his jaw and cheek puffy. His lip had been split, a nasty dark scab across it. It had to hurt each time he took a puff on his cancerstick.

That didn't stop him from doing it.

He looked tired.

Tiff stood. She had been kneeling beside Sophia. The Were-dog was wiping red-rimmed mismatched eyes. The look on her face wasn't sorrow, it was anger. Raw, unbridled hatred. Pale European skin flushed a dark red that made her russet hair seem shinier. Her hands were shaking as she smeared the tears on her face.

Standing beside them was a little towheaded boy with cowlicks and his momma's eyes. He was all alone. A chubby hand patted his mom on the arm. I closed my eyes deliberately, opening them slowly.

The kid was still human.

I filed it away as Tiff stepped to me. She was dirty again, soot smudged across her skin and clothes in abstract, almost tiger-stripe patterns. It did her no good to have showered earlier.

The thought of the shower sent a twinge through me.

She was still wearing her black leather jacket. It had protected her from the explosion. Her hair was wild, tossed out around her face like a mane, but other than that she could have been going out on a Friday evening.

Her face turned to me, voice soft. "How are you, baby?"

"I'm fine."

"How's . . . ?"

I raised my voice. I only wanted to say it once. "Kat's dead."

The words hung in the air, filling the room. They swelled in the silence, racing along cracks in the walls like water soaking a sponge as everyone absorbed what I said.

Father Mulcahy looked slapped by the news. His head dropped in prayer.

Tears began to flow down Sophia's face again, dripping off her chin, soaking into her hair.

Boothe's face became stoic, bland, folding away in pain.

Josh hadn't worked with Kat for the last few months like Boothe had. He pushed up, wrapping his arm around the big man's neck, pulling him close in comfort.

Ronnie stopped rocking and stared at me with wide, unblinking eyes.

Special Agent Heck gave a small nod of sympathy.

Tiff's face broke just a little, jaw tensing and her bottom

lip quivering to hold it together. She blinked tears away from her eye and stepped into me. I put my arms around her, holding her, trying to comfort her around the wide hollow place inside me.

After a moment, she pulled away.

No one spoke. One by one their faces turned to me. I didn't have any inspiration. No comfort inside me. The only thing I had at the moment was the desolation of my friend's death.

That and the twisted snake of hatred for the witches responsible burrowed deep in my guts.

I cleared my throat, looking at no one in particular.

"Kat is dead because of Selene and her people. I don't have time to mourn my sister. Right now, you don't have time to mourn her either. This thing we do has a cost, a price that is sometimes too hard to bear. But we don't have a damn choice. This is the deal. This is the gig. This is the job. Push your pain aside and man the fuck up because we've got work to do."

As I watched, they pulled themselves together. Shoulders squared, tears dried, resolve hardened. They all, in their own way, did exactly what I told them to do. Some pushed their pain away so they could carry on. Some embraced it, drawing it close to act as fuel.

"Okay. We're two people down and they were our best researchers. Now we have to figure out how we're going to find these damn witches."

Boothe raised his hand. "Larson?"

My voice sounded cold and hard in my own ears. "Larson's never coming back." No one else said anything. "Any suggestions?"

Movement in the corner of the room drew my eye. Sophia was trying to hold her son, but he had squirmed free and now was walking my way on his little bowed legs. She started after him but stopped and sat back down when I held up my hand. The child kept walking until he stood in front of me. His shirt was blue and made the one blue eye he had surge out of his chubby-cheeked face. *Samson.*

I knelt down so that he and I were nose to nose. "What is it, Sammy?"

"I can help you find my brothers, Unca Deacon."

My scalp started to tingle. "How can you do that, little buddy?"

He closed his eyes. A tiny line formed between his brows, a crease of concentration. His chubby hand lifted up. It hovered in front of my face. I watched it only an inch or two away from my skin. A tiny gold spark flickered across his fingertips. My lips went numb.

That tiny hand descended, four chubby fingers warm on my face. A spark zinged through my skin, racing along my optic nerve like a ragged fingernail down a chalkboard. My mind's eye blinked to life and I was somewhere else in my head.

The connection was dim, the edges fuzzy like a bad movie effect, like someone had smeared Vaseline around the lens of my mind.

Dark. Lights flickering. Yellow. Fire. Thin bars of my cage cutting between pads of my feet. Muzzle full of dead blood long dried. Soaked into wood of floor. It stinks with it. Figures move in front of me. Raised up. The ones who took me. And brother. Two women move around, pointing at things. Big hairy monkey stole us carrying things. Sounds are funny. Everything muffled by thick gray stuff coats almost everything. Air is weird. Hurts.

I reeled back to reality. My head spun, knocking me on my ass. Samson stared at me, both mismatched eyes lit with a slight gold light. His chubby chin dipped and he looked at me under wispy thin eyebrows. "You see, Unca Deacon?"

I nodded, mouth dry as sand. I swallowed just to be able to talk. "I see."

"Bring us back together, Unca Deacon."

"Will do, kid."

The boy nodded once, turned, and toddled back to his mother. I stood up. I knew what the witches had planned. I knew where they were and I had been there before. I should have made the connection sooner.

"Father Mulcahy."

The priest looked up at me.

"I'm gonna need to get inside the vault."

45

Sister Mary Polycarp's hands wrapped around the thick handles of the wheel lock. She paused, not moving.

"Are you sure about this, Father? We aren't supposed to open the vault without direct permission from the Holy See."

"We have the dispensation of discernment, child. We're charged with the care and keeping of the items inside. It is a duty laid upon our immortal souls. It's why we were appointed here. You are going to have to learn this. One day it will be your responsibility to decide." The priest adjusted himself on his crutch. "*One* day, but not *to*-day. If the Holy Father has a problem with *my* decision, he can call me tomorrow. Now, open the vault, child."

She began to spin the wheel, leaning back and pulling hard to get it started.

It was hard to hold back from stepping up to help, but I'd been firmly instructed that I could not be part of opening the vault. It was something only clergy and the "professed religious" could take part of.

I know from Father Mulcahy that what I do is Vatican approved, but I am still just a normal Catholic like everyone else.

Okay, not normal, but when it comes to matters of the Church, I am no different, no better than any other Catholic son.

So I didn't help as Sister Mary Polycarp yanked on the handle. I let her struggle. It took minutes of work to break the wheel free. Once started, it spun in a circle of silver making small clicking noises until it clanged to a stop.

Sister Mary reached out and tugged, pulling the door forward on oiled hinges out into the hallway. It was massive, a foot thick. Father Mulcahy crossed himself and stepped inside, using the crutch. I followed, pausing to cross myself like he had before stepping over the threshold.

My foot hit the floor.

My power ripped me open, spilling out.

It was like being gutted with a lightning bolt. The world went black and empty, everything wiped away in one supernova flash. I was drowning, choking, sensations crashing into me like a tidal wave. I fought my power, yanking, pulling, wrestling it back inside me. It fought me like a live thing, writhing and whipping through my body.

My mind's eye opened and I saw my power. A dragon of energy clawed its way out of me. I grabbed it by the tail as it passed. Rough, horned scale sliced my palms, cutting into my skin like a pattern of broken glass. I yanked, pulling the dragon back in.

It turned, snarling at me. I shook it. It was *my* power, by God. My will slammed into it like an iron hammer, beating it down. Hand over hand, I hauled it inside me and shoved it down, locking it away.

My vision came back a laser, burning into my retinas. Everything too bright, too sharp, hard edged. A headache blossomed in the back of my skull. I blinked, my eyes beginning to dull, pupils constricting so that light wasn't an acid bath on my corneas.

Father Mulcahy had only taken one step.

All of that had happened in a blink, in a split second. I shook my head. I should have known. I've had this power inside me for five years now, living in my blood since that Angel of the Lord had resurrected me. I knew that it was triggered by all things occult.

What the hell did I think would happen when I walked into a vault full of the most dangerous occult objects on the continent?

I should have been prepared. Sonnuvabitch I was off my game. I had been all damn night.

In that moment I knew I had to get my shit together. That was a rookie mistake. A mistake that would have been made by past Deacon who had first started hunting monsters. A mistake that could get me killed or worse, could cost me the life of someone else I loved.

Tiff. Father Mulcahy. Ronnie.

Fuck *that*. The only people dying from this moment on were the people I was going to kill.

Father Mulcahy was talking. I shook my head to clear it and paid attention. His eyebrows were pulled together.

"Are you all right, son?"

"I'm fine. Just needed to adjust to the atmosphere for a second."

Father Mulcahy knows how my power works. I looked around. The inside of the vault was brightly lit with the flickery cold-white light you only get from florescent tubing. It looked like the bank vault it was originally planned to be.

The walls on each side were filled with steel security boxes like a bank's safety deposit box system. Even with my power shoved down as far as I could shove it, there was a dark, prickly energy coming from the left-hand side of the room.

The symbology wasn't lost on me.

On the back wall sat an ancient book on a wooden stand. A raven feather quill stood beside it next to a sealed ink pot. The book was huge, too big for a grown man to hold in both arms. The paper looked like thin sheepskin, aged a yellow that was almost brown.

Stepping up to it, I was hit with a waft of book. Before my life went to shit, I was a reader. One of my favorite things about reading and owning books was the smell of them, the older the book the better. It's a scent you can't really describe other than saying it's the scent of story and paper. Book.

"Do you know what you are needing tonight, son?"

"You tell me. I need the most powerful weapon I can use."

He limped over to the book, crutch making a small squeak on the cold marble tile of the floor. I thought he was going to flip through it, search the listings, and find a weapon.

Instead, he used his free hand to reach under the edge of the book. The top of the table it sat on hinged up silently, revealing a hollow spot under the book. He lifted out a ring of keys. They jangled against each other as he hobbled over to the middle section of the wall on the right.

Bending, he studied the fronts of the drawers. Stepping closer, I saw that writing was engraved roughly on the front of it. It looked like it might have been done with an awl instead of any kind of modern implement.

Gladium Paladinus Caroli.

The words were Latin. I knew enough from Mass to recognize the language, but not enough to translate. Father Mulcahy studied the keys, selecting one, and inserting it in the lock.

He left the keys to dangle. "Kneel."

I listened to my priest, lowering myself to the ground on my knees. I bowed my head. I felt his hand move over me, carving the sign of the Cross from the air. His voice fell heavily as he prayed.

"More than ever we feel the need of having Thee close to us. At any moment we may find ourselves in battle. However rigorous the task that awaits your servant Deacon Chalk, may he fulfill his duty with courage. If death should overtake him on that field, grant that he die in the state of grace. Forgive him all his sins, those he may have forgotten and those he may recall now. Grant him the grace of perfect contrition."

I knelt there under his hand and felt that weightless presence that I know is God, Him giving His acknowledgment. I never know what it means, if He approves or disapproves, I just feel that He hears me. That's the faith part. The not knowing, just moving on, acting as if.

"All right, son, get up. You have work to do."

I stood. Father Mulcahy looked at me, something in his eyes. "I'm proud of you." He said it, turning to the drawer and opening it with a twist of the key before I could say anything.

The drawer slid out silently, extending almost four feet. Inside lay a sword on a bed of blue-black velvet.

It was breathtaking.

The blade was double-edged, about two fingers wide, and the polished steel gleamed in the light. The handle was gold, intricately wrought into a basket of vines and flowers. A clear glass dome nestled in them, inset in the crossbar. It was filled with a dry brown powder that looked like rust.

The rest of the hilt was wrapped in a blue cloth, a net of fine black strands knit around it. The hilt was lacquered with a dull sheen. The pommel was a round bulb of steel with a small, misshapen square of ivory inlaid in the center. Father Mulcahy crossed himself.

I did it since he had.

"Is that Excalibur?"

A look crossed his face. "Oh ho, you think you're King Arthur now, do ya?" He chuckled. "Why would Excalibur be in America?"

"Oh, sorry, I forgot that we had broadswords here in America. This one must have belonged to George Washington. Or was this one Benjamin Franklin's?" We both shared a small laugh. It bounced off the hollow bubble inside me from Kat's death.

"That is Durendal. The Peerless Sword of Roland, given to him by Charlemagne."

I looked at the sword, then looked back at him. "I don't have any idea what that's supposed to mean. I haven't had a World History class since high school."

"It's a holy sword, said to be indestructible. The hilt contains the blood of St. Basil, the hair of St. Denis, a tooth of St. Peter, and a piece of the Blessed Virgin Mary's raiment." He crossed himself again.

"You couldn't get Excalibur?"

"Excalibur is in the Holy See."

"America always gets the damn leftovers."

He indicated the sword with a wave. I reached out, slipping my hand around the hilt. The second my fingers closed my power began to bubble deep in my blood. The Angel blood in my veins called to the holy sword.

I took a deep breath, centering myself, and lifted the sword out of the drawer. It was lighter than I thought it would be, balanced in my hand. The blade was springy, like a tai chi sword instead of a broadsword. The handle was tight in my grip, the cross hilt and the pommel pressing in against the sides of my palm. Stepping back, I swung the sword in a quick arc. As it crossed me it tugged toward the left-hand wall, the blade pulling slightly. I tested it, swinging that way again. The blade tugged toward the wall where evil artifacts were stored.

Interesting.

Father Mulcahy had lifted the velvet, pulling out a brown leather scabbard and sword belt. They looked ancient and well-worn but still whole and serviceable. He held them out to me. "You'll need this to carry the blade, son."

I nodded, my fingers sliding along the hilt in my hand. My fingertip rubbed the smooth enamel square. This is from the mouth of the first Pope. A shiver went up my spine. My mind tripped on a memory of teeth. I looked at Father Mulcahy.

"There's one more thing I need from in here."

46

"You are staying here, dammit. I don't have time to argue." I stood up from securing Durendal in the front seat of the Comet. Tiff helped me click the lap belt in place around it. The holy sword was sheathed, ready for me to belt it on. It leaned across the seat, point toward the floorboard.

"You aren't leaving me behind."

My fist slammed into the roof of the car with a loud *BANG!* I turned, anger sparked deep in my chest. I stuck my finger in her face, words coming out between clenched teeth. "You are not going. That. Is. Final."

She blinked at me with mismatched eyes. "It's my sons."

"Sophia, get your ass back inside. I know you want to save your boys, but I've got this." I indicated the car full of people. "We've got this. Let us work."

Her face thinned with anger, paring down to skin and planes of bone. Blue and brown eyes bright and feral. "Those witches have to pay for ever touching my children. The flesh must be torn from their bones and their bones must be cracked open so the marrow may be sucked out."

Lycanthropes always get formal when their children are in danger. The animal part of their brain kicks in, tapping into the hereditary, genetic memory of whatever species they are.

"Stay with Samson, with your son that is here." I grabbed her arm, making her look at me. "I saved your children before they were ever born. I'll do it again now." I gave her a little shake, just enough to get her attention. "Trust me."

She stared at me for a long moment, not blinking. It was a predator stare. Her head moved in a quick nod of assent. She turned and walked away, stepping between Sister Mary Polycarp and Josh. She took her human son and went through the door of the church without a backward glance. Samson waved a chubby hand at me before disappearing in his momma's wake.

"Well, that was awkward." Father Mulcahy lit a new cigarette from the still-burning stub of the one he had just finished.

"I'm not going to have the same problem with you, am I?"

"Not tonight. I'd just slow you down." He shifted on his crutch. "You've no use for a crippled old man tonight."

"Don't say that." My chest was tight. "You can still kick my ass, even with a busted leg."

His mouth opened, hesitated, then closed. He glanced over his shoulder at Josh and Sister Mary. Turning back, his mouth opened again to speak. He stopped himself. The tightness in my chest made it hard to breath, an iron clamp around my lungs. After a second, he cleared his throat.

"Remember that Durendal works best when you don't doubt yourself. God's very hand is on you tonight, son. You're doing His work, so stay strong." He flicked the ash off the end of his cancerstick. "And be sure to bring it back. I don't want to fill out the paperwork if you don't."

I smiled. I had a snappy comeback prepared. It was on the tip of my tongue. A real smartass comment that would have kept the mood upbeat until I could get in the Comet and go.

It was right there, waiting to be said.

And that was the very second a vampire stepped out of the bushes.

47

I yanked the MAC-10 up, swinging the barrel away from Father Mulcahy and toward the bloodsucker. Tiff boiled out of the passenger seat, racking the slide of the shotgun in her hands. Boothe and Special Agent Heck were a step behind coming from the backseat. Both men showed their similar training, guns up and pointing forward. Ronnie stayed in the car, spinning to look out the back window. Four of her spiders popped up on the roof of the Comet.

Blair stood ten feet away, head down, honey-blond hair fallen around her face. Her hands were up and empty in the air. The only movement from her was a slight shifting from one foot to the other. Tiny curls of smoke rose around her toes as each foot touched the consecrated ground. Her face tilted up, wide blue eyes meeting mine. The marks on her throat pulsed crimson, red-lighting the bottom of her jawline, and I could *feel* her.

It was different than it normally was with a vampire. Hell, it was different than it had been with Blair before. The connection between us was alive and electric. She still felt like a vampire, all cool and prickly, the smell of snakeskin and the itch of shedding, but the connection was like a hundred thin strings tying me to her. Strings I could pull. Strings I could control. I dropped the submachine gun to my side.

That's when Boothe pulled the trigger on his pistol.

Blair was a blur, moving so fast she almost blinked out of existence for a split second. She fell to the ground, the bullet splitting the air where her head had been. She fell flat, every inch of skin that touched the consecrated ground began to sizzle and smoke.

She bounced up inhumanly fast, face knotted in a snarl as a scream ripped out of her. Fangs burst out of her mouth, and talons peeled back the tips of her fingers. She sliced through the air in front of me, flying at Boothe like she was on wires, moving too fast for him to get off another shot.

Twisting, I swung the MAC-10 up and around, smashing the square metal gun into her chest. The jolt of it shuddered up my arm, clacking my teeth together. The vampire banged to a stop, crashing to the ground at my feet. I swung the submachine gun, pointing it at her face. Shoving power behind my words, I made them a command. "Stay. Down."

Tendons stood like cables on Blair's throat and arms as she fought to get up. The marks on her throat pulsed like a heartbeat. I realized they were in sync with my heartbeat. Smoke began to rise off her, undead flesh sizzling as it pressed against the holy ground. It smelled like rancid bacon. "What are you doing here? I thought you blew up with my club." Anger trickle-charged through me at the thought of Polecats.

Blair swallowed, drawing a breath she didn't need so she could talk. Her voice still had the molasses-thick Southern accent, but it was threaded with pain. "I don't want to be here, Sh-Sh-Sugah, but this is where you told us to meet you."

My hand swept around toward the people standing in the

parking lot. My people. "I told *them* to meet me here. How did you get out of the club? I had you frozen on the bar when the . . ."

I stopped short. I had yelled for everybody to get out. Apparently that had included the bloodsucker at my feet. My mind tripped back to noticing she was gone off the bar as the magick that destroyed my club built in intensity. My eyes narrowed as something occurred to me.

"Do you have one of those orbs in your chest?"

Her hand slid up, fingers hooking the hem of the too-small T-shirt that strained across her chest. She had to lift it up over the bottom swell of breasts that defied gravity between silicone and undead flesh. Below her sternum was a line of scar tissue. I concentrated, pushing my power at her. It slipped down the connection between us, swirling around it like oil on a cable. It took no effort for my power to sink inside her.

Satanic energy crackled at me like feedback. I could almost *see* the orb inside her chest like a smooth globe of malignant magick. It called to me, whispering in my head. Just one small nudge of my power and I could set it off. I could trip the switch and move on. It nestled under her heart, rocking slightly with each beat, a dark temptation.

Wait.

"Why is your heart beating?"

"It's been doing that since we fought." A pink tear rolled down her cheek, soaking into her hair. "It's making my blood rush through my veins, filling my head. It's all I can hear."

A hand touched my arm. I looked over, the connection to Blair in my head like an echo. Tiff stood beside me.

"What's going on, baby?"

"Weird shit." My mind chewed on an idea. "I'll fill you

in when the night is over." I stepped away from Blair, moving Tiff with me. "Stand up."

Blair rose to her feet like she had been picked up by an invisible hand and set upright. A roil of rotten bacon smoke swirled from being trapped between her back and the consecrated ground. It made my eyes water and set Special Agent Heck to coughing.

She stood there, back to shifting from one foot to the other. "What are you going to do with me?"

I fished out my keys, my thumb pushing a button on the key fob. The trunk lid popped up with a dull thunk. I stepped over, lifting it up. "Get in."

Blair came over, hotfooting like a barefoot kid on Georgia asphalt when the summer sun bakes down making the tarmac boil. She rolled inside. There was plenty of room for her. The Comet has a six-body trunk—you could fit six bodies inside with no problem.

Trust me, I know.

"Stay put until I let you out."

She nodded, blond hair falling over her face. She rolled over on her side, pulling long spray-tanned legs up to her chest and curling into a fetal position.

I closed the trunk. "Let's go."

Special Agent Heck held up his hand. "Wait a minute."

I stopped.

He pointed at the trunk. "You're taking a vampire with us? One of the vampires who attacked us earlier?"

"She's in the trunk, isn't she?"

"And this vampire has one of those balls of explosive magick that blew up your club and almost killed us all inside her?"

"Yep."

"And she just attacked me," Boothe said.

I put my hands up. "Like it or don't, this is what we're doing. Now get in the fucking car."

Special Agent Heck took a step toward the backseat. He stopped. "Do you at least have a plan?"

Tiff laughed. "Sorry, I forget how new you are to the group."

Boothe stood, one leg in and one leg out of the backseat. "Even I know there's no plan." He slipped in, folding long legs as he sat beside Ronnie. She was facing forward again, holding a basket on her lap. A soft skritching sound came from inside it as her spiders jostled for position.

Special Agent Heck climbed in the other side. Tiff and I pushed our seats back together and fell into the car. Special Agent Heck spoke from the back. "I'd feel better if we had a plan."

I looked into the rearview mirror.

"Where would be the fun in that?"

The Comet roared in agreement as I turned the key.

48

An hour of balls-out driving carried us a hundred miles away and about sixty minutes shy of dawn. I could *feel* the sun hanging below the horizon, coming, but not here yet. I can feel the rising and the setting of the sun in my blood. It pulls at me like the moon pulls the tides.

In this business, you damn well better learn the comings and the goings of the sun. It can mean the difference between winning and losing, between living and dying.

The sun is the greatest advantage humanity has going for it. It's the thing that keeps the monsters from rising up and slaughtering us wholesale. We can walk in the light, we can hunt in the light. We go in at night, locking ourselves behind our thresholds and hoping that is enough to keep the monster outside the door.

Sunrise breaks the back of magick, wiping it away and starting the word fresh and clean.

I didn't know when Selene and her crew were going to try whatever it was she had planned. Probably tomorrow night. They had a window of a few days to fall in the celestial convergence. I knew they were doing a Black Mass. It's a major working and requires some prep time.

The Black Mass is the most unholy ceremony there is. It's pretty much what it sounds like, a satanic version of Mass, full of blasphemy and bullshit. Those usually happen at midnight, which was hours gone. I looked at my watch. 4:41.

Had it really been less than nine hours since this night started?

It had been a long damn night. We were all loaded up on caffeine pills to keep us alert, the stimulant giving the night in my headlights a surreal, jittery feel to it. The colors passing by were either washed out or lurid in their intensity.

The road had been empty for the last half an hour, just the occasional truck on the other side of the divided highway, headlights flashing by like desolate will-o'-the-wisps. It felt like we were sitting still inside the Comet and the world was being dragged past us in a blur. The music on the stereo was a low, mournful blues rendition of a Hank Sr. song about the Battle of Armageddon.

It was a spooky little spiritual and the singer really drew out the harrow in the marrow that Hank Sr. brought to his original. The music was turned down, barely cutting through the roar of the big block engine that wrapped around us like a cocoon, insulating us from the thing we were going to do.

The exit came up on us in a rush at the speed we were going. I pushed the brake, spun the chain-link steering wheel, and slid sideways off the road. The hot rod bitched about slowing down with a whine of tire and a crackle of exhaust through the pipes.

I blasted through the Yield sign and onto the swayback country road off the exit. I kept our speed reasonable, the sound of the motor quiet enough now that we could talk.

I looked over at Tiff. She was slid down in her seat, legs disappearing into the darkness of the front floorboard. She sat still, calm and not moving except for her thumbnail. It was flicking the zipper tab of her jacket back and forth, back and forth, back and forth. Not nervous, just burning off the caffeine jitters. She couldn't see me looking at her, I was on her blind side.

I reached out and touched her leg, my fingers sliding over the firm muscle of her thigh. She turned and her smile was a quick, short burst on her pretty face.

I broke the silence. "How're you holding up?"

"I'm all right. Pretty amped up." She looked down at her thumb and it stopped suddenly. "Still a little shocky about Kat."

I gave her leg a squeeze. I didn't say anything because there was nothing I could say, but I knew how she felt. I had the same scooped out spot inside my chest. Another hole bored into my heart next to the rest of them, punctures left by the loss of people in my life. Realization fell on me like a ton of bricks.

"You ever lost anyone before, little girl?"

"No, my grandparents died when I was a kid. I don't even remember them, not really. My G'ma used to smell like oatmeal cookies, and my G'pa had these little wire glasses that were always crooked, but that's about it."

"Your parents are still alive?" I had never heard anything about them.

"They are. They live in Florida because of my mom's job." Her hand fell on mine, tightening on my fingers. "I haven't really talked to them since we met. I wonder why that is."

"It's because you've been ass-deep in monsters little girl."

"It's not that." Boothe leaned up from the backseat. "I've watched you doing this job. You found something that you've been looking for your whole life. This is what you are supposed to do." His hand came up over the seat and patted her shoulder. "Soldiers don't tell their family about the war. They don't understand, they can't, and it would only frighten them if they were told. It makes a distance between you and them because there's a part of you that now they can never know."

"That makes sense." She smiled at the Were-rabbit. "It kinda sucks, but it makes sense."

He slid back into the seat.

Special Agent Heck spoke up. "You are quite good at this, Miss Bramble. The O.C.I.D. could use someone like you in the agency."

Tiff blushed, her skin darkening in the dashboard lights. The thought of her being offered a job doing this gave me a surge of pride that was immediately drowned in a swamp of worry about her out there without me next to her.

Hell, being with me had cost her an eye.

I pushed it all down as I wheeled the Comet onto the backcountry dirt road. Immediately the car was enveloped in a cloud of red dust cutting my visibility in half. Riding the brake, I slowed us even more. The car swerved left and right, bouncing us against the doors and each other. The rosary on the rearview mirror swung crazily. Rocks pinged off the quarter panels.

Dirt roads are rough, rain and wind cutting away the red clay we have for dirt into something resembling a cheese grater. This one had gotten worse since the last time I had driven on it. The pine trees were still thick on the edges of the road, and bushes had grown wild, hanging out and slapping against the windshield.

After several minutes the road straightened under the wheels, spilling us out into a clearing.

The world opened up as the pine trees stopped abruptly. We were in front of a set of hills that the road cut between, swinging back and forth as it climbed. The moon was gone this close to dawn, leaving the sky dark, the only illumination from the brightness of the Comet's headlights.

Last time this space had been filled by a broken trailer park. Single-wide trailers had dotted the hills, broken and washed out from being baked in four decades of harsh Southern sun. They had housed an army of vampire slaves, keeping them safe from that hated sun.

It looked like a tornado had come through.

The trailers had been torn apart and scattered like broken toys in the wrath of an angry child. Trash littered the ground, cheap plywood furniture, shredded insulation fluttered in the night breeze like cotton candy. Big chunks of manufactured homes were strewn across the road, blocking us from driving any farther. The abandoned cars, rusted out hulks of twisted metal and broken glass, were now lined along the ridge, forming a fence across the top of the hill. The taint of magick thrummed in the air.

This had been done on purpose.

I shifted the Comet into Park, killing the engine. Grabbing Durendal and pulling the door handle swung the door out and away. I stood, moving aside so Boothe could clamber out. Tiff was already outside the car, stretching lithe arms over her head and shaking them out to loosen up. Special Agent Heck stepped out, pulling on his jacket, settling it on his shoulders. Ronnie came out holding her basket. She was moving smoothly, but stiffly, spine straight as an arrow, every motion precise and controlled. It took me a second of watching her to realize she was moving like my friend Charlotte, Were-spider and mother of the ghost spiders that were bonded to Ronnie.

Durendal hung heavy on my left side, leather straps creaking as I pulled them tight. The hilt jutted forward on my hip. On the other side I hooked in a leather contraption that had a mess of thin straps. It held a huge crucifix. The cross was made of silver, covered in a delicate filigree. The figure of Christ that hung on the face of it was masterful, the carver using an attention to detail that let you see every line of agony and every drop of sweat on the representation of the suffering of our Lord. The end caps on each of the four arms had small, polished pieces of ivory that weren't ivory at all. They were the teeth of St. Peter, the very first Pope. Along the back of the crucifix was an inscription:

ḥEXE AUFGABEBRECḥER.

The Witch Breaker.

I was hoping tonight it would live up to its name.

Under my arm hung an old-ass Colt .45 1911 that Father Mulcahy had given me. The steel was gunmetal blue paired with well-worn cherrywood grips. It was a sweet gun. It felt like something that had sentimental value to the good Father, but I didn't ask, he didn't tell, and it didn't matter at the moment. It was a damn fine pistol that fired a big-ass bullet, which I had plenty of. It rode under my left arm in the spring steel holster. Both knives were still tucked in the shoulder rig, handle down for quick draw.

I walked over to the trunk, punching the key fob. It sprang open with a click. Blair still curled around herself, knees to chest. The connection between us hummed to life the second I saw her. Her hand flashed, sweeping blond hair off her face. A big blue eye rolled up at me.

"Get out." In a flash she was up, out, and standing on the ground next to me. Reaching in the trunk, I spoke to her over my shoulder. "Stay right there."

Moving stuff around in the trunk, I found a few things I thought we could use. A stun baton, a machete made of razor-sharp spring steel, a silvered bowie knife that was damn near a foot long with a palm-wide blade, and a jar of blessed salt. I passed them around, keeping the stun baton for myself after making sure it still had juice. A flick of the

On switch arced a purple blue spark between the contact posts. Yahtzee.

Tiff took the machete, strapping it around her waist so that it slung low on a rounded hip. Boothe tucked the bowie knife in his belt. I handed the jar to Special Agent Heck.

"What is this?"

"Blessed salt. Breaks enchantments, repels the supernatural. It'll probably come in handy."

He shook the jar. The salt wisped around the glass. "Seems a little unwieldy."

I held my hand out for the jar. He put it in my palm. It was a mason jar, thick clear glass topped with a screw-on metal lid. Pulling a knife, I jabbed the point into the lid seven or eight times, twisting it as I did, making little ragged holes. I handed it back to him. He looked at it, looked at me, and cocked up an eyebrow in question.

"Now it's a salt shaker."

He nodded, flicking his wrist quickly from side to side once. Grains of salt scattered on the ground at his feet. A few of them bounced up, hitting Blair's bare feet. They began to smoke and dissolve, sinking into her undead skin. She hissed in pain but didn't move from where I told her to stay put.

"Sorry," he said.

I felt bad for Blair. "Shake them off," I told her.

Hold the fuck up. Did I just feel bad for a vampire? A bloodsucking fiend from hell? What was wrong with me?

She kicked dirt over her feet, wiping away the salt granules, sighing with relief.

"Thank you."

"Don't thank me yet. I've got a lot of work for you tonight. But we need to get a few things straight before this breaks off."

She nodded.

I pushed my power into our connection. It pulsed between us and I felt a *pull* toward Blair, like a physical, gravitational thing. The marks under her jaw began to glow, pulsing in time with the heart beating in my chest. My voice was deep, authoritative. I made my words a command.

"Do not hurt anyone standing here with me. You are to fight at their side and save them if you see them in danger. To hear them command is to hear me command. You will help me save the children inside first, second to that you are to help me kill the witches and whoever or whatever they have working for them." I leaned in, locking eyes with her and driving my power down that connection. It sank into her, a barbed hook that wouldn't be easily removed. "Have I made myself clear?"

She nodded.

I took a deep breath and turned toward the line of cars at the top of the hill.

"Let's go kill some witches."

49

"What the hell is that place?"

We stood beside the rim of car bodies that had been twisted together like a wad of bread dough. Boothe's finger was pointing at the church on the other side of them.

It was a small country church, the kind that dotted thousands of back roads in the South. It used to be a Baptist Church, but that didn't matter. Baptist, Presbyterian, Methodist, hell, it could have been a snake-handling version of Pentecostal when it was in service.

Now it was a giant pit of blasphemy.

It squatted on top of the hill, somehow darker, even more tainted than the last time I was here. It had the same red-brick walls, the same busted-out stained glass filled in with moldy plywood, the same steeple with the cross that had been yanked off and replaced upside down.

There was a perimeter of stainless-steel crosses that Father Mulcahy had planted to save my ass when I went up against that hell-bitch Appollonia. They had all been up-rooted and shoved top down into the ground. The church, which used to be a consecrated place to worship God

Almighty, now seethed with the taint of corruption and blasphemy.

It was exactly the type of place three witches needed to hold a Black Mass.

"It's a blasphemed church."

Wide hands rubbed his muscular arms. "I don't like it. It gives my heebies the heebie-jeebies."

Ronnie's footsteps were completely silent. The basket was still in her hands, but several of the ghost spiders had crawled out and were riding on her arms and chest. They all bounced up and down on translucent legs, moving in sync like they were tied to the same string. It was creepy.

Slowly, she turned to face me. "We remember this place. Our mother was here. She was not happy then."

What the hell? Ronnie was being mega freaking creepy. She lost a bunch of spiders in the explosion at Polecats and ever since had been becoming weirder and weirder, acting more and more like a spider. I knew that they were tied to her psychically, and that they affected her but she was acting like she had in the beginning.

The first two weeks after the spiders imprinted on her, she was a big ball of crazy. She swung wildly from catatonic to frenzied. There were long periods where she would find a dark cubby and crawl in it. We would find her tucked away somewhere, squeezed into a small space, just her and the spiders. Back then there were hundreds of the damn things, all about the size of a quarter. Charlotte had helped her through the transition. It had taken weeks for her to be able to function. She still wasn't right and maybe never would be, but this was super spooky to a whole next level.

Tiff waved her hand in front of Ronnie's face. "Are you all right, honey? You don't have to come?"

Her head snapped around, faster than human. "We'll be fine. We are going in there."

Tiff's hand was on her gun. It's okay, mine was too. She eased back a step and glanced over at me quickly. I shrugged. What the hell did I know? Ronnie had been all right up until now, coping with the spider thing, weird, but okay. She had lost a lot of spiders in the explosion. Maybe there was a psychic backlash and her connection was being fried. I had no idea. I would keep an eye on her, make sure she didn't flip out on us.

I spoke to the vampire to my left. "Blair, you go first."

I felt her push back against the command, fighting to not obey. "Why am I going first?"

"This line of cars isn't all Selene and her crew have planned. If there's a witchy version of a land mine, you get to find out first." I put a push of power behind my words. "Now shake your ass, sister."

She looked at me, anger scrawled across her face. When a vampire gets pissed, you know immediately.

Blair's face was knotted into predator mode, fangs extended, eyes gone blood and black, skin thinned over a bestial face. She snarled in my direction but dutifully began to climb up on the hood of the wrecked car in front of us. Slowly, she crawled across the dented metal, really putting a lot of effort into it, shifting her hips in a rocking motion that made her denim shorts ride up. Her face turned to look back over her shoulder. Her features were human again as she gave a wink and wicked smile.

Special Agent Heck made a small sound. I looked over and he had turned his eyes away. In the low light it was hard to see that his cheeks were red.

Tiff stepped closer to me. She didn't take my hand or say a word, just bumped me with her hip ever so slightly so that I knew she was there.

She had no idea that I would never forget that, no matter

what Blair did. Her theatrics had as much effect on me as it did on Boothe.

I flicked my fingers at Blair in a "hurry up" motion. Flipping around, she hopped off the car, standing on the ground. We all held our breath, waiting to see what would happen.

Nothing.

"Walk out about six or seven feet." Blair did what I said, stepping carefully in bare feet. She stopped at six feet precisely, spun around, and did a curtsy.

Still nothing happened.

Fuck it. We didn't have all night. The two kids in that church didn't have all night either. I stepped up onto the car hood, took two strides, and stepped off the other side. I stood for a second, waiting again. I felt nothing. Nothing moved. Nothing happened. I waved the rest of my people to follow me.

I watched the darkness around the church. I could hear them come over the metal hood, their shoes and body weight making it protest by buckling and popping hollowly. Tiff came up beside me, followed by Special Agent Heck, Ronnie and her spiders, and finally Boothe bringing up the rear.

The Were-rabbit's boots had just hit the soil when the first noise crept from the shadows.

A low, sinister mix of a wet, strangled cluck and a dry, sibilant hiss. It was the sound of a python eating a live chicken, slithering and the rustle of feathers. The moist sound of bone popping from cartilage.

The nerve under my eye twitched.

Boothe whispered loudly. "What was that?"

Ronnie's spiders scrambled down her body, forming a half circle around her feet. Their spindly, translucent legs began to wave in the air like sensory antennae. Her voice was singsong. "Something rotten this way comes."

My hand itched. I scratched it by filling it with gun.

A pair of yellow dots broke the darkness around us. Two glowing spots about three feet off the ground. Pair by pair, the shadows began to fill with unblinking yellow eyes. The darkness moved toward us. Boothe flicked on the flashlight from his belt.

The LED light cut through the dark. Its white-hot circle showed a creature that should never exist. It was about four feet tall, standing on two scaled legs. Three horned toes scratched the dead dirt, clawing marks. Its body was slick-scaled. Thin, brackish green reptile skin hugged a skeletal body under a short pair of rotten, black-feathered wings; jutting ribs, swollen joints, and protruding vertebrae. Its spine ran down into a long, bony tail that whipped behind it making small tornadoes in the dust.

It herky-jerked forward in a strut. The head was covered in brilliant feathers that hung long down around its shoulders and chest. They made a brightly colored headdress of reds, greens, and whites. A blood-red comb cut up from its narrow skull and from the center of its feathered face jutted a vicious hooked beak lined with needle-like fangs. Corruption-yellow eyes stared as it slowly walked toward me.

The darkness broke, revealing a pack of them.

I stepped back, guns pointed. "Anybody got an idea what we're dealing with?"

"Cockatrice." Special Agent Heck held a small square device that looked like a smartphone. He was pointing it in the direction of the creature and looking at the display. "Known as the Witch Hound. They have venom in their teeth and claws on par with an Arizona Bark scorpion. One dose won't kill you, but it will make you sick, and multiple exposures may prove deadly."

"All that information is in that device?"

He nodded, slipping the device back in his jacket pocket. "I've got to get one of those."

The flock of cockatrices continued to strut toward us, more and more of them coming from the shadows. They were filling the space between us and the church. It was a lot of demon-bird-lizard-things.

I spoke over my shoulder. "We cut our way through these damn things and get inside that church. We've got two scared boys who are counting on us."

I pointed the .45 at the closest, biggest cockatrice. The others pressed to its back as it drew tall, opening greasy, ragged wings. Its chest expanded, beak yawning open to reveal a tongue the color of pollen. It whipped around, slinging venomous spittle in a wet swirl around its feathered head. A damp, hoarse caw came from its throat in a mist of poison.

I squeezed the trigger. Feathers burst apart like blood-ied confetti, choking off the sick cry of the cockatrice as the headless body slumped to the ground. The rest of the pack jumped away from their fallen leader in a slither of scales and a rustle of greasy feathers. They clucked and cawed around the body before, one by one, they turned unblinking yellow eyes toward us.

With an ear-piercing squawk, they charged.

Hey Chicken Little, the sky is falling.

50

My foot lashed out, snapping into the chest of the monster lunging for my balls. Ribs caved around my boot. Clawed feet snagged my jeans and a long, bony tail whip-cracked across my hip in a line of fiery pain. I shook the crushed animal off my foot. It fell away with a squawk, twitching in the dirt.

Another one sprang up, leaping off its fallen brother toward my face in a bundle of feathers and teeth and venom. Beak snapping for my face, its legs wrapped around my chest, claws digging in my skin. Venom slapped across my neck in thin strings from its mouth of murder, burning like lines of acid. Breath that stank of rotten fish and mildew misted my cheeks.

My hand closed on its neck, fingers clamping around greasy feathers and the bone underneath. I gave it a twist, wringing its neck with a *clickity clackity* ratcheting noise. I pulled to the left, trying to yank the damned thing *off* me.

The head popped free in my hand.

Gore shot out of the neck stump in a gout, splashing over me. I closed my eyes in time to keep that shit out of them, but it still washed my skin in a cold spray that stunk to high heaven. The body spasmed, falling away in a tear of claws.

My head swam in a hot, sticky rush as the venom soaked into my skin through the holes left by the claws. I wiped my eyes with my right arm, the other one holding the still-snapping head away from me. Vision cleared, I saw the body of the cockatrice stumbling to and fro, falling and getting back up. Running around like a cockatrice with its head cut off.

Excuse me, torn off.

The head in my hand jerked, fanged beak snapping, looking for a mouthful. I threw it away from me. It sailed through the air, still snapping. The body had fallen and lay quivering.

My hand closed on a rail to steady myself. The venom burned in my veins, making my stomach feel like it was full of boiling oil. I was at the bottom of the steps to the church.

Boothe was about ten feet away. He stood on two crooked legs, feet burst out of his boots into big, paddle-sized paws. Massed with muscle and damn near seven and a half feet tall, eight with the ears, every inch of him was covered in short gray fur except his white chest. Big pink eyes rolled in his oval skull as he lashed out left and right, crushing unholy beasts with each strike. He had the bowie knife in a clawed hand. It flashed pneumatically in the waning light, stabbing his attackers over and over again. Blood ran freely from scratches and bites, staining his fur. He had waded in, taking the brunt of the first wave, and he had paid the price for it.

Blair was a flurry of action, blond hair swirling as she spun like a ballerina. Her hands taloned, she tore into the little creatures like they were stuffed animals. She was the personification of liquid, graceful death. Her fangs glistened in the moonlight, and she was covered in the gore of dozens of fallen cockatrices.

Special Agent Heck had one cockatrice that danced in front of him, hopping from leg to leg, a hissing bundle of homicide. His gun was locked open and laying on the ground. His suit was tattered, bloody slashes showing under on his legs. He stumbled. The cockatrice struck with a hiss. It leaped, claws out as it flew.

Special Agent Heck righted himself, flinging his arm out. Blessed salt struck the cockatrice in a slicing arc.

It looked like he had struck it with a Louisville Slugger.

It flailed, tumbling to the ground as he scrambled away, thin reptile skin boiling with smoke. It writhed, holy salt eating through it like burning embers through toilet paper. Special Agent Heck stepped over it, turning the jar upside down. He dumped salt on the smoldering beast until it stopped twitching.

Ronnie had a cockatrice on the ground, held under one foot. A dozen ghost spiders had latched on to the thing, fangs sunk deep. It twitched and whipped like it was being electrocuted. Bits and pieces of cockatrice lay scattered around her like garbage strewn by stray dogs. She was covered in dirt and gore, but looked whole and unharmed.

She was staring at the cockatrice under her foot, hair hanging in a thick ringlet curtain around her face. She looked up, meeting my gaze. Her eyes were glowing red, casting shadows under her cheekbones.

What the hell?

I pushed it away, my eyes searching for Tiff. A gunshot behind me spun me on my heel. Tiff stood on the top step, pistol in one hand, machete in the other. A cockatrice tumbled down the stairs, thumping along in a flurry of shed feathers like a molting volleyball. It bounced to a stop at my feet.

A second cockatrice perched on the railing of the stairs, horned claws wrapped around the rusty metal. It leaped with a ripping squawk, yellow tongue lashing around, toothed beak spread wide and full of venom. My heart cramped as it flew toward Tiff. I swung the gun in my hand up. Too close, I might hit her.

Tiff spun on one heel, machete held close, blade out, slicing the air in a wicked arc around her.

The last cockatrice split in two, falling in halves around her to plop wetly on the brick porch of the church.

She wiped her hand down the front of her zipped jacket, sluicing off the gore splattered there. She flicked it away from her fingers. "Gross."

"You looked pretty good there, little girl."

She walked down the steps. "I had a good teacher."

"True that."

My eyes searched for cuts and scratches. There was one across the back of her hand. It was red, puffy, and leaking a yellow fluid, but other than that she was unharmed, her leather outfit was apparently tougher than cockatrice claws.

Thank You Lord.

Turning, I found Boothe staggering over. His muscles were spasming, gray fur receding. His ears shrank. The bones of his skull shifted, re-forming. I could hear them grind together. He stumbled as his legs broke and reknitted into human formation.

He knelt where he had fallen, bent in half. His ribs flared as he tried to suck in air.

I went over, grabbing his shoulder, keeping him from falling on his face. His skin was ice, so cold it burned my palm. He was whole, all his cuts and scratches healed with his shift. He looked up at me. His eyes were solid red, the crimson pupils dilated to cover his pink irises; every blood vessel in the whites had burst, spilling out to stain his cornea. Sweat ran down his waxy skin in rivers. Jaw muscles bulged as his teeth ground together.

I knelt beside him. The ground was wet with cockatrice blood, soaking through my pants. He looked at me, eyes unfocused. Unseeing. "You all right, man?"

He didn't respond, just ground his teeth louder.

Ronnie's eyes had bled back to their normal almond brown. Her head tilted as she looked at Boothe. I realized they were nearly the same height with her standing and him kneeling. "He's taken too much of the cockatrice venom. His change has sealed it inside his body."

I looked her up and down. There were scratches along her arms and legs, thin crooked lines where cockatrice nails had cut into her. Blood crusted her forearm where it had run from a double row of punctures that circled it. I nodded at the bite. "How are you holding up?"

She looked down, turning her arm slowly. "Venom does not hurt us." Her arm dropped to her side. Ghost spiders sat on her shoulders, staring at me with pinprick red eyes. "He needs to rest. He will recover, but it will take a while."

"I'll take him back to the car." My hands slipped under the big lycanthrope's arms. Ronnie reached over, stopping me.

"We can take him."

I looked at her. She was five foot even and voluptuous. She had a good shape, but other than dancing, didn't do anything to exercise. Boothe was six foot seven and covered in meaty bodybuilder muscle. He was going to be a struggle for me to move.

Bending my knees, I prepared to lift with my legs. I was going to put him in a fireman's carry to get him back to the Comet.

Ronnie pushed me away with one hand.

I stumbled back two or three steps. The tiny dancer

hooked Boothe under his arms, straightened, and scooped him up like a newlywed groom carrying his bride over the threshold. "I'll take him to the car and we will watch him. We will keep him safe."

She turned and started down the hill. Boothe's fingers trailed the ground with each step. She moved fluidly and gracefully, as if she were walking across a room unhindered instead of carrying three-hundred plus pounds of unconscious Were-rabbit over rough terrain. Two rows of ghost spiders marched behind her in a line of translucent death.

"That's something you don't see every day," Special Agent Heck said.

"It's not the weirdest shit I've seen on this job."

I took in his torn suit. I couldn't see any blood on the suit, the black material wicked it away into hiding, but where the material gaped there were scratches. "How are you?"

"My head is pounding, but the blessed salt did a good job absorbing the cockatrice venom before it could do too much damage. If it wasn't for that, I'd be in worse shape than Mr. Boothe."

"So you're ready to rock?"

He nodded. I turned to Tiff, her hair was drying stiffly into gore shellacked curls. "How about you, little girl?"

She lifted the machete. "Born ready."

I slapped a fresh clip into the .45, settled my shoulders, and turned to the steps. "Let's roll."

I had taken one step when a southern accent broke the night. "Can I go back to the car?"

I stopped short. Blair was looking at the ground, blond hair a curtain over her face, hands skimming up and down her arms. The connection between us was buzzing, humming with . . . worry?

"What did you say?"

The vampire shifted from foot to foot. "I want to go back to the car. I don't want to go inside that place." Her finger stabbed toward the church, little flakes of dried cockatrice viscera drifted down. "It's almost dawn and I want to get back in the trunk of the car."

Anger tipped over inside my chest. It trickled down, spilling into my bloodstream. "Get your undead ass in gear and get moving."

She resisted, struggling with the command I sent down the line of our connection. The marks on her throat blared out with crimson light and began to bleed. Thin trickles of hot, bright red, *living* blood ran down her collarbones, soaking into the thin cotton of her T-shirt. Her jaw clamped tight as she forced words through clenched teeth. "I haven't taken blood tonight. The thirst is driving me mad."

The second she said it I became aware of it. My throat began to burn from tonsils to stomach like I had swallowed a mouthful of ground glass. The sides of my throat stuck together like Velcro. I tried to swallow and came up empty, but the effort ripped a burning pain from the top to the bottom of my esophagus. The thirst began to beat against the wall of my sanity. Chipping. It. Away. One. Tiny. Shard. At. A. Time.

Enough.

I reached down and grabbed my power, pulling it up from my core. It washed over the thirst like a rush of cool water, quenching the fire, soothing the shredded flesh of my throat. Twisting and pushing, I folded the thirst like origami, shoving it back at Blair through our connection and ramming it deep inside her. I buried it as far as I could inside the vampire in front of me.

She stumbled, falling on her ass in the blood-soaked dirt. My voice was hard, eyes cold as I looked down at her. I had almost forgotten what she truly was.

Bloodsucker.

Undead.

Creature of the night.

"There. Problem solved. Now get up."

"Please don't make me! I know what you have planned!" Crystal blue eyes filled with pink tears. They shimmered on the edge of thick fake lashes, threatening to break and run. "Deacon, I don't want to die!"

I stepped up, looming over her. My voice was harsh through a tight throat. "You should have thought of that before you helped these assholes take two scared little boys."

"I didn't have a choice! I was under that warlock's spell!"

"Don't you dare sit there and act the innocent with me, bitch. You might not have done *that* on your own, but you have survived at the expense of others. You are a vampire, a heartless killer."

Anger was the struck match, my power the gasoline. I shoved it through our connection, ramming my will against hers, overpowering it. "Now you will do exactly as I command and help us save those two boys."

I mounted the steps, each footfall like thunder in my bones.

"Besides, you're already dead, so what the hell does it matter?"

51

The wide wooden doors swung open with a short jerk of my arms. No locks, no chains, no way to secure them at all. Sometimes I'm amazed at the megalomania that monsters have. The more powerful they are, the more prone they are to it. It's like their supernatural ability feeds directly into their psychotic narcissism. This is why the bad guys always tell you their plans. It's like they can't fucking help it. They get even the slightest edge and an audience, and all of a sudden they start blathering on about what they're going to do.

Whatever, it helps me do my job. Pride goeth before a fall and all.

Stepping into the church was like taking a bath in bees. The air was swollen with magick, constricted like a throat under a strangler's hands. The skin on the back of my skull tightened, burning hot and tingly with witchcraft. There was a spell going on, some kind of ritual that was building power. Spellcraft layered on spellcraft like concrete blocks in a wall.

The vestibule was just how I remembered it. Dark, gloomy, dank . . . pretty much one of the most depressing places I had ever been. Tatters of spider silk still hung to the walls and ceiling, wisping around like ghostly curtains. The walls still had satanic sigils painted on them, blasphemous symbols of arcane power. They looked wet, fresh, as if they had just been repainted. A deep sniff confirmed. I inhaled the chemical peel of paint with an undercurrent of blood. The symbols glistened in the low light, surrounding us with eldritch magick that pressed against my skin like buzzing, biting insects.

Tiff's voice bounced around the empty room. "Welcome to Creepsville, population us."

In front of us were wide double doors that led to the sanctuary of the church. Muffled voices carried through the wood. I couldn't hear the words, but they were rhythmic, rising and falling in cadence.

A chant.

The bees buzzed against my skin.

Leaning back, I planted my foot against the doors, smashing them open. They banged against the walls on either side revealing a scene straight from Hell.

The pews of the church had been smashed and tossed aside. They piled in heaps of kindling and splinters against the long walls of the sanctuary. The wood plank floor had been swept clean of debris and painted with a giant pentagram. The lines of it were wide and black and solid, smeared on the floor in what looked like tar. At each point stood a child-sized candle, flame guttering at their wicks, tallow running and pooling at their base. Sooted black smoke rose from each of them, curling toward the high-pitched ceiling. The smell of burnt hair and bacon frying slapped my nostrils.

My mind glitched back to the sensory memory I had gotten touching Ahriman's pendant. Human fat and braided hair wicks. My stomach lurched, trying to crawl up my throat.

In the center of the pentagram stood Selene. Her arms

were healed from earlier, whole and chubby again. Her dress had been switched for a long dark robe with a silver hem. Silver stitching formed more sigils on the cloth. She held a dagger long enough to be a short sword. It cut the air in her plump hand, wavy blade gleaming on both edges in the sputtering candlelight.

Both of Sophia's sons were bound and gagged in front of her on an altar made of rough-hewn granite. For a split second I wondered where they had gotten all the stuff needed to set this ritual up but shoved it to the side of my mind. I didn't know how long they had been setting this up before making their first move at the restaurant, and right now it didn't fucking matter.

I had work to do.

She was shouting, words tainting the air inside the pentagram. In the space above her the spell boiled, roiling and shimmering, turning the color of a ripening bruise.

Athame and George stood on the edge of the circle. The Were-gorilla had Ahriman's pentagram hung around his neck and his arms were up in supplication as his monkey mouth spat out the guttural incantation. With the bang of the doors he stopped chanting.

Head jerking toward us, his eyes opened. They were rolled back in his head, gleaming out of his monkey face in a dull worm white. The Keeper was still driving that train.

Athame was also draped in a dark robe, the edges of her hood trimmed in red cloth. More twisty symbols writhed around the trim in silver thread. Her hands were up and she continued chanting as the Keeper began to lumber our way.

He dropped down, swinging bowed legs and using leathery knuckles to drag him along. The planks of the floor shook under my feet, vibrating into my shinbones as he picked up speed.

I shoved the gun back in its holster, hand closing on the

grip of the stun baton. Flicking my thumb over the switch jolted the baton to life. The possessed Were-gorilla roared, stinky breath washing hot over my face. My foot slipped back, bracing. I leaned in, hunkering down as he closed in.

A foot away I rammed out with the baton and spun. The device jabbed into George's chest, just below his nipple; 1.5 million volts stuttered into his pectoral muscle, twisting it like a used napkin in a fist. The impact drove me back, pain flaring from my shoulder as my arm was jammed backward.

The Keeper roared and swung George's big gorilla fist at my head. I fell to the side as it grazed my cheek, big monkey knuckle skinning away the top layer of flesh. It felt like I had been hit with a piledriver. The floor came up in a rush. I tried to get out of its way, but it ran into me before I could. The stun baton clattered away from my fingers.

Special Agent Heck stepped up. The jar rose up over his head and he smashed it down on George's skull. Blessed salt crystals spilled down, scattering through wiry gorilla fur. Immediately it began to smoke and crackle. The Keeper lashed out. George's fist drove into Special Agent Heck's chest, sending him flying through the air. He bounced off the floor, rolling away out of sight.

Tiff stepped up, twisting from her hips. She swung the machete at George's face. The flat piece of steel smashed into his wide nose, drawing blood.

"Blair!" I screamed, pushing my power at her. "Grab him!" Blair zoomed over, moving at vampire speed, knocking Tiff down as she flashed past her. I scrambled to my feet. The blond vampire wrapped slender arms around the possessed Were-gorilla. Her hands didn't touch across his chest. Blood welled in dark fur as she dug taloned fingers into his skin to keep her grip. She screamed as the grains of holy salt burned her arms, but she hung on. The Keeper jerked around, trying to get his arms free from the vampire on his back.

My foot lashed out, heel driving under the Were-gorilla's sternum. Air blasted out of George's lungs, driving him to his knees. The Keeper continued to struggle, but the body he inhabited had been weakened. Blair pulled out her fingers with a squelching sound. She hooked her arms under the Were-gorilla's, leveraging them up to hold him down.

I was impressed that she knew the hold. It showed that somewhere Blair had some kind of training in combat. Vampires are wicked strong, in that hold she could have torn George's arms off.

I stepped up. The Keeper was sucking air into George's lungs, working them like a pair of bellows. Fish-belly eyes turned to look at me. The voice of the demon grated in my ears. "I'm not going to give him up. You will have to kill him to free him from me."

I said nothing. My fingers were numb as I pulled my St. Benedict medal out of my shirt. Holy white light flared, making both the demon-possessed Were-gorilla and the vampire holding him flinch. I pulled the medal over my head, holding it in my hand.

The Keeper began to fight, jerking George's shoulders back and forth trying to get free. Blair snarled, yanking up on the Were-gorilla's arms. His left arm slipped out of the socket with a loud, wet pop of bone separating from gristle. The demon riding him kept fighting, not caring about the damage done to George's body. The dislocated arm slid farther down Blair's grip as the Keeper lunged, snapping George's teeth at me.

"He's going to get free!"

My fist crashed into George's skull, the thick bone ridge over his eye splitting like rotten fruit. Monkey skull snapped to the side and I tossed the saint medal over it. The blessed object fell, bouncing off the chest once before settling into place. The Keeper began to scream as holy light blazed. My fingers swiped my cheek, the skin raw and wet where George's knuckles had torn it open. They came away red and sticky slick with my blood.

Blood that had been mixed with Angel blood long ago.

My hand snaked out, smearing that Angelic blood over the thrice-blessed holy relic of a medal that pressed against demon-possessed flesh.

The effect was instantaneous.

Holy light exploded in a lightning crack of power. It washed over me like a tidal wave, crashing against me, breaking, and washing past. I was ready for it, eyes shut tight. The world still went bright orange as the light blasted into my lids. It lasted less than a blink and the light was gone.

I opened my eyes. Blair was airborne. She sailed across the room, blond hair streaming as she did. Etheric energy crackled as she struck the edge of the pentagram on the floor. She bounced away like she had struck a force field, slamming to the floor face-first.

She didn't get up.

George's head was thrown back, mouth open. Yellow smoke poured out of his open maw in a boil of sulfur stench. The Keeper being evicted. The last of the smoke wisped out and George slumped. Shoulders bowed, head slung down to his chest, he began to shudder and shake. Thick slabs of monkey muscle spasmed, charley-horsing all over his body. His bones pulled, changing shape, not far off human. Black fur thinned into a pelt of human body hair, still thick, but not all-encompassing. He fell over at my feet.

George had turned human.

Brown eyes blinked up at me. "Deacon, what happened? Why do I hurt all over?"

"Demon. You were possessed. You're better now." My eyes began to cast around, looking for Tiff. "Tell you later."

I found her.

Tiff was across the room, swinging the machete in an arc to block Athame's soulsword. The witch was in her devil form, robe tattered from her transformation. The two blades clanged together. Tiff was driven back by the impact.

I stepped over George, my hand closing around the handle of the sword that hung on my side. I didn't look down as I spoke, just kept moving. "Get up and fight if you can. If not, stay out of the way and whatever you do keep that medal on."

He didn't get up and I didn't stop. The holy sword sang free from the scabbard as I stalked toward where my girlfriend was fighting a devil-witch.

Tiff was on the floor, right leg twisted out to the side painfully. Athame loomed over her, soulsword raised to strike. Durendal swung back, its weight pulling against my shoulder. Pain stretched as the blade pulled. Twisting, I swung it at Athame's head. The edge sliced the air, singing as it arced.

The devil-witch leaped out of the way, the tip of my sword just catching the spaded end of her tail. It flew away in a spray of black gore, skittering on the floor where it flopped and twitched like a fish out of water.

Athame spun on hooved feet, hissing at me through triple-rowed teeth. Her wings flapped, keeping her upright. Lashing out, her soulsword licked toward me like a serpent. I drew up on my toes, swinging the greatsword in a downward arc. It kerranged against her unholy blade with a shower of sparks.

She came up, ebony blade a swirl of death. I stumbled back, keeping Durendal between me and the edge of her soulsword. She screamed, howling in satanic glee as she pressed toward me. Each strike I blocked jarred pain up my arm, burning my nerves. She was stronger than a normal woman, stronger than me and better with a sword. She beat me back, step by step.

"You will die tonight!"

I didn't argue, just kept shoving the sword between us. My arm was a hunk of lead, and her blade kept driving closer and closer to me. She lunged, soulsword slipping over my blade. Time shrank around us and I watched it stab forward. Twisting, I tried to get out of its way, but the blade ripped through the skin on my side, bouncing as it grated along ribs.

Athame's yellow eyes narrowed as she leaned in, pressing against me, holding the magickal blade in my side. Every muscle I had was locked, spasmed into immobility. She was so close I could see every pore on her boiled red skin, every drop of oily sweat that coated it, every strand of blood-red hair that stuck to it. Blackened and chapped lips curled away, sliding wetly over razor-sharpened enamel. Breath that smelled like a bloated corpse misted out, filling my nose as she spat one word in my face.

"Etacoffus."

Fire blasted through my chest, burning away every drop of oxygen in my lungs. I was drowning, lungs shriveled and empty. I gasped silently, trying to draw air into my clotted throat. Everything went gray and buzzy, static scattering across my vision. Panic clawed at my mind, frantically chewing at my sanity like a starving rabid dog on a bone.

The world disconnected with a wet pop and began to fade. Strength drained from me, running down my legs, spilling onto the floor.

My eyelids weighed a hundred pounds, dragging down over my eyes. My bones threatened to haul me under the darkness. They tried to pull through my skin.

Darkness swept over me.

52

"Get the hell off my boyfriend, you bitch!"

Air rushed into me bringing the world with it. My lungs inflated like dry-rotted wineskins being filled for the first time in forever. The pain was a firestorm in my chest. Oxygen a cold burn on the inside lining of my lungs, ice crackling with each gasp.

I was on my knees, the edge of the stage creasing across my kidneys. A sharp pain punched deep in my side with each breath. Reaching, my hand touched it. The skin was whole but felt soft, mushy like a bruised apple. It was fever hot under my fingers. Strength flowed back into me in fits and starts each time I drew air.

Tiff was on Athame's back. She had the machete across the devil-witch's throat, edge in. Her other arm was hooked around it, trying to cut the bitch's head off. One leg wrapped around Athame's waist, the other flopped limply as the witch thrashed around.

Athame's taloned hands were locked under the machete, holding it away from her neck. Brackish blood ran down her arms. The goat-headed medallion sat on her chest, eyes glowing with satanic power as it protected Athame from harm.

I pushed off the stage. Athame forced the machete away from her throat. It swung out and away, loosening Tiff's hold on her.

I snatched up the holy sword I had dropped as Athame reached back and took hold of Tiff's hair. With a wrench of unnatural strength, the devil-witch drug Tiff up and over her shoulder, flipping her over to thud against the floor. Tiff lay there, sprawling boneless and limp.

Athame raised both hands above her head. The talons lengthened, becoming razor-sharp daggers long enough to go straight through Tiff from one side to the other. Wings spread, she shouted down at Tiff. "I am going to flay you alive and devour your skin while you watch! I will eat you raw strip by bloodystrip."

No! Not Tiff!

I batted her wings away. My fingers snarled deep in a tangle of blood-red hair, pulling hard. Durendal slipped into her back and burst out of her chest in a shower of black gore. The goat-headed medallion fell to the floor with a hollow sound.

I held her there, pinned by the sword while she convulsed, *ghuk ghuk* noises coming from her throat. There was the sound of wet paper tearing as wings and horns sheared away, tumbling off of her to wither on the floor. The red of her skin boiled back to the pale white tone of human. A tremor ran from her heel to her head, ending with her slouching, folded around the holy blade. My arm was shaking from the effort of holding her up. I let it drop and the witch slid off the sword to lay dead in a widening pool of her own blood.

A spin of my wrist flung witch blood off the holy blade in an arc. Stepping over Athame's body, I dropped the sword into the scabbard. It sank home with a hard pull on the leather belt around my waist.

Kneeling beside Tiff, I gently pulled her up, supporting her with my arm.

Her lovely face was ghost-white pale. Sweat beaded her upper lip and along the edges of her cheekbones. Her eye was bright, pain making it shine. Softly, I moved her hair out of her face. It was stuck to her skin with sweat. "Hey, little girl. Thanks for saving my ass."

She coughed. "Thank me later, we've still got work to do."

"Settle down. You don't have to be tough anymore; I've got it from here."

"That's good, 'cause I think my leg is broken. It hurts like a bitch."

I looked down. Her leg was bent unnaturally. There weren't any lumps under her leather pants that would have been a compound fracture, but it didn't look right.

Movement caught my eye. My hand was on my gun as Special Agent Heck staggered from the shadows. One arm was across his chest, holding his ribs, the other was snapping a cell phone closed. He came over, standing.

I looked up at him. "I thought you were dead."

His voice was strained, words coming on shallow breaths. "Broken ribs. Maybe sternum fracture."

He was tougher than I thought. Broken ribs are no joke. Everything you do—breathing, moving, hell, even thinking—feels like it's tied in with your body core. It hurts constantly, a sharp, grinding pain that keeps a knife edge against your nerves. Every tiny sip of air is torture. He looked over my head, behind me.

"That's a problem."

I turned. Selene was still inside the pentagram. The spell bubble had turned a sickly violet, crackles of corruption magick zipping through it like miniature lightning. Selene was raging inside, still casting her ritual. It was all contained in the bubble of the spell, including the sound. Her poison green eyes pinned to me, fury naked on her chubby face. Both boys lay on the altar, still bound.

It was the air over them that was the problem.

It had split, rent open like a jagged wound. The edges of reality peeled back like the lids of an empty eye socket. Inside, a miasma of magick roiled, spitting sparks of witchcraft. It split wider as I watched, tearing and ripping.

I pulled Tiff to her feet quickly, gently as I could. She sucked in a deep breath when her heel struck the floor and became even paler. Fat droplets of sweat popped on her forehead. Definitely a break. I moved her toward Special Agent Heck.

"I know both of you are hurt, but you have to get each other out of here."

"I'm not going anywhere. You need my help."

"Don't make me carry you out and toss you down the stairs, little girl." I transferred her arm from around my neck over to Special Agent Heck's shoulder. "Get your asses out of here so I can deal with Selene and finish the job we came for."

"But—"

"No buts. Go."

Her mouth formed a hard line. "Same deal as always, lover, you bring your ass back home to me."

"Yes, ma'am." I turned to Special Agent Heck. "Get all the way to the car. I want her to the doctor ASAP."

"Backup is on the way."

"Not my backup."

"The O.C.I.D. has people coming."

"Good, they can clean up my mess. Now get moving and try to take George with you, he's by the door."

Tiff reached out, touching my arm. "Love."

"Love."

She nodded and they turned to the door, leaning on each other.

I turned away and went back to work.

My fingers felt thick and dull as they fumbled with the straps of the holster on my thigh. It took a few seconds for me to work enough of them free so I could pull out the cross it held. *Hexe Aufgabebrecher.* The Witch Breaker. Damn near two feet long and twenty pounds of anti-occult kick-assery. It filled my hand and began to glow with a pure, righteous, blue-white light.

Time to finish this.

53

Stepping to the edge of the pentagram, my skin felt like it had been scoured. It was raw with stinging magick, the nerves pulled too close to the surface, open to the air, sore to the touch. The spell made a dome that was solid. I could see Selene through it, but I couldn't hear her.

I edged my foot toward the dome, sliding my boot forward slowly to touch it. An inch away one of the sickly yellow crackles arced over, zapping my toes.

The whole thing went numb and cold up to my calf muscle.

Reaching down, I dragged my power out of my guts, unfurling it and pushing it toward the bruise-colored dome of light. The Angel blood in my veins began to boil, pushing my power *hard*. It rose, spilling out and crashing against the spell in front of me.

And broke.

My power ricocheted, bouncing off the spell, and slamming back into me. It bent my knees and sent my stomach into convulsions. I took a deep breath, settling myself. The gulp of air sent a stab of pain through my rib cage where Athame had stuck me with that damned soulsword of hers.

Selene's eyes cut over at me. Magick continued to spill out of her mouth as she chanted. A pudgy hand reached down, tangling in the mane of the child in full animal form. He began to jerk, fighting until she lifted him up with a sharp yank of her chubby arm.

The wicked curved blade began to move down toward fur-covered throat.

Dear God, let this work.

I leaned, swinging The Witch Breaker back over my head. Every muscle pulled as I drove it down like a hammer, smashing it against the dome of magick. Cankerous, aurulent witchcraft flashbanged under the strike, backfiring up the cross. It jolted through my arms. The muscles of my hands seized and locked around the cross, clenching it in a death grip. A peal of thunder rolled through the sanctuary, reverberating like a gong had been struck.

The curved blade hesitated in the witch's hand.

I pounded the cross against the skein of magick. With each strike, acid boiled up my nerves, climbing and crossing my chest. Yellow witchcraft crackled under the blows. Anger fought agony inside me becoming rage that clawed its way up my throat, tearing out in a roar.

The skein of magick rippled, splitting with the wet rip of an animal being skinned. Through the tear I could hear Selene chanting strangled consonants never meant for a human throat. The Witch Breaker clattered to the floor as I ripped Durendal out of the scabbard and shoved the blade into the hole. Twisting, I tore the blade up, the edge cutting through eldritch magick and parting a way.

The air was malignant as I stepped through.

I pointed the sword at her. "Stop what you're doing right now."

Selene stopped, pausing in her chant. The spell hung noxious in the air in front of her face. She pulled the pup closer, knife edge to his throat. Tears rolled down plump cheeks, shimmering on her soft jawline and dripping onto the head of the child in her arms. Her voice cracked with desperation.

"You're ruining everything! Stop and let me finish."

"That's never going to happen, witch."

Her eyes were desperate. "Wait, wait, look at the portal."

My eyes followed her finger, sliding up above the altar.

The air yawned open, images flashing across the gape. It tugged at me, like the hole had a gravitational pull. It was like looking through a hole in a tent if the universe were a circus. The images rouletted around, settling on a scene in a home.

It was dinnertime, the table set with three places. The table was a hand-me-down, the top of it scarred from generations of children doing homework and craft projects there, discolored after an uncountable number of meals taken there, heat stained from years of Thanksgiving turkeys carved and Christmas hams sliced.

We always meant to refinish it and never did once our children started adding to the scars.

My heart locked in my chest as two people came into the scene. One was a boy who was stretching toward manhood. Midteens, he was just starting to fill out, still almost painfully thin from a growth spurt, but you could see his shoulders were widening. His hair was cut close and gelled into a short upkick in the front.

The girl was in the first bloom of womanhood. Her hair was thick, honeycomb brown, and bone straight. It bobbed behind her in a ponytail. A dash of freckles ran across her nose, and her lips were made for laughing.

Both of them had the same wide gray-blue eyes. Both of them were older. I hadn't seen their faces in over five years.

They sat down. The girl looked up as someone else stepped into the scene.

Holy Mary, Mother of God . . .

My hand slammed over my mouth.

The woman was gorgeous. Long midnight hair that swung wild and free to her supple waist. She sat at the remaining place setting. Quick brown eyes danced behind thick-rimmed glasses that framed her face, her lovely face, thick lips pulled up into a smile. She reached out for her glass, a wide band of diamonds glittering on her slender finger.

It was the one piece of jewelry of any value she'd ever wanted, the one piece she had loved the moment we found it at the little jewelry store in town.

The pain in my chest intensified, sliding all the way through me. It hooked under my heart, barbs of memory digging in, tearing as they pulled. Tears ran hot and salty down my face.

My family. I was looking at my family. They were older than my memory.

About five years older.

They were alive.

The image wavered, edges breaking, flaking away like desiccated reptile skin. The scene dimmed. Fading. Going away.

I lunged. "Bring it back!"

"The spell is fading. I have to finish it to keep the portal open."

I stopped, torn in two. My eyes cut to the image of my family. It was sliding away like water in a drain. I looked at the Were-child in Selene's grip, knife to his throat. His eyes were wide over the muzzle that held his jaw closed.

The witch spoke. "I can give you what your heart desires most, Deacon Chalk. You see them *but I can bring them to you.* Your family can be with you again." Her voice dropped, breaking. Tears welled in her poison absinthe-colored eyes. "I know the pain of a lost love. The hollow, empty feeling. I know what it is like to wake up in the dark of the night and reach over to touch the cold space beside you. The loneliness that gnaws at you, grinding away at your sanity while leaving you cold and dead and hard inside."

"That's not my family." My voice was hollow in my own ears. The words dragged through me like regurgitated ground glass.

Absinthe eyes glittered fever bright. "But it is! That *is* your family. They live in another version of this world. In their version, it was you who died that night so long ago, not them. They live together, still missing you every day. They would gladly join you here if they knew they could."

Oh, God. My family. To be with them again.

"Could you really bring them here? Do you really have that much power?"

"Yes! This world is the knot in the stitch. Every time a world-changing event occurs here on this plane of reality, it ripples out in different variations across the multiverse. We can't go there, but I can bring them here." Her voice dropped. "I can take away your pain, Deacon Chalk, but only if I finish the spell."

"What else will come through?"

"My husband. I will only bring him and then I can rid myself of the pain I carry too."

"And then you'll close the rift?"

"Once open I cannot close it, but does it matter? You can have your heart's desire. You can be whole again."

My family. I could see them, they were so close. My heart ached, driven through with nails of memory. I could have them back. All I wanted was only one word away.

I looked up. My wife laughed at something one of the

kids said. She held a napkin over her mouth, her body shaking with laughter. Everyone was smiling as they ate. I remembered that. Being at the dinner table, in a kitchen full of love and care.

Peace.

One word. Just a nod. Just not stopping Selene and they could be mine again.

They could come to my world, to my life.

My life of monsters.

My life of pain and blood and fear.

My life where they had already been killed by what I fought every day.

I looked Selene in her poison green eyes.

"Fuck you."

"What?"

The sword blade rose in front of me, point toward her. "I said fuck you. No."

"You *want* this, Deacon Chalk. I can feel it. You want to be with your family again."

"More than you know, bitch, but I'm not willing to drag the rest of the world to hell to do it."

Selene seethed at me, anger pouring off her in waves. It spilled from her rounded shoulders and down her arms in jaundiced rolls of sorcery. Her voice was a harsh, grating hiss.

"I am."

The curved knife began to slide across the child's fur-covered throat, blood spilling across the wicked sharp blade.

54

I lunged, thrusting the sword in my hand toward Selene's head, aiming for one of those damned absinthe eyes. The witch ducked, knife coming away from the child, swinging up to whack into Durendal's steel. She dropped Sophia's son, dancing back, chanting the entire time. Sorcery spilled out of her mouth in malignant syllables. Magick began to gather inside the dome like a thunderstorm, pressing with an intensity that was barometric.

The Were-child she'd held hostage rolled off the edge of the altar, landing on the floor with a thump. The movement loosened his bindings and they slipped off his front paws. He immediately set to clawing at the muzzle on his face, mane shaking and whipping around. It broke after a few swipes of his lycanthrope claws, falling away. It hit the floor and he drew in a long breath that he let out in an ear-piercing howl. Blood darkened the fur on his throat and chest, but the cut was already starting to close. The blade wasn't silver. He shook off the rope around his back paws, turned, and clamped his jaws on the ropes tying his brother, gnawing on them.

Magickal lightning crashed inside the dome as Selene

brought her spell to a crescendo. The blade in her hand was painted in bright blood. Lycanthrope blood. The Blood of the Trinity.

A flick of her hand slung blood through the air. It spun, arcing toward the rift in reality. I dove, stretching, reaching, trying. My hand rose up as the blood tumbled through the air in five fat droplets.

Four of them splattered against the skin of my hand and arm.

The last one hit the rift like a bullet through glass.

I fell to the ground as Selene screamed in triumph. "Come to me, my dark darling! Chernobog, black god of depravity, I call to you. Heed me, join me in this world ripe for your plunder."

Movement caught my eye as I began to stand. Sophia's kids were both free. They stared at me with wide eyes. They still held their forms. I jerked my head toward the cleft in the dome I had come in by. As one, they scrambled across the floor, darting through the hole in the magick.

I stood up.

The rift in the air had solidified. My family was gone, now the inside of the rift was a tide pool of inky darkness. It swirled, flashes of sorcery cutting through here and there. Something moved deep inside it. Something drawing closer.

Something powerful.

55

A tentacle curled over the edge of the rift, slapping on its rim of magick. It pulsed there, suckers sucking on solid air. The underside of the slimy thing was a raw pinkish red, the red of skinned flesh. The topside was a liver-spotted moss green that dripped ichor on the floor. A second tentacle slithered into our world, squirming into our reality. It hung in the air like dog's nose sniffing, testing it. The raw flesh suckers on the underside opened and closed like tiny, toothless mouths. Flexing and bunching, they began to pull.

A man's head and shoulders pushed out of the rift. Blue-black hair hung around a face carved from granite by a heavy-handed sculptor. It was rough-hewn, a wide nose, heavy jaw, a brow that jutted over deep-set eyes the color of an eclipse. Wiry hair covered a thickly muscled bare chest. The tentacles were attached to his shoulders in place of arms. Wide eagle wings filled the space behind him.

Chernobog.

He set the air on fire with sorcerous potential. Witchcraft broiled off him in seething streams of acid-flavored power. His eyes fell on Selene. White teeth flashed in a wide smile.

He was still smiling as I whacked his head off with the holy sword.

The severed head fell in a flurry of shorn hair that fluttered around like confetti. It tumbled to the floor, bouncing once before rolling to a stop at Selene's feet. The body slipped backward in a spray of gore, falling away into the potential of the multiverse.

Selene's mouth hung open in shock. Turning, I swung the sword at her, the holy blade sliced toward her head. Her hand flashed up, clamping over the blade in an iron grip. Eldritch black flame licked her chubby arm, sizzling around the sword steel in her pudgy fist. She held the sharpened metal inches away from her face.

"You think you have stopped me? You've stopped nothing! There are more of him out there. More of him waiting on me like I have waited on him."

She yanked down on the sword, wrenching it away from my hand. It pulled me forward, stumbling close to her as it left my hand. She threw it behind her contemptuously. Poison eyes narrowed. "I will go retrieve your family, Deacon Chalk. I will call forth every version of them and I will bring them to this world and kill them slowly in front of you. I will summon every monster I can to have their way with them. They will know pain and torment unimaginable. And you, you will watch every moment of this before you die at my hand."

My fingers wrapped around the goat-headed medallion that hung between us. I yanked it forward, stretching the cord that secured it around her neck. The tendons in my hand seized as magick burned along the skin of my palm. The knife under my arm filled my other hand. Slashing up, the razored edge sheared through the cord. The medallion came away in my hand.

She looked down as the sorcerous fire sputtered out on

her arms and the dome of magick over us began to dissolve like a popsicle on a summer sidewalk.

"What . . . ?"

I slashed the knife in a vicious backhand. It sliced up under her soft chin, parting the high lace collar of her dress and the pudgy skin underneath. Blood sprayed out over my hand in a hot arterial wash. Her legs went out from under her, dropping her to the floor in a tumble.

I stood over her as she crawled through the pool of her own blood. One hand clutched her throat, crimson welling up around pudgy fingers. This made her list over to one side as she pushed and pulled, trying desperately to get away. Long, once-glossy hair now hung limp, dragging through her life's blood, sticking in clumps to the rough wooden floor. Her eyes rolled up at me. They were wide, corrupted green pupils shining fever bright. Her jaw worked, trying to speak, trying to conjure words through her ruined voice box. It came in a wet rasp.

Pulling out my pistol, I knelt down to hear.

Air wheezed in through both her mouth and the gape in her throat. It had an undertone of wet bubbling. "I . . . I . . . curse you . . . De-Deacon Chalk."

"Funny words coming from a dead witch."

Her laugh caught in the blood in her throat, coming out in a big blood bubble that burst on her face like a child with a wad of chewing gum. She choked air back inside. "It . . . is . . . done. Things . . . can-cannot be . . . undone." Her voice sputtered, growing thicker, more guttural. Her witch voice. "You will . . . face . . . yourself and . . . on that . . . day . . ." Her voice had lost all humanity, becoming a growl. Magick rolled out of her in a mist of corruption that made my power jangle inside my skin. Lips pulled back to show teeth stained with her own blood, she spat, "On that day *Death* will stalk you."

The barrel of the Colt .45 pressed against her temple. Poison eyes rolled around, trying to look at it. "Maybe so, but you won't be here to see it, you bitch."

My finger pulled the trigger.

The gun roared, bucking in my hand. I let the jolt of the recoil make me stand.

Damn I was tired. I staggered out of the pentagram. Durendal and The Witch Breaker both hung heavy around my waist. My feet dragged through the blood on the floor, squelching and sticking. Adrenaline was dumping out of my system in a rush, leaving behind a queasy stomach and a woozy head. My blood sugar was *gone*. My side was a spike of agony where I had been stabbed by a soulsword. Everything hurt under my skin, all my nerves burnt and inflamed. Micromuscles all over my body were twitching and spasming.

I felt like I had been cut apart and stapled back together.

I was halfway to the door when it slammed open. Light from the dawn outside poured in with twenty people in blue windbreakers. They all had guns pointed at me. One guy stepped to the front, his gun shoved forward over a rounded paunch. What little hair he had was gray over an unlined face the color of bitter chocolate.

"O.C.I.D. Hands in the air!"

The calvary had arrived. Right on time.

Yippie-ki-yay.

56

The door shushed closed behind me as I flicked on the overhead light. Blair jerked awake, sitting up in a blur of inhuman speed. Her head twisted unnaturally, crystal blue eyes widening as she saw me. The connection between us jolted to life, sliplocking into place.

In a blur of motion she was on her feet. A wrist-thick steel chain slithered off the bed, links clinking together onto the floor. It was attached to the cross-covered steel ring clamped around her waist, the other end to a ring in the floor. The weight of the chain dug the edge of the circle into her lush hips.

I held up a Tupperware bowl. It sloshed. "I brought you dinner."

"Thank you." Blair's fingers brushed over mine as she took the container and the spoon from me. Her touch was cool. Not cold, room temperature. Vampires are cold-blooded; they take on the temperature of the environment they are in.

She pried open the lid, filling the room with the smell of rich and rusty iron. She used the spoon to gently poke at the chunks floating in the bull's blood. "What's in here today?"

"Liver and raw sirloin. How is it going with keeping solid food down?"

"I still need the blood, but I haven't thrown up in three days."

Vampires don't eat solid food. They subsist only on blood, preferably human. Blair had been craving food, raw meat specifically, for the past two weeks, so we had been including it in her daily feedings. It wasn't the only strange thing that was happening. Her fangs were shrinking, drawing up into the roof of her mouth. Her own blood ran red instead of black and dead like most bloodsuckers. Her heart continued to beat; I could hear it in my head if I spent too much time around her.

She was still a vampire, but since she and I had been linked she had been changing. The connection between us remained, even though the symbols that had been carved into her throat had healed over and were now dark pink scars instead of cuts and slashes. She still obeyed direct commands, which is why I kept her chained in a locked room instead of outright killing her.

"Can I ask you something?"

"I might not answer, but you can ask."

"Why didn't you do your original plan?"

I looked at her. During the showdown with Selene and her coven, I was going to get the kids free and then use my power to set off the bomb inside Blair's chest. I was going to use Selene's weapon against her. Blair had read this through our connection. "Things just worked out differently."

"You didn't change your mind?"

"No."

Her head dropped, big blond curls falling around her face. They hung low enough to almost brush through the bowl of blood on her lap. She looked down at the floor.

"Where does this put me? What are you going to do with me now?"

"I don't know. I'll probably keep you around as long as I can control you."

"You don't think that's dangerous?"

"I know it's dangerous, but dangerous is what I do." I looked at her, hard. "I will never forget what you are, Blair. No matter how useful you are as a weapon, I will not hesitate to dust you if I think for even one second that you could be a threat to one of my people."

"So I'm not one of your people?"

"You're not people at all, you're a vampire."

If she had been human, the look on her face would have broken a tiny part of my heart. I walked away, shutting and locking the door behind me.

Ronnie stood in the hallway.

She was wearing pajama pants and a sweatshirt. Thick, brunette ringlets piled on top of her head, held there by a wide headband. Her face was scrubbed free of makeup. Two translucent spiders sat on her shoulders, the others were somewhere out of sight. "You know, you don't have to be a dick to her."

"And you don't have to be nosy, but for some reason you are."

"She's different now, Deacon; surely you see that."

"She's not different *enough*. Don't ever forget that. She's still a vampire. Vampires are not to be trusted. They're deadly creatures, and you would do well to remember that."

She stepped forward, forcing me to look down at her. She was over a foot shorter than me. The spiders scurried away, zipping up hair-thin web lines to the ceiling as she drew close. "She's not the only deadly creature you have living in this house."

She was right.

Ronnie had changed too. She had lost a lot of spiders in the explosion at Polecats. Now she was down to only a dozen or so of the little murderous yo-yos. Since the other spiders died, Ronnie had shown signs of abilities that were not human. She was stronger than she should be. Not as strong as me, but a lot stronger than a human woman her size should be.

She was fast too. Not run a mile in a minute fast more blink-your-eyes-and-you'll-miss-it fast. It showed up in small ways, just everyday movements that she would perform so quick it was spooky. Way faster than human. Faster than me. Her movement had also taken on a rigid kind of grace that reminded me of Charlotte, my friend the Were-spider.

I would have to call her soon and get her opinion of what was going on with Ronnie.

George lived here too. He had cleaned up and was going to AA, staying sober one day at a time. He was back at work, being an engineer of all things, and took regular confession and Communion with Father Mulcahy. We weren't risking him being open to possession again. Next time I might have to put a bullet in his head, so we were taking preventative measures.

Those three plus me and Tiff in a house on the outskirts of town and we made one strange family.

Family.

Ronnie rose up on her tiptoes, planting a quick kiss on my cheek. "I just feel sorry for her. Think about being nicer to her for my sake. I'm off to bed."

"Where's Tiff?"

"In the kitchen."

"Good night, nosy."

"Good night, mean-ass."

She moved past me, heading down the hallway. Reaching the end, she went inside her bedroom, shutting the door.

I didn't turn to the locked door behind me when I spoke.

"I know you heard that. I'll admit you're changing in ways I don't understand, but I stand by what I said. She might be right about you one day. One day, but not today."

It was silent behind the locked door.

Turning on my heel, I walked away and down the hall.

Rounding the corner, I entered the center of the house. It was a square meeting of the three hallways. It wasn't a big enough house to call them wings, just hallways. One to a set of bedrooms, one to the master bedroom, and one to the common areas like the kitchen and living room. It was a nice house, older model, brick, set on a few acres far enough out to not have visible neighbors. In my line of work, neighbors are just potential innocent bystanders.

I stopped at a little table that sat in the corner. It was a small thing, hardly taking any room at all. Tiff and I had found it at Goodwill when we were furnishing the house. It had a smooth top over a small drawer and the legs had small rosettes carved into the wood. I had painted it black and varnished it.

On it sat a Sacred Heart of Jesus candle, a small statue of the Virgin Mary, and a small framed picture of Kat.

It was a picture that one of the girls from the club had taken. Kat had been captured in front of her computer screen, leaned forward, brows pulled together, bottom lip captured as she concentrated on figuring something out, hunting down and ferreting out some piece of knowledge the Internet was trying to hide from her. I had seen that look on her face countless times. It wasn't a glamour shot, it was a real shot. It was the essence of Kat.

Because of how she had died, and with the club gone, there wasn't anywhere else to memorialize her.

It had been two months since the chaos with Selene. Two months. I missed my sister, and even though we were putting things back together, there were still moments that I would turn, expecting to rely on her, only to realize she wasn't there. On the job, my fingers still hit the button on my phone to call and ask her a question, ringing before I would realize Kat wasn't going to answer.

My fingers touched the edge of the picture frame.

Eternal rest grant unto Kat, O Lord, and let perpetual light shine upon her. May she rest in peace.

I made the sign of the cross.

Amen.

I turned toward the kitchen.

Warm, yellow light spilled through the doorway. From inside came the sound of movement and the smell of coffee being brewed. I crossed the threshold to find a beautiful woman in a well-tailored suit.

Her back was to me as she leaned into the refrigerator looking for something. I stopped short, admiring. It was a *very* well-tailored suit.

Standing straight, Tiff turned, holding a container of milk. She smiled at me, moving to the counter to set them down. Her suit was black, matching tie stark against the white shirt she wore. The jacket was open, revealing the handle of the Taurus Judge that hung under her arm.

"How are you tonight, Special Agent Tiff?"

"I'm fine, and it's Agent-in-Training Bramble, thank you very much." Stepping over, she slid into my arms.

"Sorry, I forgot, you just look like you would be in charge."

"Soon I will be."

"Oh, I don't doubt it."

Her lips were warm against mine.

After the brouhaha with Selene and her coven, we had all

been taken in for questioning by the O.C.I.D. Once the dust settled we walked away with job offers. I turned them down flat, I don't play well with others, but Tiff had said yes.

She had been training with them the last few weeks, as soon as her leg had healed. Now we both worked mostly nights. Sometimes we even worked together.

"Is Special Agent Heck back on the job?"

"Yep, we went to the site earlier today."

"Any luck on tracking the rift?"

"Not so far, but we have people on it."

The rift that Selene had opened stuttered in and out of existence. It kept moving, sometimes only a few feet, sometimes miles and miles away. The O.C.I.D. was trying to find a way to close it and, until then, to track it.

"Anything else come through it?"

"A flock of blood-drinking butterflies and an undead squirrel. Nothing big or unmanageable. If that happened, the agency would call you."

"They better."

The O.C.I.D. had taken me on retainer, available to help them when my expertise was needed. It let me be there whenever Tiff had a really dangerous case. It wasn't a perfect solution, but for now it worked just fine.

Tiff stepped back, not far, just enough to turn and pour two cups of coffee. Her hip still touched my thigh in a warm, gentle curve. Handing me a cup, she pushed the sugar my way.

I love coffee but only with cream and sugar. In my opinion, coffee smells amazing and tastes like crap. Cream and sugar make coffee live up to the promise of how it smells. Tiff disagreed, taking it black and bitter.

I added three spoonfuls of sugar and a healthy splash of chocolate-flavored almond milk. Once it was right, I took a sip. "I heard from Sophia today."

"How are her and the kids doing?"

"Fine. The boys still haven't switched forms yet."

"They could come down to the agency and have one of the lab guys look them over to see if that's a good thing or a bad thing."

"I don't think Sophia would trust them to a lab."

What I didn't say was that I didn't blame her. Tiff may work for the O.C.I.D., but that didn't mean I trusted them completely. Her? With my life. Them? About as far as I could throw them collectivly.

My cell phone buzzed in my pocket. I pulled it out just as Tiff reached into her pocket for hers. We both looked at our screens.

She looked up at me. "Silas?"

"Oh, it's Silas now?"

"Don't be silly. Special Agent Heck, then."

"Yep."

"Want to ride in together?"

"Only if we take my car."

"Of course."

I chugged down my coffee, burning the roof of my mouth. Tiff dumped hers in a travel cup.

"They tell you what we were going to be dealing with?"

"The message just said 'mummy.'"

"I'll grab the charcoal starter fluid from the garage, then."

This job never ends.

Thank God.

Dear Loyals and True Believers,

Well, we have had a helluva ride, haven't we? Thank you so much for your love and support. It is really heartwarming how much you all love this series.

This book was CRAZY, wasn't it? This book is the game changer. From here on out things only get wilder in the Deaconverse. I definitely want you to hold on tight.

Thank you for all the times you have mentioned this series to your people. I appreciate it, I truly do. Thank you for all the times you have spread the word. You are the greatest.

You keep reading, keep reviewing, keep spreading the word about Deacon Chalk and these books, and I will keep writing all the mayhem that is the Deaconverse.

You mean the world to me.

James R. Tuck